Best WOMAN

Best
WOMAN

A Novel

ROSE DOMMU

BALLANTINE BOOKS
NEW YORK

Ballantine Books
An imprint of Random House
A division of Penguin Random House LLC
1745 Broadway, New York, NY 10019
randomhousebooks.com
penguinrandomhouse.com

Copyright © 2025 by Rose Dommu

Penguin Random House values and supports copyright. Copyright fuels creativity, encourages diverse voices, promotes free speech, and creates a vibrant culture. Thank you for buying an authorized edition of this book and for complying with copyright laws by not reproducing, scanning, or distributing any part of it in any form without permission. You are supporting writers and allowing Penguin Random House to continue to publish books for every reader. Please note that no part of this book may be used or reproduced in any manner for the purpose of training artificial intelligence technologies or systems.

BALLANTINE BOOKS & colophon are registered trademarks of Penguin Random House LLC.

LIBRARY OF CONGRESS CATALOGING-IN-PUBLICATION DATA
Names: Dommu, Rose author
TITLE: Best woman: a novel / Rose Dommu.
DESCRIPTION: New York: Ballantine Books, 2025.
IDENTIFIERS: LCCN 2025019340 (print) | LCCN 2025019341 (ebook) | ISBN 9780593975688 hardcover | ISBN 9780593975695 ebook
SUBJECTS: LCSH: Weddings—Fiction | LCGFT: Queer fiction | Romance fiction | Humorous fiction | Bildungsromans | Novels
CLASSIFICATION: LCC PS3604.O48 B47 2025 (print) | LCC PS3604.O48 (ebook) | DDC 813/.6—dc23/eng/20250422
LC record available at https://lccn.loc.gov/2025019340
LC ebook record available at https://lccn.loc.gov/2025019341
International ISBN 979-8-217-09452-3

Printed in the United States of America on acid-free paper

randomhousebooks.com

1st Printing

First Edition

BOOK TEAM: Production editor: Cara DuBois • Managing editor: Pam Alders • Production manager: Katie Zilberman • Copy editor: Sheryl Rapée-Adams • Proofreaders: Alissa Fitzgerald, Megha Jain, Katie Powers, Tess Rossi

Book design by Kim Henze Walker

The authorized representative in the EU for product safety and compliance is Penguin Random House Ireland, Morrison Chambers, 32 Nassau Street, Dublin D02 YH68, Ireland. https://eu-contact.penguin.ie

For Maddy and Alex

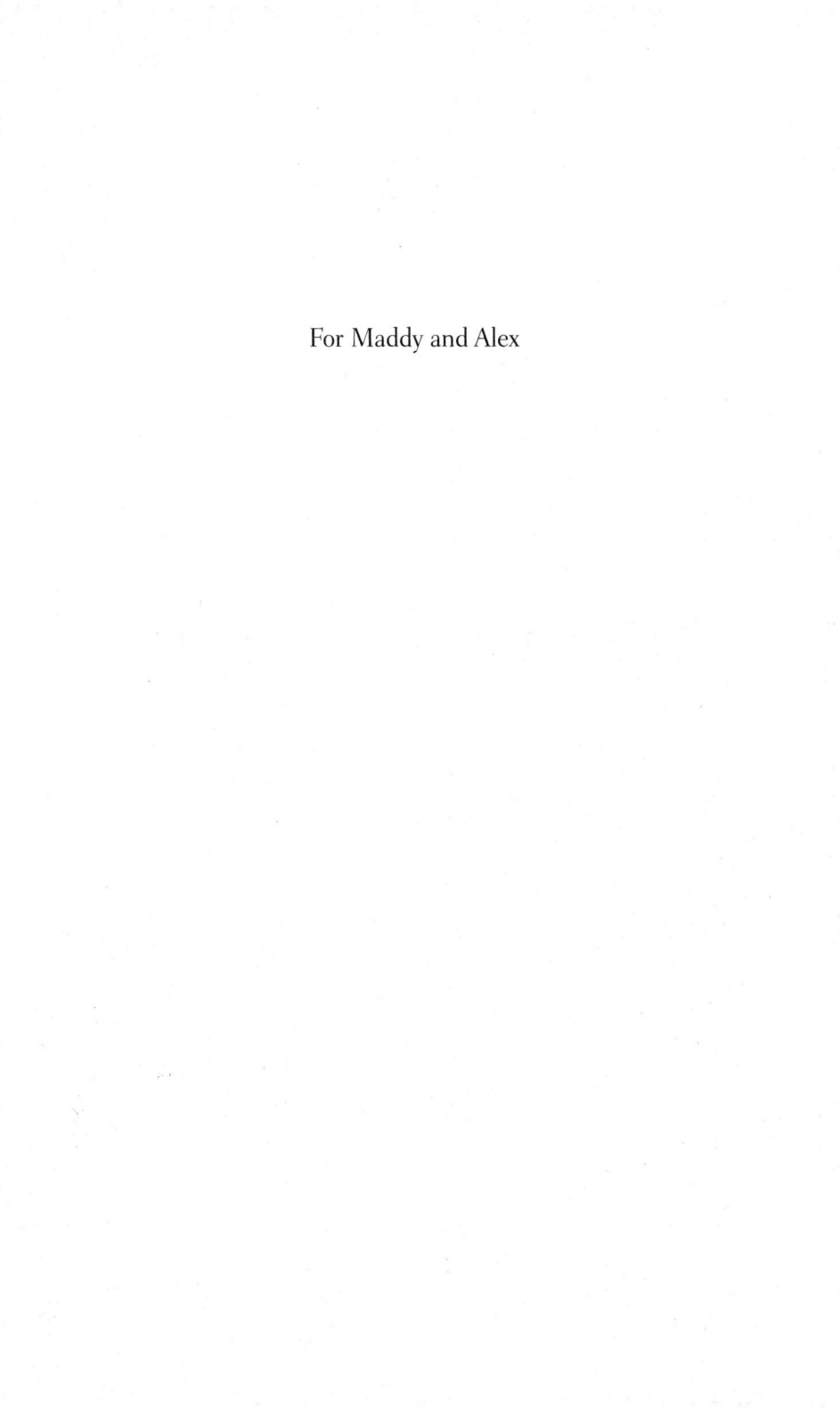

"This is my one chance at happiness. I have to be ruthless."
—Julia Roberts, *My Best Friend's Wedding*

I want to be the girl with the most cake.
—Hole, "Doll Parts"

Prologue

IT'S SO HOT inside the club, the walls are dripping.

I'm not a very good dancer, but tonight isn't about dancing. I'm on the prowl, but I'm no sexy feline. I'm a bumbling, bipedal animal and evolution has not been kind to me. I watch everyone around me pair off in twos and threes—the first orgy on Noah's ark, after the flood.

Suddenly, like light breaking over the horizon, I see her. She stands alone, nursing a drink long turned to ice, leaning against the sticky wall in jeans and a black tank top. Her messy mullet is meant to look effortless, like she took a pair of shears to it herself, but I'm guessing it's the work of the lesbian-run salon in Williamsburg that specializes in sapphic shags.

I bob and weave through the heaving mass of bodies, mumble something loud enough, charming enough, to catch her attention. We join the other dancers. Her arms are strong where they wrap around my waist, and her hair is slick with sweat that drips into our eyes as we kiss.

In no time at all, we're shoved inside a bathroom stall, furiously making out, hands in each other's hair. I don't know her name, but I don't need to. She doesn't know mine either. She doesn't know anything about me.

After, when I'm back out in the sea of bodies, I don't feel any different than before. My feet are beginning to hurt from these shoes. Just another night, another party, another nameless stranger. Another train ride home alone.

Better luck next time.

CHAPTER One

THERE ARE NO malls in New York City. As a recovering mall goth, I find this sad. Malls are my favorite kind of liminal space, a portal to a bygone era that smells like Auntie Anne's cinnamon pretzels and credit card debt.

On occasion, a woman finds herself in need of a garment so special in its mundanity, so particular in its ubiquitousness, that it can only be obtained in a large, air-conditioned building where one can also buy ill-fitting cargo pants made of microplastics, expensive body lotion that smells like rotten bananas, thigh-high boots that were trendy four years ago, a sleek new laptop, lipstick in one hundred nearly identical shades of mauve, vinyl records that will end up in a landfill when their owner has moved on to a new hobby, and designer perfume. I am a woman who has found herself with this particular need, meaning that after three subway transfers and one sojourn on the Long Island Rail Road, I am at a mall.

The skylights, soft pop music, and power walking senior citizens remind me of home. I spent enough of my adolescence in malls to know that they are all fundamentally one shared space stretching across the fabric of reality. This mall is my childhood mall, the mall of my ancestors, my children's mall, etc.

I pass a department store full of middle-aged women returning jeans they've already worn twice, a fast fashion chain selling fetish wear to teenagers, and, of course, a Starbucks.

"New phone case?" The pimply teenage salesman stares at my chest, not that he'll find much there.

"Try our new falafel recipe!" I spit out the overcooked ball of fried chickpeas as soon as the kind-eyed woman who forced them on me is in the distance.

"You'd look gorgeous with some extensions." The pretty girl running the kiosk probably means that I'd look *better* with extensions, as the rain and humidity have both flattened my hair and electrified it with frizz, but alas. I check my boring brown bangs in my phone camera, but they're beyond repair.

After walking what feels like miles, I finally reach my destination. Born to Bride is tucked away in an older corner of the mall that clearly hasn't been renovated to keep up with the newer additions. While there are, according to the Born to Bride website, thirty-five locations across the country, this was the only one in New York State. Headless brides clutch plastic flowers in the windows, which seems like a bad marketing strategy—how are they supposed to sell veils that way? Do brides still wear veils, or is that outdated?

I text Aiden. **Is Rachel wearing a veil?**

nah he replies right away. **fuck that purity culture bullshit. she might be doing a flower crown though. very early lana.**

I can't deal with my twenty-seven-year-old heterosexual

brother knowing who Lana Del Rey is, so I drop my phone back in my bag and head inside the store, passing through the archway molded to look like a chuppah—Born to Bride being a chain primarily marketed toward Jewish women—and into a scene straight out of *Say Yes to the Dress,* but with uglier dresses. In one corner of the store, a girl with frizzy hair—I raise a mental fist in solidarity—is hissing at a woman who can only be her mother, who is in tears. At the other end, a sales associate bearing a shocking amount of cleavage for a Thursday morning seems to be talking down a woman who can't zip up the back of her dress.

"I'm so *fat,*" she wails. "My wedding is in *six weeks.*" So is mine, incidentally. I thought everyone got married in the spring, but autumn weddings are seemingly de rigueur for East Coast Jews.

"We can try the next size up!" The sales associate's face is braced for impact. The gaggle of friends circling the bride-to-be starts shaking in fear.

"I will *not* wear a size fourteen on the most important day of my *life.*" The bride is not quite blushing, more tomato red with rage. She whips out her phone, presses a button, and raises it to her ear. "Hello, I need to make an appointment with Dr. Roth for CoolSculpting next week." A momentary pause, her face cracking with rage. "I don't *care* if he's boogie boarding in Corsica, I am getting married *next month.*"

As fun as it would be to watch her meltdown progress, I am on a mission. I shoot a sympathetic glance toward the sales associate and refocus my attention to the register, where a woman around my mother's age is perched, assessing the space like a large bird. The kind of bird that reminds you birds are descended from dinosaurs. There are dark, puffy circles under her eyes barely hidden with concealer that's far too light and far too yellow for her. She has clearly been on her feet far too long today, or this week, or this life. But she plasters on a smile as I approach. According to her name tag, she is Lorraine.

"How can I help you today?"

"I'm attending a wedding next month." I'm a bit sweaty from my trek through the mall, and it's warm under the bright lights. Every pearl and scrap of lace glimmers in this overstuffed store. "It's in Florida, but I called customer service and they said I could come to any location and pick up a dress with the model number."

Lorraine nods, eyeing my sweaty upper lip. I give her the number and she checks their system. "Yes, we should have it in stock. What size do you need?"

"Well, here's the thing," I say. "I need that dress in a fourteen, but I actually need it in a different color."

She sneers. "The order has no additional color options attached." Her face smooths into something resembling customer service. "Listen, honey, I know you might not think"—her eyes flick to the screen—"*burnt sienna daydream* is your color, but . . . I'm sure you'll look lovely." She's not really selling the compliment.

"And after all," she says, clacking away at the keyboard, "it's not about *you,* darling. You're a bridesmaid."

Big smile. "A groomsperson, actually."

She nods, eyebrows raised. "I'll see what I've got."

A few minutes later, Lorraine leads me into a sumptuously appointed dressing room.

"Thank you." I toss my bag on the ground and look around,

realizing something is missing. It takes me a minute because I've only had one cup of coffee today and there's currently an Adderall shortage in New York City. "Where's the mirror?"

She crosses her arms. "All the mirrors are out here," she says, pointing toward the pink hallways branching out into dressing rooms. "People usually come here with friends and family and want to share the experience."

"How fun for them," I manage through clenched teeth. There is nothing I hate more than trying on clothes in front of a communal mirror and fielding commentary from salespeople, other shoppers, and the odd security guard trying to get my number. The last one is mostly wishful thinking; *nothing* is more gender-affirming than being desired by people you don't want to have sex with.

"I'll be back in just a moment." Lorraine marches off to a hidden back room, stiletto heels sinking into the blush carpet with every step.

"You're being such a BITCH." The frizzy-haired bride stands in the doorway of the dressing room across from mine, the skirt of her dress as wide as the doorframe. Her mother cowers before her. "I can't deal with this. I can't deal with you! Go get me a cinnamon pretzel with the cinnamon scraped off and an iced almond latte and don't you dare come back until you're ready to lift your fat ass off Daddy's life insurance money and buy me the dress I deserve."

The mother stalks past me, something shattered behind her eyes. I can't look away from her daughter, which proves to be a mistake. She catches my eyes and mistakes loathing for sympathy, giving me a look I recognize from my face, reflected in the windows of every restaurant my mother has ever embarrassed me in. It's a look we Jewish girls grow up with, permanently beneath the surface, never far from emerging. It says *Can you believe her?*

"Sorry you had to hear that." She is anything but contrite, walking over to the mirror between our two fitting rooms. "Weddings, you know?"

Shrug.

"My mother keeps going on and on about keeping the cost down, but I told her if we swing this thing for under 150 she's getting a deal. And how could anyone say no to *this dress*?" Her eyes glaze as she runs her hands down the mass of white chiffon.

I would, in fact, say no to the dress. It has lace in places lace simply should not be, and is at once baggy and too skintight. It's a mess.

"You look beautiful." That's safe enough, right?

"I know," she tells her reflection. Unfortunately, she's not quite Narcissus, because she catches my eye in the mirror. "Mine's in December, a Hanukkah wedding. When's yours? And where are your bridesmaids? Or your mother?"

"Uh, I'm not getting married. I'm here to pick up a bridesmaid dress." Kind of.

"My bridesmaids hate their dresses." An ugly smile splits her face wide open. I feel another swell of sympathy for her mother, who is hopefully getting a drink at the last TGI Fridays in America or drowning herself in the food court toilets.

"I haven't seen mine yet."

"I'm sure you'll look . . . great. You have nice"—the strain on her face is Herculean—"hair."

"Yeah, I'm sure my hair will look great in whatever nightmare my future sister-in-law picked out."

"Hmm."

That's Lorraine, standing behind me, holding the nightmare in question.

"Good luck," says the bride, nasty grin fixed firmly in place. Perhaps her mother has walked into oncoming traffic.

I'm hustled back into the dressing room, a space draped so aggressively in pink it feels almost vaginal, which is probably the point.

Lorraine hangs up the dress and leaves me to it. Resting on a hanger, it's benign, harmless. The dress is strappy, and slinky, and has a slit up one leg that promises to show off some of my best assets. But I understand clothes and the ways they lie, and also the truths they uncover, ones we are desperate to hide. The low, curving neckline would look fabulous on someone who could fill it out. I can't, and my breasts are likely to look small and pointy and very, very sad sitting in it. The tiny straps might make me look delicate if it weren't for the span of my shoulders.

At least mine will be black. Burnt-sienna-whateverthefuck is *not* gonna work with my complexion.

I strip off my clothes—also black, my urban armor—and prop my phone up on the small stool nudged against the wall, opening the camera app to use as a mirror. I'm not going outside until I'm sure it won't be humiliating.

There, on my tiny screen is my body. And it's just that: a body. Despite all the time I spend thinking about it, all the tears I've cried over it for the past twenty-nine years, and all the opinions people seem to have about it, it is still just a body. It is pale and freckled and imperfect. My hips are too square, my thighs too dimpled, my stomach too curved, my ass too flat. But as I normally do, I try to find the parts of it I like, the parts I see as mine: My collarbones jut in a way that is almost delicate, the freckles on my shoulders left over from summer are sweet and girlish. Eyes wide, neck long, lips full—thank you, Juvéderm. And Bridezilla was right—I have great hair. Even when I had nothing else, I had great hair.

I slip into the dress, which looks . . . all right on the tiny screen, so I cautiously drag open the dressing room curtain, flinching at the screech of curtain rings. I step barefoot into the padded hallway and turn to face the large gilt mirror at the end of the pink-tunneled dressing area.

It's not great, but it's not terrible. The color washes me out, but I won't be wearing this color, so that's fine. The draping does nothing for the places I'm curved correctly and emphasizes the places I'm decidedly not, but in the grand scheme of bridesmaid monstrosities, I've gotten off with relative ease.

"And how are we doing here?"

Lorraine is behind me in the mirror, and I catch an unguarded glimpse of her face, and a look of naked curiosity on it as she takes in my broad shoulders, my knobby knees, my face under the harsh overhead lighting.

I meet her eyes in the mirror.

"I'll take it."

I have to split the dress on two different credit cards at checkout, and Lorraine sighs audibly. Bridezilla's mother and I lock eyes from across the room. I almost ask for a bite of her pretzel.

YEARS AGO

"*WHY DID YOU* let me drink so much Manischewitz?"

I'm on the floor of my grandparents' guest bathroom, toilet full of regurgitated gefilte fish and wine mocking me. The gefilte fish does not look very different after its brief sojourn down my esophagus.

Aiden is looking at the photos on the wall and nervously folding hand towels. "You're the one who said the ritual four glasses of wine were 'merely a jumping-off point' and you wanted to 'imbibe the blood of our ancestors.'"

"I *hate* Passover."

"You *love* Passover. When we were kids you used to find the afikomen in like, five seconds, hide it again, and find it again just to gloat that you found it twice."

"I can't help having the nose of a bloodhound and the competitive drive of Tonya Harding!"

Even the mention of matzah turns my stomach and I hurl again, but I feel better for having expunged more sweet wine and pureed fish. I haul myself up and clean out my mouth with the essentials my grandparents keep stocked for whenever one of their kids or grandkids is visiting. If I'm lucky, there may be some old Valium rattling around in the drawer next to dental floss from the Bush era—the first one.

Aiden wrings the towel between his hands, clenching and unclenching. "Do you have a problem with Grandma's design choices," I ask, "or can I use that? I know she hasn't redecorated since the late eighties, but I'm into the new romantic vibe she's got going on in here."

"I don't think it's appropriate for her to have all this African art," my brother says, handing me the towel.

He's followed me in here for a reason, but as always, I have to be the one to start the conversation. As I wipe chunks of fish from around my mouth, I find his eyes behind me in the mirror.

"Rachel seems nice," I say, opening a toothbrush sealed in plastic. "I'm glad I could spend more time with her. We didn't get to hang out for long when y'all were in New York last year."

He smiles, grateful. He and Rachel have been dating for over a year, but this is the first big family event she's joined. Passover is taken seriously in our family. My grandpa does the long version of the seder—long for Reform Jews at least, so still under two hours—and my grandma makes sure she gets the best brisket delivered from the deli and takes compliments on its tenderness as if she had not only cooked it herself but also butchered the cow. Possibly gave birth to it too.

"She is nice. She *really* likes you. It's cool that y'all have so much in common."

"Yeah, it's great that we both love . . . music." My head is ringing a bit too much to come up with anything better.

"And her family is great too." They wanted her to be home for Passover but were excited for her to meet my family."

"That's great." A rumbling. There may be more gefilte fish in my system than previously estimated. Or maybe it's the charoset I hoovered up despite my lifelong raw apple allergy. What was I supposed to do, *not* eat the delicious nutty treat that symbolized the backbreaking labor of my enslaved ancestors?

"You should stay with us the next time you're here. We have an extra bedroom and I know it's chaotic at Mom's with the twins."

"The new futon in my old room is very comfy." Now that I've added a memory foam pad, at least. "And she always wakes me up for Pilates." Something is rising inside me, using my esophagus as a ladder. Or a hose. "Whether I like it or not."

"I'm gonna ask her to marry me."

"How Oedipal of you," I say, eyes watering. Aiden shoots me an unimpressed look in the mirror. "That's amazing, Aiden. I'm so happy for you." I'm clenching my hands into fists, nails biting into my palms, hoping the pain will distract me enough to keep the food of my forefathers in my stomach, where it belongs.

"You'll be best man at the wedding, right?"

Chunks of fish, matzah, apples, and hard-boiled eggs, all tinged the dark pink of kosher wine, spray my grandmother's art deco mirror and culturally insensitive tchotchkes. "Fuck!" Aiden runs out to get help, or at least escape my shame and pass the responsibility of handling me to someone more qualified.

I kneel at the porcelain altar, the warbling soprano notes of my grandma singing "Dayenu" wafting in through the open bathroom door. I don't know what makes me feel sicker: the smell of my puke, the snot dripping from my nose, or the thought of the unopened vial of injectable estrogen buried deep in the backpack currently sitting atop my mother's pretty fucking uncomfortable futon.

CHAPTER

"YOU'RE WEARING *THAT* to the wedding?"

The weight of River's nearly biblical judgment, the horror dripping from their voice, has me gulping down a rather large bite of salmon Benedict, without chewing it. Thankfully I have half a Bloody Mary left to wash it down with. I roll my eyes and lock my phone, hiding the evidence of the blurry photos I took at Born to Bride. "All the bridesmaids are doing the mall princess fantasy. At least I get to wear black and match the rest of the groomsmen."

River, wearing a strappy, asymmetrical tank top so complex I can't begin to comprehend how they shimmied into it, looks appropriately distraught at the mention—or mere existence—of a mall and that someone would procure a garment for a formal occasion at one. "Are you *sure* you don't want me to pull something for you? Hannah G has a few red carpet castoffs that could always 'fall out of an Uber' on their way back to the showroom."

River is constantly stealing designer items from the B-list pop star they style and is convinced she has no idea. The reality is that River's uncle is the head of Hannah G's label, and she'd rather release her questionable tweets from 2011 than risk offending her boss by finding a stylist who won't pawn her Gucci castoffs at Beacon's Closet for coke money or schedule their top surgery for the same week as the Grammys.

I'm currently wearing a skirt Hannah G once wore to a Marvel movie premiere and River once wore to "cocktails" with a married senator. River is *very* generous about sharing the wealth, especially when they're feeling guilty about missing a lunch date or forgetting my birthday, something that has happened almost every birthday since I've known them, five years and several sets of pronouns ago. I'm mostly lucky that I'm Hannah G's size and River isn't. The pop star and I share a similar build: flat ass, no chest to speak of, but long legs. Meanwhile, River is tiny, maybe five foot four in the Margiela boots they favor, with light-brown skin and a shock of dark hair currently parted down the center and smoothed down with gel like the world's sluttiest English schoolboy.

I grimace. "While the thought of transporting stolen property across state lines thrills me, I'll pass. It's going to be a disaster anyway. I should just lean in."

River rolls their eyes, spots Kyle, and begs, "Please talk some sense into her!"

"She still complaining about the wedding?" Kyle asks, effortlessly hauling a case of champagne behind the bar—he never skips arm day. Or leg day. Ignoring his actual paying customers, my buff bestie refills our Bloody Marys with a long-suffering sigh. "At least they *invited* you to the wedding. Your family is so annoyingly PFLAG. Your mom sends you Pride care packages and, like, watched every episode of *Glee* because she thought it was supportive. You're basically Lady Gaga to them." As usual, he is dressed entirely inappropriately for food service, shirt unbuttoned nearly down to his navel to show off deep-brown skin and a furry chest that sends bears, otters, and cubs alike into a feeding frenzy. He props his head on his arms on the bar, the better to show off his biceps. "*My* family has spent most of my life desperately trying to figure out something to get me for Christmas that isn't a coupon for conversion therapy."

"And *I went* to conversion therapy," says Daytona, swanning in from the door, late as usual. "Hey, dolls," she coos, blowing us air-kisses.

Kyle, River, and I give each other a look, the *is she being serious or joking or* ***both****, yikes* look we end up giving each other whenever Daytona references her family. Daytona doesn't notice, too busy tossing her trench coat on a stool and hopping up onto the bar, which Kyle keeps telling her to please not sit on lest the health department make a surprise inspection. She shakes out her long dark hair, adjusting an eyelash and the rhinestone below it in the reflection of her phone camera, contour dark against the fading summer tan on her ivory skin.

Kyle picks our thread back up, because if every conversation halted to give Daytona a dramatic entrance, we'd never have time to talk about anything. "What did *your* parents get you for the holidays last year?" he asks me.

I squirm on the barstool. "Laser hair removal."

"Amen to that," says Daytona, leaning back over the bar, hair dipping into a carafe of orange juice that will no doubt still be served to customers, phone outstretched in hands tipped with hot-pink claws. "Kyle, baby, plug this in and cue up my track. I just need to piss and then I'll start the first set." She hops off the bar, landing with ease in six-inch heels, and struts toward the employee restroom she's been asked repeatedly not to use.

Daytona Bitch is not officially booked to do drag brunch at Tony's, the chic little Italian restaurant Kyle rules with an iron—yet limp-wristed—fist, but since we're here every weekend anyway and Daytona will start performing something from *Blackout* within two hours of entering any given space, That's Amore has become an "if you know you know" brunch event for our extended social circle and the twenty lesbians who follow Daytona to every gig she books, rain or shine. Last Sunday she performed "Memory" from *Cats,* Celine Dion's rendition of "O Holy Night" (it's September), and a Nickelback song I secretly loved in high school.

River turns their attention back my way, though I've been attempting to make myself invisible on my barstool. "Seriously, Julia, we can't have you at this wedding in something off-the-rack. This is your big *I'm a gorgeous woman with amazing hair and a fabulous life* moment with your entire extended family. You need to be in ready-to-wear *at least,* if not couture."

"River has a point, babe." Kyle's phone is sitting on the bar and he sends some horny hopeful a photo of his penis with zero attempt to disguise what he's doing. "You've been hyping yourself up about this official debut for literal years, why not pull a real stunt?" He smirks at the photo he receives in response, ignoring a straight couple at the other end of the bar passive-aggressively trying to get his attention.

The twisting feeling in my stomach that has nothing to do

with the freshness of Tony's smoked salmon intensifies. "You should know better than to believe my bullshit when it comes to my family."

This is deeply, painfully true. When I first came out to my friends, I ranted for months to anyone who would listen about just how much I didn't care what my family thought about me, all while I was avoiding their emails and video calls so I wouldn't have to *tell* them. My dad had to start the conversation by sending me a screenshot of my most recent Instagram post and the words **anything u want 2 tell me???**

Kyle hands me a mimosa and chucks my empty Bloody Mary glass into a bin. I take a slug, steeling myself for judgment.

"Honestly, I feel lucky that they're including me as much as they are. And I'm already going to stand out as the only groomsperson wearing a dress. It should at least match what the other girls in the bridal party are wearing. It could be worse, Aiden could've made me wear a tux."

"Oh, a tux could be superchic," River says, eyes lighting up. "Very *Victor/Victoria*."

"I don't feel quite femme enough to wear menswear in public," I shoot back. "And it would probably confuse my grandma. 'What, are you a boy again now?'" I ask in an approximation of her Long Island drawl.

"Could you at least let me dress you up for the rehearsal dinner?" River says. "I need to start building a styling portfolio outside of Hannah G and you're the only person I know with her measurements."

"Can you *please* convince her to get bigger tits so I can finally start enjoying the fruits of your attempts at labor?" Daytona, back from the bathroom, asks. While I share Hannah's modest chest, Daytona spent six months' worth of tips becoming a double G.

"I'll see what I can do."

"You're a doll." Daytona stretches her legs in anticipation of the twirls and dips she's likely about to execute. I say a prayer for the structural integrity of the tables—she has been known to leave broken furniture in her wake. "And *you*," she says, pointing a claw my way, "are going to *be* a doll and let River give you the full *Pretty Woman*. Don't you want to fuck a bridesmaid?"

"Or a groomsman," Kyle says.

"Who says I'm worried about getting laid? Maybe I'm going to focus on my brother and this beautiful moment of two souls becoming one!"

Crickets.

"Good luck with that, honey," Daytona flips off the overhead lights, another thing she has repeatedly been asked not to do, on her way toward a tiny corner where a table has been moved out of the way to create an impromptu performance space. Kyle finally decides to take the straight couple's orders—the woman, who had looked mutinous, changes her attitude immediately. I think I hear her call him "girlfriend." River accepts a call and begins to talk Hannah G down from her latest fashion crisis. "Of course you can't wear *real* fur, you fucking idiot," they hiss.

And then, just as Daytona starts to writhe to the opening chords of "Black Velvet," my own phone vibrates with a call from **Aiden Rosenberg**. His ears must have been burning.

"Hey, future groom!" I'm trying so hard to sound cheerful that it's bordering on shrill. "How's it going?"

"Hey, best woman! Is that Alannah Myles I hear in the background?"

"It's very strange that you know that."

"My taste is both eclectic *and* impeccable. Listen, I wanted to call and give you a heads-up that Rachel's maid of honor had to drop out of the wedding."

I rack my brain trying to remember what I know about the minion in question. I vaguely recall a blond girl with a J name and overbleached hair smiling next to my future sister-in-law in the bridal shower photos. "Why, she didn't like the dress Rachel picked out?"

Aiden and I have always been, as much as possible, brutally honest with each other. It might have started when we were kids and Aiden was so confused as to why our parents were getting divorced. "They hate each other," I told him. "They fight every night after you go to sleep." It had hurt, but he'd eventually appreciated that I hadn't lied about it, and since then we'd always more or less told each other the truth.

Which is why he doesn't hesitate to tell me what he's calling about. "No, she, uh, didn't want to walk down the aisle with . . . you."

"One moment, please." I slide off the barstool onto suddenly shaky legs and head outside. Fort Greene is busy on a Sunday afternoon, even though it's starting to rain, crowded with attractive young families. MILFs and DILFs as far as the eye can see. I shelter underneath an awning for the laundromat next door, but even seconds in the rain has my hair erupting in frizz.

"Wait, so . . . what?"

"Yeah, Jenna's been Rachel's friend since kindergarten and

I guess they made some promise to each other that they'd be maid of honor at each other's weddings. Jenna got married last year and honestly, the vibe at the wedding was *weird*. Her dad was strapped at the reception."

"Like, with a *gun*?"

"Yeah, can you believe it? Florida, dude. So Rachel was already feeling weird considering some of the stuff we heard last year, like she knew Jenna was pretty conservative but only recently started realizing *conservative* was code for *bigoted asshole*. Then I guess Jenna made some pretty gnarly comments at the bridal shower and Rach uninvited her on the spot."

"Fuck. I'm sorry she had to do that."

"Don't apologize, Jules. *I'm* sorry that you even have to hear this, but I thought you'd want to know who you're walking down the aisle with now."

This is all so much so quick I haven't had time to think about the inevitable replacement. "I'm sure whichever of the Rachels has been moved into first position will be fine," I say, referencing my future sister-in-law's squadron of identical besties.

Aiden laughs. "No, it's uh . . . you actually won't believe it. It's Kim Cameron. You know, from high school?"

Kim Cameron.

Thirteen
YEARS AGO

"DO YOU NEED a ride home?"

I look up from where I'm surreptitiously reading the *Buffy the Vampire Slayer* fan fiction I printed out at home last night, dazed by the muggy Florida heat. Standing in front of me, haloed by the August sun, is *her*. Kim Cameron. My eyes catch on her legs in their ripped fishnets for a moment.

"Me?"

"Do you see anyone else out here?" She has a hand on her hip and looks like she's already regretting this.

"No." Everyone else is gone, rehearsal having ended almost an hour ago. I've been waiting for Aiden to pick me up. Sharing a car and splitting the monthly payment was a great idea in theory *before* he got his license, but since I'm always at rehearsal after school and he's out the gate the second the final bell rings, I am constantly waiting around for him. He hasn't responded to my last three calls and I've resigned myself to withering away in this parking lot with nothing but my forty-seven pages of smut and a Luna Bar.

But here *she* is, currently starring as Cinderella in the fall production of *Into the Woods*, while I, who barely made it on to the props crew, dangle paper birds over her lovely head during the prologue. Today I accidentally hit her in the face, scratching a tiny paper cut into her nose. Is that why she's offering me a ride, so she can murder me and dump my body on the side of the road? It's a diabolical plan, and there's no chance she'll get caught—I doubt anyone at home would miss me. The twins are firmly in the terrible twos and our entire house has fallen under the thrall of the Wiggles, whose videos and CDs play at top volume all hours of the day and night.

"You live on the west side, right? I've seen you at the Publix on Powerline."

"Yeah." I've seen her there too, buying sushi with her friends to take to the beach as I trail behind my mom, who insists that I need to start drinking the diet Arizona iced tea instead of the regular.

"Come on, it's so fucking hot out here."

Feeling almost disconnected from my body, I get up, sling my messenger bag over my shoulder, and follow her to her black Honda Civic. It smells faintly of pot and the floors are dirty, sprinkled with sand and empty water bottles. At least she doesn't have to share it with anyone. She's an only child.

I give her my address and she starts the car, exiting the school parking lot. The late-summer sun hits her face through the window and I try not to stare at her glowing profile.

"I'm sorry about hitting you with those birds today," I blurt out, immediately wishing I'd stayed quiet. I read somewhere that being cool is about waiting for other people to ask questions and answering as vaguely as possible.

She laughs. "It's OK, you didn't do too much damage. Just don't let them peck out my eyes like they do to the stepsisters."

We laugh, and I realize that I'm in *Kim Cameron's* car. With *Kim Cameron,* a year ahead of me, the girl who received a standing ovation in the cafeteria last year for punching a guy in the face when he called her a dyke.

She powers on the radio and flips through a few stations, evidently finding them lacking. She reaches behind her seat when we hit a red light, and her T-shirt rides up as she twists. My eyes are stuck on the curve of her back and I shamefully whip away as she turns back around, CD case in hand.

"Find us something to listen to?"

Oh god, the pressure! I unzip the book and flip through pages of albums I've never heard of, mix CDs with esoteric titles like *Beach Vibez* and *Mike's Hot Jamz Vol 69.* There are a few Broadway cast recordings mixed in, but I'd rather throw myself from the moving vehicle than suggest we sing along to *Wicked.*

A name catches my eye. "Who's Ani DiFranco?"

She gasps, eyes wide. "What kind of question is that?" She's overdoing it a bit, but she's not the star of the school play for nothing.

I shrug. "One someone who has never heard of her would ask?"

"Put it in, put it in!" she insists, turning up the volume. We listen in silence for a moment to something that sounds more like poetry than music, and then a plucking guitar arrives. "I like it," I tell Kim after a few verses.

"I can't believe you don't know who Ani DiFranco is," she says, making a left turn past the complex where my pediatrician's office is. "Are you sure you're gay?"

My breath catches. "I'm not gay."

She looks over at me, mortified. "Oh my god, I . . . I'm so sorry. I thought . . . I heard some people talking at rehearsal, they said you came out over the summer."

I turn my head to look out the passenger window, hands twisting in my lap. "I did. I'm, uh, bisexual?" I hate the way it comes out as a question.

"Oh," she says. Over the speakers, Ani is scatting little "aahs" and "ohs." We listen to her sing about drowning for a moment before the girl beside me sighs. "I'm sorry. I shouldn't have assumed."

I still can't look back at her. I don't know why I feel so embarrassed. "It's OK. I know a lot of people think it's basically the same thing, or that I'm just . . . pretending I like girls too so I don't have to like, *actually* be gay." I turn toward her, weirdly angry and maybe a little hurt. "But if I was gay, I would have said I was gay. I don't care what anyone thinks. I'm bisexual."

"Use your education, and take an educated guess, about meeeeee . . ."

She turns in to my neighborhood, drawing up to the security gate. I give the guard my name and he waves us through. We drive by golf courses, a canal full of ducks, and rows of identical houses with identical cars parked outside. An old woman grips a walker as she makes the journey from her battered Cadillac to an open front door. We pull up to my house, and as I expected, my car is sitting in the driveway. I'm sure Aiden is upstairs taking his daily post-school nap, and my calls and texts are ignored on his phone.

I grab my bag. "Thanks for the ride." Before I can open the door, her hand is on my arm.

"Hey," she says. I look back at her. It's golden hour and the sun is streaming through the window, illuminating her face. She is the most beautiful girl I've ever seen. "Thank you for correcting me. I'm sure it's fucking annoying to have people . . . get you wrong."

My throat is tight. Her hand is so hot on mine. "Yeah. Um, you're welcome?"

Something lingers between us for a moment. But then I remember that she is older, is into girls, and whatever camaraderie she just extended about me isn't really about *me,* but about something that's shared between us. And right now, that's enough.

CHAPTER Three

"IT'S ONLY TWO million, can you believe?" Everett says, without a hint of irony.

"What a deal."

The apartment is on the upper part of the Upper West Side, and Everett complained about how long it took to get here from Chelsea for the entire Uber ride.

"The floors will need to be replaced, and the ceiling too." He sashays through the open space, a general surveying the battlefield. "The exposed brick will have to go too. No one is doing exposed brick anymore. New appliances, new lighting. We'll tear down that wall"—he points toward the living room—"and go for something open concept. So with renovations, maybe . . . three? That would barely cover the closing costs if I was buying downtown, can you imagine?"

I cannot. My rent is $1,200 a month, with two roommates, and we steal my neighbor's wifi, which they should have thought about before hanging a photo of Susan Boyle on their door, naming the wifi after her, and making the password "IDreamedADream."

"Can you start taking notes? I want to get as much of this down as I can while I'm in the moment and unfettered by the ugly financial details."

I take notes on my phone as Everett moves through the brownstone he and his husband are buying, jotting down random phrases like "urban pastoral," "sensory deprivation tank," and "Stephen Sondheim's sex dungeon." When I'm back at our office, I'll attempt to translate all of this into a mood board and begin scouting pieces. It's usually fun to shop with rich people's money, to fill their homes with lovely expensive things I will never be able to afford.

"There are two guest rooms, so you can spend the night whenever you want when we're working late. I can't imagine how long it would take you to get back to *Chinatown* from here!"

And he means it. If Everett had things his way, I would move in with him and his husband, an endless slumber party of billable hours. He loves to say I'm his friend first, protégé second, assistant third.

"*What* is *this*? Julia, I told you I wanted golden beets, not red ones." Everett cracks open one of the floor-to-ceiling windows overlooking Riverside Park and chucks the $17 juice I purchased for him into the trees. I'm pretty sure there's a scream from the street below.

"My bad." I'm ninety-eight percent positive the voice memo he sent me this morning specified red beets, but Everett doesn't pay me to tell him he's wrong. He pays me—off the books—to drop off his dry cleaning, pick up upholstery samples for couches that cost more than a year of college tuition, and buy artisanal poppers for the sex parties he hosts every summer on Fire Island.

"I need to be alone in the space for a bit. Can you grab me an iced macadamia nut latte? And get yourself something, of course. It's going to be a long day."

"Sure, I'll be back in twenty." When I get back he'll probably insist he asked for his latte hot and equal parts soy milk and half-and-half, but that's a problem for future Julia—and whoever he drops *that* drink on.

Everett's brownstone sits on a quiet, tree-lined street, the kind of street you can only afford to live on if your net worth is at least eight digits. Everett's would be even if he didn't design the homes of the rich and famous—not the rich and famous anyone has heard of, of course. We're talking people with *real* money, the kind of money that makes it both possible and preferable to be mostly anonymous. Everett has access to them because he's one of them, a trust fund baby with good taste who fills the summer (and winter . . . and spring . . . and fall) homes of the elite with vintage vases that probably belong in museums and oversees the contractors who soundproof their private screening rooms.

I met Everett through River. They went to the same prep school and bonded at alumni events over being the only queers who came out, despite most of their classmates having canoodled with them. Everett is ten years older than me, though he and his dermatologist would disagree, and hired me after fifteen minutes of conversation and two vodka martinis.

"What interests you about interior design?" he'd asked.

At the time, the real answer had been "Eight hundred dollars a week." But I didn't say that.

"I like the idea of transforming a space, that the things you've decided to fill your home with say something about you." Bullshit, but bullshit I've come to believe. I love walking into one of our clients' homes when it's raw and unfinished and seeing the possibility of what it *could* be. In the year and a half that I've worked for Everett, he's slowly handed me more and more responsibility. He listens when I weigh in on cabinet finishes or paint colors and has even started sending me out to oversee installations when he's busy snowboarding with Anderson Cooper.

A text from Everett: **Can you grab some wet wipes at CVS? This place doesn't even have a bidet :/ and pls start sourcing rose quartz countertops for the Thompsons' meditation room.**

Waiting in line at the coffee shop, I unlock my phone and scroll through my recent calls to find a contractor's number. At the top of the list is Aiden's call from the day before.

Kim Cameron. Kim Cameron. Kim Cameron.

In CVS I find the most expensive wet wipes possible and grab two packs, plus a moisturizer some beauty influencer convinced me to buy, charging it all to the company credit card Everett would rather *literally* die than check the statement for. And a pack of gum. And a phone charger.

Back at the brownstone, Everett accepts his latte. "I asked for almond milk, Julia, but it's fine. Is everything OK with you today? You seem a bit off, babe."

I hand Everett his wet wipes and smile beatifically. "Everything is fine."

CHAPTER Four

BORN TO BRIDE is nearly empty.

I spent the entire train ride praying it would be full of brides and the staff would be so busy that my transaction would be handled with brutal efficiency. More than anything, I prayed Lorraine would not be working today. I wanted to be in and out of there as quickly as possible. If I wasn't saving literally every penny for this damn wedding, I would have paid the exorbitant delivery fee, but I'd checked my bank account balance, winced, and started applying winged eyeliner, which heavily flags *girl* on the days I can't be bothered to wear something feminine.

There's no one behind the register, and the only sales associate I can spot is helping a middle-aged woman choose between garters. I wait for her at the register, texting Kyle about our movie plans for this evening and replying to the selfie my mom just sent me, identical to every single selfie she's ever taken. Beautiful! Did you do something with your hair?

"Picking up?"

Shit motherfucker fuck shit. Lorraine is behind the register, her smirking lips painted a shocking pink. "Hi, yes, I got a notification that my dress was ready."

She nods and starts clanking away at the ancient computer terminal. "Ah yes, the Rosenberg wedding."

"You must get a lot of those."

She glances up at me, unmoved. "Weddings?"

"Rosenbergs."

Her mouth purses. "That sounds a little anti-Semitic."

"Rosenberg is *my last name*. The groom is my *brother*."

She makes a *hmph* noise and clacks away at the screen. "Here we are. *Julia Rosenberg*," she draws out the name, the *allegedly* all but audible under the words. "I see you've already paid the base price, but there was an additional tailoring fee. We had to let it out in a few places to suit your . . . unique proportions." She makes *unique* sound like a slur, and I'm sure the word she'd rather use *is* one.

"Why wasn't I informed about these fees at my fitting?" Perhaps she can be reasoned with. Or bullied. I channel my mother and slip into my best *I'd like to speak to the manager* voice. "Since I'm just finding out about this now, I'm sure you can do something about waiving them."

"I wish I could." There's not a single ounce of sincerity in her voice. Her pink lipstick has cracked into the lines of her mouth, and in one place it's smudged over her teeth. She's narrow and hawklike, spends her days bullying brides for minimum wage plus commission, and probably goes home at night with aching feet. She's enjoying this little bit of power she has over me, probably hoping I'll cause a scene so she can have mall security escort me out.

"Fine," I say through a smile as nasty as I can make it.

"Excuse me, I think I need the next size up."

The voice has come from the door to the dressing room, and as annoyed as I am to be interrupted when all I want is to get the hell out of this store, this mall, the entire situation . . . something in it makes me turn.

It's Kim Cameron. Shit motherfucker fuck shit.

Kim Cameron is standing at the entrance to the dressing rooms, wearing a burnt sienna version of the dress I'm picking up. I can see why she's asking for a different size: she is spilling out of it, clasping the back closed behind her. It's not necessarily a bad look. The color offsets her dark skin remarkably, the slit shows off a shapely leg, and her long braids are loose over bare shoulders. She is even more beautiful than I remember.

In high school, Kim Cameron was *that girl*. Everyone knew who she was but no one was really *friends* with her. She was simply too cool to be something as banal as an active participant in the high school social structure. She skipped class to smoke cigarettes in the abandoned Chase Bank down the road but was always near the top of her class. She starred in the school play but never came to Denny's with the rest of the cast on opening night. She came out halfway through freshman year, dated a sophomore at the local community college, *and* hooked up with the homecoming queen. Until I moved to New York City, Kim Cameron was the coolest person I'd ever met.

She was also, of course, the biggest crush of my adolescence.

Then I remember Aiden's call. Kim Cameron is my future sister-in-law's maid of honor. We're walking down the aisle together at their wedding.

Rachel is a year older than me, making her three years older than Aiden. She met Kim in college, where they roomed together freshman year. Aiden was friends with Rachel's brother and the two hit it off at a party. The only memorable conversation Rachel and I ever had was at my twin brothers' b'nai mitzvah, when we got drunk and gushed for an hour about how cool Kim Cameron was. It was the first time I saw what Aiden saw in her—she had good taste.

And now Kim Cameron and I are standing in a shitty bridal store in a shitty mall as I have one of the shittiest interactions I've had in months.

Recognition is blossoming in her eyes, with the customary momentary adjustment I'm used to from everyone who knew me *before*. "Julia? Julia Rosenberg?"

"Hey, Kim. It's been a while. You look . . . I guess that's for the wedding."

"Yeah, I *really* shouldn't have left it until the last minute. Can we . . . I'm about to burst out of this dress. Give me a minute." To Lorraine: "I need the next size up."

Lorraine checks her computer for a moment as Kim and I wait in that awkward silence that you want to fill but have no idea how. "Unfortunately I don't have the next size up. I can order it for you, but it'll take three weeks."

The wedding is in three weeks.

"And I don't have a sample for you to try. We only carry up to a ten in store."

Was this woman grown in a lab for the specific purpose of mortifying future bridesmaids?

"That's pretty fucking stupid considering the national average dress size in the U.S. is a sixteen," Kim says. It's the same tone she used to take with football players in high school who called her "Black Ellen," a cruel but deeply unimaginative insult.

Despite having spent the last few minutes trying to disappear, I unfold myself into the conversation, which is now bordering on confrontation.

"Kim, my dress is the same style, just in a different color, and it's a fourteen. Maybe you could try it on and make sure the size is right and they can rush order you something?"

Lorraine scoffs. "We can only make orders based on one of our sample dresses, this has already been altered."

Kim turns to her.

"Ma'am"—which is just about the cruelest thing you can call a middle-aged bridal sales associate and not be thrown out of the store—"perhaps you can make an exception *just this once* so that I can try the dress on. I'm the maid of honor and I wouldn't want to have to call another store, or corporate customer service, and let them know how . . . challenging it was to order my dress."

Kim glances down at the woman's ugly pink name tag, clearly taking note. "Lorraine."

Oh wow, I did not expect Kim to channel her own inner Karen, but needs must.

Lorraine huffs, shoots me a look dripping with acidic disdain, and heads to the back, ostensibly to grab my dress.

"Julia, if you don't mind sticking around for a minute, maybe we can find somewhere to grab a drink?" Kim's smiling. I'm trying hard not to look at the places where her dress is straining to cover her skin.

"Well, I *did* see a Cheesecake Factory on my way in . . ."

"Perfect."

CHAPTER Five

KIM CAMERON AND I are sitting in a booth at the Cheesecake Factory, sharing a bread basket. If my high school self could see me now, she'd scream.

Well, if we're being technical about it, *he'd* scream. And then ask why I have boobs, and if he could touch them.

The waiter drops off our drinks—Pineapple Moscow Mule for me and my insatiable sweet tooth, whiskey ginger for Kim—and encourages us to take our time with the menu. We'll need it, considering it's roughly as thick as a *Twilight* book. We're talking *Breaking Dawn*.

"So—" we say in unison. I sip my drink to make it clear she can go first. I don't know what I was going to say anyway, having used up all my small talk on the trek through the mall from Born to Bride.

Kim's teeth are very white and sharp when she smiles, dark-pink lips fuller than filler could ever make mine—and I've done the research. Kim was pretty and aloof in high school, the kind of emo waif I always imagined myself with. Now she is devastatingly hot, her face more angular, her body immaculately curved but *solid*. She was a bit more delicate in high school, but now she's hardened into steel. She looks like she could tear me apart. I'd let her.

"How've you been? It's been a long time. I've heard things here and there from Rachel and, you know, the internet."

Another enamel-eroding gulp of my cocktail. "I'm good. Fine. I don't live in Florida so . . . there's that."

We both laugh. I've met more than a few Floridian expats in New York and we all have the same story: weirdos who escaped as soon as we could. Among my friends who have left the Sunshine State are a burlesque-dancer-slash-mortician, a baker who only crafts cakes shaped like vulvas, and a nonbinary software developer who dresses exactly like Trinity in *The Matrix*.

Lounging on her side of our booth, whiskey in hand, Kim somehow looks like she is at some horrifically exclusive after-hours party. Even in the unflattering overhead lighting, she glows.

"Not being in Florida is certainly a win. Have you lived here since high school?"

"At the Cheesecake Factory? Yeah, I've got a lovely little studio set up in the walk-in freezer."

Another laugh, her eyes crinkling. "I've been in New York since college," I continue. "Floundered around for a couple of years figuring things out after I graduated. Not that I *have* figured anything out."

Her eyebrow raises. "Well, you figured *one* thing out."

I laugh. "The girl thing, yes. Everything else, not so much. I somehow fell into interior design, which I like and am weirdly good at."

"That makes sense." She rips off a piece of brown bread and starts to butter it. "You always had a very clear sense of style, even in high school."

I attempt to duck behind my bangs. "I'm not sure my *Hot Topic sale rack* vibe was all that stylish."

"You had a point of view. That was pretty rare where and when we grew up."

"And likely why I left. What have you been up to since then?"

She shrugs, swirling her drink. "This and that. I wanted to make music for a while but was never all that good. Then I dipped my toes into event production, but I hated always smelling like secondhand cigarette smoke. Did corporate marketing for a bit, but the money is *not* worth how psychotic everyone is. Now I mostly consult."

"So you're what, professionally *cool*? Sounds about right. You were like, the most interesting person I met until I turned eighteen."

She laughs. "Don't sell me short, I'm still the most interesting person you've met."

We clink our glasses in mock cheers.

I suppose it's time to address the elephant in the Cheesecake Factory. "You'll certainly be the most interesting person at the wedding."

"Maybe not. After all, you'll be there."

"Aw, shucks." I take another swig of my drink. "Being *interesting* is not all it's cracked up to be. A wedding is inherently a family reunion."

"But one with ice sculptures." Kim knocks back the rest of her drink and waves over the waitress. "Last week Rachel told me over FaceTime that they're having a hard time deciding what kinds of animals to do. Swans are *so* 2012."

We order another round of drinks from the waiter.

"That's nothing." I tear viciously into the bread between us. "Last I heard they were trying to rent a replica of the couch from *Friends* for wedding photos."

"Why?"

"I don't know. Straight people?"

"Straight people."

"How's your sudden promotion to maid of honor going?" I ask. "It's a lot of responsibility in such a short amount of time."

"Honestly, it's been a nightmare. I love Rachel, but you know what she's like on a normal day."

"The first time I met her I tried to buy Adderall off of her because I assumed she was on, you know, a lot of it."

"Right," Kim says. "I still don't know why she needed me to step in all of a sudden. She and Jenna were always so tight."

How to handle this? If Rachel didn't tell her, it was probably for a reason, although if I'm being generous, that reason was probably to spare my feelings.

"Jenna didn't want to walk down the aisle with me."

Kim's brow knits in confusion. "But you're Aiden's sister. You're the best woman."

"Yeah, but I *used* to be Aiden's brother and I was *supposed* to be the best man. Jenna is pretty conservative." That I refer to myself even in the past tense as male is a testament to how the drinks are hitting me. It's no secret that I'm trans, that I haven't always identified or presented as a woman, but in the current landscape of trans politics, it's not exactly the *done* thing to admit to ever having been a gender other than the one you are now, or always were, or whatever.

What I'm *supposed* to say and think and believe with every fiber of my being is that I am a girl, have always been a girl, was born in the wrong body, and that my transition was a righteous victory in my lifelong battle against the assignment forced on me against my will at birth. And no matter how true or false or *complicated* that may be when applied to my real lived experience, I at the very least should not hand ammunition to the millions of people ready and willing to call me a wolf in women's clothing.

"What a cunt," Kim says, leaning back against the vinyl booth. "I'm so sorry. Did Jenna say something to you?"

"No, my brother told me."

"Damn, that's shitty. Why did you even need to know that?"

I guess I understand why she'd think that, but she doesn't know my relationship with Aiden, that our closeness was born out of our willingness to share the ugliest parts of ourselves and our lives. Two children of divorce so used to being lied to by their parents that the only way to survive it was promising to never lie to each other.

But I don't know how to put that into words Kim will understand. This is a girl who, if I remember the gossip correctly, spent most of her senior year living with her grandmother after her mom found out she was gay and kicked her out. I don't want to throw in her face that my brother is such a good, ugh, *ally* that he wouldn't stand for having a bigot at his wedding.

And the sympathy swelling in Kim's eyes is a little patronizing, sure, but it's also kind of nice. It's the same way she looked at me when she saw me sitting alone outside the auditorium. That sympathy is the reason she gave me a ride home, and let me get close to her for long enough to set my heart—and hormones—on fire. Maybe... there's something in that. A chance to get a little more of Kim's attention.

Not that I'm desperate or attention starved. I have plenty of fulfilling sex with hot people, but this is Kim Cameron, my unattainable first crush suddenly thrust back into my life, the first person I ever wanted so bad I thought I'd die from it. Maybe it's the mall, or whatever preservatives are in the Cheesecake Factory bread, but that old teenage obsession is roaring through me all over again and I'm as desperate for her as when we were dumb gay teenagers. *You have an angle,* some reptilian part of my brain hisses. *Use it.*

I shrug and cast my eyes downward, trying not to oversell it. "I don't know. I guess they were a little upset about the whole thing." And they had been, but *on my behalf.*

"*Dealing* with me in the context of their wedding has been, I don't know, a constant source of tension," I say, feeling stupid as I say the words but also enjoying the opportunity to ham it up. "Aiden and I aren't even that close," I say, surprised my tongue doesn't trip over the lie. "When he asked me to be his best man it was honestly kind of surprising."

Kim nods. "I thought it'd be Ben Otsuka."

I truly cannot deal with the thought of Ben Otsuka right now, so I just let my mouth run. "Well, it was me. And when he asked me, I was just like, figuring the girl stuff out, but I wasn't ready to talk about it yet, so I just said yes." That was all true, but once I *was* ready to talk about it, Aiden had been kind and supportive. He'd done the work to educate himself, to admit that it might take him some time to get everything right while assuring me that he wanted to.

"We've all spent the past couple of years *not* dealing with it." Also technically true: everyone had been so cool there hadn't been much to deal with.

"OK, so you're my best *woman*," Aiden had said, arm around my shoulders. "Big whoop."

"Anyway," I say, attempting to project the deep inner fortitude of someone *rising above it*, "I just have to make it through this wedding." I finish off my drink and set it down on the table, and Kim makes the world stop when she puts her hand down on mine. It feels like a live wire.

"You deserve so much better than that, Julia."

My insides twist like the snakes my cousin Max used to keep in a terrarium, making them fight for dead mice. I'm ecstatic and ashamed all at once. It's *working*.

Our second round of drinks arrives and we order a few small plates to share—I don't think my stomach could handle an hour-long train ride full of Cheesecake Factory food, no matter how bad I want to see if Evelyn's Favorite Pasta is as good as I remember. I ask the waiter to make sure there are no carrots in anything—I'm intensely allergic and do not need a swollen face when I'm trying to woo my high school crush into a pity fuck— and he nods without really looking up from his notepad. "Sure, man, no problem."

Ouch. Not ideal, but whatever. This is the kind of casual misgendering I'd usually brush off. This guy has been checked out the entire time he's been helping us, probably counting the minutes until his shift ends, and has likely inferred, in that unthinking way most cis people do when hearing my husky voice on the phone or from the back seat of an Uber, that I'm a dude. In the early days of my transition, I would have made a stink and corrected him, maybe even asked the manager to comp us a round of drinks. But almost four years in, I've learned that it's so much less work to just let it go because the only person who is going to be embarrassed in that situation is me. This is a random waiter at the Cheesecake Factory who I'm never going to see again. Who cares if he assumed I wasn't a woman?

As it turns out, Kim cares.

"It's *miss*, dude." Miss Dude. Good drag name. "Her pronouns are she, her, hers." She says it with such condescending disdain it causes the waiter to finally break out of his disaffected haze and take us in. He gulps.

"I'm so sorry, uh, ladies." His cheeks are turning red. Kim corrected him in a way that made *him* look like an idiot, something I've never been able to manage. He flees.

"He's a clueless asswipe, Julia." Kim is looking at me with concern that I'd find condescending from anyone else, but she rests her hand on mine again, and the electricity of her touch is just as intense the second time. She looks even more open and sympathetic than she was a few minutes ago. "God, that guy, your family . . . cis people suck. I apologize on our behalf," she says. It could be a joke but she says it seriously, and I'd love nothing more than to roll my eyes, but they're too busy looking down her shirt as she leans over the table.

Snap out of it, Daytona's best Cher voice chides in the back of my mind.

"Don't worry about it." I'm doing my best trans martyr drag, a woman struggling to be above the constant cruelty of a cisheteronormative society. This is true, in a way, but I've conditioned myself as much as possible to be unaffected by it, and insulated by queer people who get it and non-queer people who make an effort to be, ugh, *allies*.

Kim doesn't know that, though, and playing it up means more sympathy. More touching. We're going to walk down the aisle together at Aiden's wedding, and the more time we spend together, the more protective she feels of me . . . maybe that hand touching could become something more.

Because that would be the real validation, wouldn't it? The final confirmation that I'd conquered womanhood: the first girl I'd ever been obsessed with, who I could never *have* because she was only into girls, being into me. All the waiters and baristas and customer service representatives in the world could misgender me, but they'd never be able to take that away. I'd at last be the real, actual, best woman.

"You deserve so much better than that," she says, echoing her words from before. She's laying it on thick, which feels like another point in my favor.

The waiter reappears and sheepishly apologizes again before telling us he's comped our entire meal. My ears burn with embarrassment, and I hate how he lingers, desperately eager to make sure he's forgiven for his mistake. But I don't hate that Kim hasn't let go of my hand. I don't hate it at all when she squeezes it as the waiter finally rushes away.

"Are you worried something like *that* will happen at the wedding?" she asks. "Like, outright ignorance and hostility?"

"No, everyone uses the right name and pronouns. It's nothing . . . obvious." That would be too easily disproven at the wedding. "They've been great on paper. To my face." I dig up that awful first year, when people were bumbling and thoughtless but, generally, trying. "There's what people *say* and then what they think, what they *believe,* deep down inside. The way people like, falter for a minute when they have to introduce you to someone. Or never call you pretty, just say you look nice. Or pretend *buddy* is a gender-neutral term." I'd rather die than use the term *microaggression,* but I don't even need to. Kim is one hundred percent the kind of girl who has read *Conflict Is Not Abuse.*

This part is true. My whole life, I've been the odd duck, not quite the black sheep but maybe . . . the gray goat. Before people knew *what* was different about me, they still knew *something* was, and that difference was like bulletproof glass between us. They could see me, and I could see them, but sound and meaning had no way to travel through. As the years went by and more and more family members coupled up, figured themselves out, and started having kids and mortgages while I moved across the country and changed almost everything about myself that I possibly could, the distance between us became a chasm, one I didn't know how to cross.

But remarkably, transitioning had been the bridge. People who'd always thought I was quiet or sensitive suddenly had an explanation as to why, and though the mechanics of it confused them for a while, it also brought into focus some element of me that had previously eluded them. I made more sense than I ever had before.

But Kim didn't have to know that.

"Have you thought about just, I don't know, not going?" She's treading carefully. "That's shitty, but it would be understandable if you bailed."

Too far, too far, now I have to backtrack. I need something a little more logical than just playing the martyr. Kim would want a woman who stands up for herself.

"If I don't go, *I'm* the bad guy. I'm a drama queen, I'm making their special day all about me. I'd be the snowflake so sensitive she skipped her own brother's wedding, and the rest of my family . . ." I trail off. I must be careful here and not say anything that will be too obviously disproven by reality. Is there a relationship in my life so inscrutable, so intrinsically complicated, Kim would never know if that person and I were obsessed with each other or wanted each other dead?

I think again of Kim's senior year and know exactly what to say. "Anyway, my mother would *kill* me."

I can't even look up to see how she takes this, but her hand spasms against mine. She shifts our palms so that we're holding hands on the cold marble tabletop.

My stomach falls directly into my ass and my head is starting to throb like it's been stomped on by the mules my drink is named after. It's a brutal combination of success, guilt, and lust.

"I get it," she says, voice tight. I am, officially, horrible. "And hey, you won't be in this alone." She grins. "*I'm* the maid of honor now, and I'm gonna make sure you have the *best* time."

I'm riding too high on my win to see it as the loss—for my conscience, my self-respect, whatever—it really is. "I'm going to show up at that wedding and be so *fucking* happy for them," I promise, which was already the plan, but now there's sexy intrigue behind it. I'm going to convince Kim that everything sucks by being completely normal. It's kind of genius. Evil genius. But whatever, it's a couple of days of little white lies to get some attention from *Kim Cameron*. "I'm going to be so fucking *nice* about it and I'm going to look *fucking incredible!*"

The warm, sympathetic look she's been giving me turns speculative, and if I'm not mistaken it . . . appraising? Maybe even . . . hungry. "I could see that," she says with a little smirk.

The waiter drops off our appetizers and scurries away as we dig in. I eagerly shove food into my mouth to stop me from running it and getting in deeper than I already am.

Kim starts putting together a Thai lettuce wrap, and even her *hands* are sexy. "Are you bringing a date?" Am I going crazy or is there a bit of sheepishness in her tone?

"I don't have a lot of prospects right now." My last relationship—if you can call three months of admittedly incredible sex with a married Park Slope lesbian a relationship—ended in August when Sharon decided she'd rather take her toddler to Disneyland than fuck me in the back seat of her Subaru. "What about you?" I scoop artichoke dip onto a red tortilla chip.

"Flying solo," she says. "Ugh, I don't know why I said it like that. I'm not bringing anyone. I'm single."

We catch each other's eyes for a moment, but the moment's broken when the hot dip burns my mouth. I squeal and spend the next few minutes with my tongue pressed against a glass of ice water as Kim laughs delightedly.

"I suppose I can save you a dance at the reception," I say, keeping my tone light but letting my interest show a bit. "The maid of honor and the best woman should be able to . . . get along."

She leans back against the booth, too beautiful to believe. "I think we'll get along just fine," she says, and I hope she's right.

CHAPTER

Six

"ARE WE ALLOWED to be here?" I ask, carefully clutching my drink so as not to spill it on the fur rug.

River, clad in leather pants so tight I'm worried about their circulation, admires their legs in the mirror. "Oh absolutely, Hannah G and I are basically family."

From his perch on said pop star's marble vanity, Kyle snorts. "How many phones has she thrown at you this year?"

River smiles, snapping a selfie. "Three. I got to keep this one when my nose cracked the screen."

We are staked out in the pop star's SoHo loft, with its floor-to-ceiling windows and the kind of furniture you only buy if you become very rich very quickly but have no taste. Maybe I should connect Hannah G with Everett and try to get a commission out of it.

After mixing a round of cocktails ("If she were here she'd *obviously* offer us a drink," River had insisted) we'd decamped to a walk-in closet straight out of a Russian billionaire's YouTube handbag collection tour. The "dressing room" is the size of my entire apartment *and* the bodega downstairs. Every wall is full of floor-to-ceiling shelves, every shelf filled with designer bags, shoes, and clothing. When we arrived, Daytona grabbed a Birkin and told us she'd be in the guest bedroom taking nudes. She's been gone . . . awhile.

Giving their leather-clad legs one more satisfied nod, River meets my eyes in the mirror. "Jules, I'm so happy you changed your mind. We are going to find you something *sickening* to wear to this bar mitzvah."

"It's a wedding."

"Sure." They walk to a clothing rack nearly buckling under the weight of what must be at least twenty gowns and start flipping through the hangers. "How do you feel about ass cleavage? Prada is all about VBC this season."

"VBC?" I ask, not really wanting to know.

"Visible butt crack. There was a *Women's Wear Daily* article about it."

"I'll make sure to mention that to the security guards as they drag me screaming from the synagogue."

They start flinging dresses onto a chaise lounge. "Wonderful, but don't let them grab you too hard. These are 'borrowed,' after all." They even do the air quotes.

I slink back toward the vanity and hop up next to Kyle. "Why do I feel like we're in *The Bling Ring* and River is Emma Watson?"

Kyle snorts. "Did you see the look the doorman gave us on our way in? I'm pretty sure he was pressing a panic button under the desk."

I take a sip of Hannah G's expensive vodka. "Fabulous, the

only way this week could get more complicated is with an arrest."

Kyle shoots me a sympathetic look. Of our little group, he's the only one with an attention span long enough for emotional labor. River is the friend I call when I need a mindless night of clubbing. Daytona will read me to filth when I need to get my shit together and then do my makeup afterward. Kyle is the person who will drop everything and crawl into bed with me when I need a cuddle. We met at a yoga class six years ago, left early, had sex, and decided we were better off as sisters. When I guiltily confessed my scheme at Tony's after I saw Kim last weekend, Kyle closed the bar early and turned up at my apartment with *Erin Brockovich* open on his laptop.

"How are you doing?" he asks. I know he wants the truth, not the bullshit—we're all a bit too self-involved for faux sympathy—but it still feels like an emotional booby trap.

"Stupendous." I sweep the hand holding my drink out to take in the room. "We've broken into the apartment of someone who currently has two songs on the Billboard Hot 100 and are stealing her extremely expensive clothing so I can con a hot lesbian into paying attention to me at my brother's wedding."

"It's not stealing," River corrects, holding up something pink and shiny. "It's *styling*. What about PVC? Though it *might* squeak when you walk down the aisle."

"I won't be walking down the aisle, remember? This dress is for the rehearsal dinner."

"Then I'll add it to the maybe pile." They fling the dress into a pile of couture whose value would likely cover the down payment on Everett's brownstone *and* a custom sectional.

Kyle tops off my glass. "Are you OK? Still feeling . . . icky?"

There's no use pretending in front of Kyle, in front of any of them. They've seen me at my lowest, the nights I cried after a co-worker called me the wrong name, or a girl I had a crush on said we'd be better as friends. Daytona gave me my first shot of estrogen, River showed me how to walk in heels, Kyle came with me to the courthouse to get my name legally changed and bought us oysters after. These are the people it's OK for me to be ugly in front of, both physically and emotionally.

"I know I should feel bad but it's just . . . twisting the truth." There is a lot of very expensive and completely terrible art in Hannah G's closet, along with a People's Choice Award and some *very* interesting Polaroids featuring a certain Oscar winner. I didn't know Hannah G was into British MILFs, another thing we have in common besides our waist-to-hip ratio.

"Yes, twisting it into a *lie*," River says, flinging a sequin skirt onto the pile.

"Maybe I've been feeling a little guilty." A lot more than a little. "Fine, I feel like dog shit."

"Atta girl," says Kyle, relieved.

"We've been waiting for you to crack," adds River, looking disdainfully at something large and covered with tulle.

"It's about damn time, bitch." Daytona saunters into the room, mercifully clothed, Birkin perched on her arm in a perfect imitation of an Upper East Side hedge fund wife. "You've been spiraling, and the only one who didn't realize it was *you*." She sidles up to River. "Would she miss the bag if it came home with me?"

"She'd hunt you down to the ends of the earth. Or at least the end of Williamsburg."

Daytona sighs longingly and replaces the Birkin on a shelf full of nearly identical bags in every shade imaginable. She turns back toward the vanity and cracks a grin. "At least the bitch won't miss the champagne." We've been chilling a bottle and Daytona pops it with practiced ease, pouring glasses for everyone. Then she fixes her deep brown eyes, always far too knowing, on me.

"You've completed step one, which was admitting that you're a mess."

I sniffle. "I don't know if I'd use the word *mess*—"

"I would. You've been quiet and moody and you keep snapping at everyone, and unless you're trying to be so unclockable you've given yourself phantom PMS, we can admit your loathsome lesbian liaison is why."

I shoot her a withering glare. "Oh no, you got me. I guess I should stop carrying tampons in my purse *just in case.*"

Kyle inspects a pair of Hannah G's diamond earrings. "I mean, they came in handy when River gave themself a deviated septum at the rave we went to under that bridge last year."

"*Do you know how hard it is to get blood out of pony hair!*" the three of us shriek in unison, cackling at the memory.

"Remind me to *never* buy ketamine from my landlord again," River shouts from the pile of chiffon they're buried under, unflappable as ever. "Speaking of, does anyone want a bump?"

"Neigh," says Kyle, and considering River's offering a horse tranquilizer, that could go either way. "Julia, we know that you've been under a lot of stress. This isn't Tumblr in 2011: no one expects you to keep calm and carry on."

"Except those breeders down in Boca," Daytona interjects. "But you made your bed, now you get to lie in it while we judge you."

"I still can't believe you've gotten yourself immersed in something straight out of a low-budget gay romantic comedy," says Kyle, pouring another glass of champagne. "I know you love a good *angst with a happy ending* AU, but this is a bit much."

"Maybe it can just be more *friends to lovers*." I can hope. "Although I've barely talked to Kim since high school, and we weren't very good friends then. We're just two queer women supporting each other during a stressful event, one of whom has lied to the other one in order to get into her pants and then marry her and adopt three children and buy a house in Cherry Grove." Even a wedding hookup seemed like a stretch, but after a few hours with Kim all of my old high school yearning had returned and taken hold. I'd been writing her name in the notebook I used at work. I thought about her every morning when I woke up and every night before I went to bed. I hadn't had a proper crush in years, not since my intense fling with a paramedic who lived with his mother on Staten Island and fucked like a sex god. And I'd never had a crush as powerful or as all-consuming as my teenage love for Kim Cameron. I felt sixteen again, and it wasn't just because of the estrogen I'd injected three nights ago. "You'll all be invited out for the summer, of course."

"Is she hot?" asks Daytona, priorities always in order.

My cheeks flush, and my lips are loose from the champagne. "She is *so* hot. In high school, she was this cool loner in Doc Martens, but now she's like, sophisticated and sexy and masc but still a little alt." Another swig of champagne. "Great tits too."

Daytona whistles. "Crunchy and curvy, *right* up your alley."

She has a point. With men, I tend to favor skinny skater boys with tattoo sleeves, thick black glasses, and stupidly big dicks. With women, I go for girls who smell like patchouli, have at one point in their lives owned a wall tapestry from Urban Outfitters, and . . . well, have nice butts.

I stand on unsteady legs and wobble over to where River is beckoning me. "It doesn't matter if she's my type," I argue, only slurring a bit. "It's just a little wedding fling. No one has to get hurt and it probably won't even happen."

Kyle and Daytona exchange a glance. It reminds me of the knowing looks my parents gave each other when I was eight and told them I didn't want to play soccer anymore because of my "allergies" when it was because the team captain, Sarah, said she didn't want to marry me, even though I'd used her favorite Ring Pop flavor for the proposal.

"If you're going to be delusional, you might as well go for the full fantasy," says River, holding something black and slinky in their hands. "Let's turn you into Cinderella."

I smile, embarrassed to feel tears welling up. I don't deserve friends like these.

"One of the stepsisters, at least," calls Daytona, wrapping herself in a silk robe.

Or maybe I do.

An hour later I leave Hannah G's building, heavy garment bag slung over my shoulder and a Louis Vuitton duffle in my hand, to make the thankfully short trek home. I live on almost the exact divide where Chinatown meets Little Italy, and at this time of night, the smell of garlic wafts from every open window. After a night spent with my favorite people in the world and six figures worth of designer clothing in my hands, I finally feel like this wedding might be OK. Not amazing. But I'll survive, and look great doing it.

My phone buzzes in my pocket. A text from . . . Ben Otsuka.

> See you in two weeks ;)

CHAPTER
Seven

SIX DAYS BEFORE my brother's wedding, I load my bags into the back of Daytona's cherry red SUV. The trunk has barely any space left inside—it contains the industrial-grade fan she uses for hair-blowing purposes at her shows, a large trunk that serves as her makeup kit, a terrifying tangled ball of hair extensions, and no less than three large duffle bags stuffed with clothing erupting through the zippers in an orgiastic explosion of sequins and satin and spandex. There's also a single Timberland platform heel perched on top of an inflatable dolphin.

"Girl, are you living out of this car now?" I ask as I slide into the passenger seat. "Your trunk looks like Hannah G's greenroom." A few months before, River had managed to get us backstage at *Saturday Night Live*. Hannah G loved rolling with a squad and we'd filled in a few times, though she never remembered the name of anyone except Daytona, who was unforgettable. Her magnetism rivaled a pop star's, and I'd felt just as starstruck around her in the early days of our acquaintance as

I still felt anytime I saw River's boss, awkward and tongue-tied, desperate to be liked.

Sometimes I still wasn't sure if Daytona liked me, even when she went out of her way to do something nice like drive me to the airport, a truly thankless task. I couldn't quite believe I'd managed to become friends with someone as fascinating and fabulous as her.

"I'm driving down to Atlanta after I drop you off," Daytona says, turning off my street and heading toward LaGuardia. "I've got a few gigs there this weekend."

My friend is kind of an underground legend, often leaving for weeks at a time to tour various queer enclaves around the country. There's something about the alchemic combination of her utter fierceness and ability to bring serious pathos to any song she performs—I've seen her bring the house down with at least three Maroon 5 songs—that hypnotizes an audience, creating an electric charge that burns right through you until you're screaming her name and emptying your wallet for tip money.

We gossip a bit, talking about pretentious parties and precarious pairings as we drive over a cemetery on the BQE. Daytona lights a joint and passes it over. I usually prefer to pop an edible after I've made it through airport security, but one does *not* turn down Daytona's weed. She always brings the best shit back with her from her travels, and soon I'm feeling pleasantly stoned as we queue up a playlist and go full Lilith Fair, singing along to "Building a Mystery."

As the next track starts up, 10,000 Maniacs' cover of "Because the Night," I'm feeling unwound enough to say, without stopping to think first: "I'm nervous."

"You'll be fine," she says flippantly, taking a final huge drag before dropping the roach into a half-empty plastic water bottle. Daytona doesn't talk about her family much, but from what I gather, she wouldn't be surprised to see them holding GOD HATES FAGS signs and tiki torches at a white supremacist rally. Family to her is something built rather than something inherent, and trust is earned, not given by default. Not for the first time, I feel a swell of pride and gratitude that somehow, I've earned hers.

In our toxic little foursome, Kyle and I spend the most time together by ourselves, and tension has lingered between Daytona and me since I started transitioning. I had a sneaking suspicion in those early days that she felt a bit as if I'd stepped on her shoe while walking behind her. Being trans was *her* thing, mostly because she relished her position as the only girl in our group. In the years since, we've sanded down the rough edges of relating to each other as women, but I've always been worried she resented me not just for moving in on her territory, but for doing it with relative ease. Or at least, ease with my relatives.

"I hope so," I say, resting my head against the window and watching the sun filter through slowly turning autumn leaves on the cemetery trees. "I can't seem to escape this feeling of impending doom."

"You're headed to Florida, the stubby little chode of America. It's gonna fuck you, but you're not gonna enjoy it."

"You have such a way with words."

I unlock my phone and begin a ritual I've taken to performing daily, sometimes hourly, almost like a compulsion: stalking Kim Cameron's various social media profiles. She's fairly active but in a cool, detached, above-it kind of way. Her latest Instagram story is a blurry still photo of a dark bar and the side of someone's head. I can't decipher a single clue about where they are and who that person is, but I'm still full of jealousy that they're with Kim.

I've got it bad.

"You've got it bad," says Daytona, who has taken the red light as an opportunity to sneak a look at my phone—and into my head. "This girl must have grass-fed organic snatch."

"I wouldn't know."

"But you'd like to find out."

She turns to look at me, but I can't see her eyes through her huge tinted aviator sunglasses. "I don't know, Jules. I think you could have saved yourself a lot of trouble and just hit on her like a normal person."

I huff a snarky little laugh. "You don't get it. Kim Cameron was a hardcore lesbian in high school. She used to run a little side hustle breaking in people's Doc Martens for them."

"That's not a bad business idea."

"When she came out, my cellphone was a Motorola Razr. And she knew me when I had acne and greasy hair and oh, *was a boy*! I need every advantage I can get."

"But don't you feel like you're *taking* advantage?" It's not judgment in her voice, but something close to it.

"I won't deny that it's a moral gray area, but look, *she* was the one who assumed I was a damaged little transsexual who needed protection from the cruel world. I just . . . let her keep thinking that."

"You're the girl who cried TERF," she says, and I can't help but laugh. "I just wonder . . ."

"What?"

She shakes her head. "I don't know, babe. What happens when a wolf does show up to blow your house down?"

"You're mixing metaphors. Fairy tales. Whatever." But she has a point. I was so eager to let Kim believe my family was a minefield lying in wait to blow up the wedding, and it was easy because it hadn't ever happened to me. There was no lingering trauma flashing red.

Which just proved Daytona wrong. Everything would work out. I'd make some sad eyes around my mother, woo my crush, and ace the ultimate test: passing for a girl Kim Cameron would date.

CHAPTER Eight

MY FLIGHT TO Florida is, of course, delayed. We sit on the tarmac for two hours as the engine is checked, the wheels inspected, and the fuel tank refilled.

I sit pressed against a window, worrying about the garment bag tucked into the overhead compartment above me. There had been no question of checking my luggage: River assured me that the clothing and accessories I was borrowing ("transporting across state lines," they'd said, an alarmingly legal description) cost, in total, about the same as the plane. So that garment bag would be staying as close to me as possible for the next week. "Hannah G *will* prosecute," River had warned. "But don't worry, you'd make friends on the inside!"

As my three-hour flight stretched into five, I decide to use my time wisely and research for my upcoming endeavor. From the extensive in-flight entertainment menu, I'm able to assemble an extremely thorough watch list: *My Best Friend's Wedding, Muriel's Wedding, Rachel Getting Married, My Big Fat Greek Wed-*

ding, 27 Dresses, Four Weddings and a Funeral, The Wedding Planner. And then I throw in Wedding Crashers as a bonus.

As Rupert Everett asks Julia Roberts who is chasing her, we finally lift off. By the time the beverage cart comes around, I'm watching Nia Vardalos fall in love with Aidan from Sex and the City. I sip ginger ale—nectar of the gods when sipped at a high altitude—as family shenanigans unfold. Their hilarious dysfunction makes me think about my own family, which is just as dysfunctional and significantly less hilarious. From the inside, at least.

My parents, Dana and Stan, divorced when I was eight and Aiden was six. From that moment, there were two sides in our family: Mom's and Dad's. I was firmly on my mom's, Aiden on our dad's. It's not that I didn't try to get along with my dad, but I don't think he ever really understood me, or maybe he never really tried. Aiden he did understand: they liked all the same things, and Aiden so clearly got that my dad needed his little buddy when I was no longer interested. Every other weekend when we'd go to my dad's small apartment, the two of them would watch baseball in the living room, fueling their grating obsession with the Yankees, while I read and drew quietly out back by the canal.

I tried to spend more time with Mom, but she always insisted that it was important for me to have a relationship with him. Maybe she just wanted me out of the house after she'd married Randy, a Texan Jew who looked kind of like Robert Redford. Randy is one of the absolute strangest people I've ever met. Once, at an Italian restaurant, he wiped the sweat off his brow with a piece of garlic bread and then *ate* the bread. "You can't waste good food," he'd told us as I struggled to keep my chicken parmigiana down. "When I was a kid we lived off a can of beans a week!"

When I was in high school, Mom and Randy had kids of their own. Brody and Brian were the cutest babies I'd ever seen, but they've always been . . . unnerving. I only had a few years at home with them before I left for college, and that was mostly spent changing their diapers and being haunted by the sound of *Sesame Street* playing on the giant TV in our living room. But every time I visited, they'd be a little bigger, a little older, and they'd look at me with eyes that were far too knowing for children. Maybe it's the twin thing, that they always finish each other's sentences and that, despite knowing them their entire lives, I *still* cannot tell them apart. No one can, except for my mom. They've got a sort of eerie, haunted quality about them, and though I've never seen them like, torturing kittens or wandering the halls of an abandoned hotel asking other children to play with them, I wouldn't be surprised.

Halfway through my next movie selection and wondering what happened to Katherine Heigl's career, I climb over my sleeping seatmates and trek to the tiny airplane bathroom. In the glaring overhead light, I stare at my face in the mirror, searching out my genetic inheritance, the puzzle of pieces that link me to my bloodline as indelibly as my memories. There is my dad's tiny sloping nose, my mother's freckles, Grandpa's bushy eyebrows, and the squinty eyes my siblings and I all share.

When I first told my mom that I planned to transition, she cried. "I've always wanted a daughter," she'd admitted as I sat curled into a tight little knot in the darkness of my Brooklyn bedroom, phone clutched in hand, terror bleeding slowly and cautiously into relief. "Whatever makes you happy," my dad had said before quickly changing the subject. Randy had taken me to the mall and bought me a shopping bag full of makeup. Brody and Brian had nodded in silent unison and then gone to set something on fire, probably.

Aiden and I had sat in silence on the phone for a full minute. "OK," he'd finally breathed out. "OK. I love you. I love you... Julia."

"I love you, Julia!" he'd said on the phone days before. "I can't wait to see you mooning over Kim in the synagogue." My stomach had twisted in knots. "Do you think the 'Thong Song' is appropriate for the reception?"

I look back in the mirror, at the eyes shaped just like Aiden's, though his are hazel whereas mine are brown. I pull my shirt up and snap a photo of my breasts in the mirror to send to the group chat with my friends when we land. When I get back to my seat, I switch off *27 Dresses* and start *Scream*, needing to watch someone die violently. Could I pull off Drew Barrymore's blond, banged bob? Probably not.

I drift off for a while and dream about a mall sunk deep underground, full of fleshy orange zombies in tracksuits who tip over a Dippin' Dots vending machine. The glass cracks and a million spiders swarm out. Lorraine from Born to Bride shambles toward me, her tracksuit an ugly teal that clashes with her skin and her putrid pink lipstick.

I jolt awake as the plane touches down. Home sweet home.

CHAPTER
Nine

THE OPPRESSIVE FLORIDA humidity settles directly under my (*itty bitty,* Daytona's voice in my head supplies) breasts as soon as the automatic airport doors slide open. I should've worn a bra. My phone buzzes, *mother!* flashing on the screen.

"Hi, sweetie. Are you outside?" Bon Jovi is blasting at full volume in the background. Mom likes to multitask.

"Yeah, I'm standing under the Delta sign. The second one."

"I'll be there in twenty minutes." Of course. Dana Esterman is perpetually twenty minutes late. In middle school, I set the clock in her car back in an attempt to trick her into punctuality, but all it did was assure her that she had *more* time to dawdle. Thanks to her, I am chronically fifteen minutes early to every dinner, date, and doctor's appointment out of pure spite and lingering trauma.

I charge my phone inside and send my saucy selfie to our group chat, Diva Coalition. River sends back an answering ass shot. Kyle sends a meme of such esoteric humor it's funnier without context. Daytona, who checks her phone maybe once every four days and mutes every group chat the moment she's added to it, does not reply.

Here, Mom texts. I drag my battered luggage through the automatic doors and there she is, standing next to her neat little sedan, completely ignoring the traffic guard loudly insisting she actually can't park there.

My mother is five foot two and about a third of that is an intricately highlighted blond blowout. She's dressed like something straight out of a Nancy Meyers movie, all cream-colored, loose-fitting linen and expensive jewelry. Her skin is aggressively tan and freckled from the sun—I don't think she's ever applied sunscreen in her life, no matter how often her dermatologist insists she's going to wind up with skin the texture of a Louis Vuitton bag. She still looks like Goldie Hawn in *The First Wives Club* on a good day, and today is a *very* good day.

She holds out her arms to wrap around me. "My baby!" Her head—well, hair—reaches my neck. She smells like Big Red gum, vanilla coffee creamer, unleaded gas, and gardenias. She pulls back to rake sharp eyes over me, her eyes—*my eyes*—warm and welcoming. I realize, suddenly, how much I've missed her.

"I can't believe you're not wearing a bra."

Well, maybe not *that* much. "Good to see you too, Mom."

"Do you need help with your suitcase?" she asks, already climbing into the driver's seat, as if my carry-on doesn't weigh more than she does and as if she'd risk an acrylic nail attempting to lift it.

She does, however, pop the trunk, alarmingly full of Nordstrom shopping bags, which in turn are full of things she's bought and likely never even taken out of the car. In six months she'll remember they're in there, return everything, and buy another trunkful of shopping bags she'll return six months after *that*.

In my tote bag is a wallet stuffed with every receipt I've acquired over the past six months, meticulously indexed and alphabetized. It's funny how we are either a reflection of or reaction to our parents.

Inside the car, Pearl Jam Radio is playing on SiriusXM. I drop into my seat, exhausted from a day of traveling and the four parties River dragged me to last night. My mom looks over at me, smiling sweetly. Something inside me that's been knotted up for months unclenches.

"How was the flight?"

"It was fine. I watched movies and slept."

"Good, you look tired."

"Thanks."

As it has for the past twenty-nine years, the sarcasm completely escapes her attention—yes, I was even a sarcastic baby. There are photos to prove it.

"I'm so happy you're home, my honeybun. *Watch where you're going, motherfucker!*" She honks at an SUV that has made the crucial error of being in a lane she wanted to enter. "Brody and Brian are so excited to see you!"

"Why, do they need a body for an autopsy?"

"Don't talk about your brothers like that! They're very sweet boys."

On the day of their b'nai mitzvah, Rabbi Hoffman had cried in front of the entire synagogue when my brothers finished their haftarah portions. Everyone chalked it up to pride at their accomplishment, but I'm guessing it was a mixture of terror and relief after three months of private lessons. They probably visited him in his dreams to tell him the exact hour and manner of his death.

"The guest bedroom is all made up for you. You're going to *love* what we did with the bathroom."

"Didn't you redo the bathroom last year? I distinctly remember you referring to it as *Under the Tuscan Sun* chic." However, in reality, the aesthetic was decidedly Olive Garden.

"Well, it turns out Tuscany isn't as chic as it used to be. We decided to go a bit more Spanish. The tile is to *die* for."

I turn down the radio, which is still at an earsplitting decibel. "I can't wait to see what country you journey to *next* year. I'll get my passport renewed."

We're soaring up I-95 approximately twenty miles over the speed limit, weaving in and out of traffic like this is an action movie and a shady government organization is after us. An air freshener in the shape of a hamsa—which likely hasn't smelled like jasmine since 2003—hangs from the rearview mirror, and a McDonald's cup with an inch of watery iced Diet Coke sits in the cup holder.

"I'll leave you my car tomorrow if you want, but I'll need you to pick my rehearsal dinner dress up from the dry cleaner's and get the boys from school. We're having dinner with Grandma and Grandpa tomorrow night, so you'll be able to see them before all the wedding festivities kick off. Grandpa is feeling *much* better, by the way."

"Was he not feeling well?"

"Honestly, Julia, you hardly ever call me, you could at least pay attention when I manage to get you on the phone." She isn't wrong that I tend to zone out, but she can go *long* about the weather, which in South Florida is some constant combination of hot and wet for eleven months of the year. "Did you bring enough socks with you? I can have Randy pick you up a pack from Costco."

"I brought plenty of socks, Mom." Already I can feel myself becoming sulky and whiny. Within under twenty-four hours of being in the same zip code as my mother, I will have fully regressed to fifteen years old.

My mother narrowly escapes causing a five-car pileup as she plows across three lanes to make our exit. "Have you talked to your father?"

"Yes, I once asked him to pass the ketchup at an Outback Steakhouse in 1997."

"Very funny, Julia. I mean, have you talked to him *recently*?"

I heave an imitation of her long-suffering sigh back at her, something I perfected before hitting puberty. "I haven't talked to him in a few weeks."

"You should call him more often, honey. He's your father."

"Hey, *you're* the one who married him."

I can't remember a time when my parents were happily married, but they must have been at some point, because once the post-divorce dust settled, Mom always insisted I try harder to get along with Dad, despite our mutual ambivalence toward each other. Still, I could tell she secretly liked that I preferred her, and her insistence that I have a better relationship with my father was more about some deference to proper parental respect.

We're stopped at a red light, and my mother turns to look at me. No matter how old I get, no matter how much I learn and grow and change, no matter how different the person I become is from the one whose diapers she once changed, this woman retains the uncanny ability to take one look at me and know exactly what I'm thinking. Is this a special kind of telepathy intrinsic to motherhood, or is Dana just supernaturally snoopy?

"I'm so happy you're here. All my babies are in one place, and one of them is getting *married!*"

She honest-to-god pinches my cheek. "You know how much I love you, sweetie."

Embarrassingly, my throat tightens and tears prick my eyes. "I know, Mom. I lo—"

Honk! "THE LIGHT'S GREEN, JERK-OFF!"

Eleven
YEARS AGO

"SURPRISE," I SHOUT into an empty house. It's a few months into my first year of college and, feeling homesick, I hoarded what I still can't stomach calling my monthly allowance—I prefer to think of my mother as a patron rather than a parent—to make a weekend trip home. I took a taxi home from the airport to really complete the surprise, imagining walking in the front door to my family gathered around the kitchen table, sadly eating their dinner and mourning my absence, only to burst into smiles (the toddler twins), fake groans that hid fondness (Aiden), pleased bafflement (Randy), and weepy joy (Mom). But the house is dark, and the alarm is going off. I punch in the code—a combination of mine and Aiden's birthdays—but nothing happens.

I drop my duffel bag to the floor and flip open the cellphone I've had for years, thinking enviously about my roommate's shiny new iPhone back in New York. Mom picks up on the third ring.

"Hi, sweetie, I can't really talk."

Then why did you answer the phone, I think, annoyed. The alarm is still beeping in the background.

"Where are you," I ask, stepping back outside to escape the noise.

"Do you want to tell your brother where we are, boys," she says, voice turned away from her phone.

"DISNEY!!!!!" Brody and Brian sound strung out on sugar and character meet and greets.

"We're just here for the weekend," Mom says. "Aiden dragged me on to Space Mountain today and my ears are still ringing, but the boys are having so much fun. How are you, sweetie?"

"I didn't know you were going to Disney." My throat feels tight. "Was it a last-minute thing?"

"No, we've been planning it for a while. Brian, do *not* put that in your mouth! Honey, I've really got to go. Is everything OK?"

"Yeah," I gasp out through inexplicable tears. "By the way, did you change the alarm code at the house?"

"What? Why? Brody, put your shoe back on!"

"Just wondering."

"It's the twins' birthday, 1104. I've got to go, honey. Love you!" The call ends.

Back inside, I punch in the code and drag myself upstairs to my bedroom. It's mostly the way I left it, although a few stray items without a proper home—the box for a new juicer, toys the twins have grown out of—have found their way in here. I bob and weave my way through them toward my bed, flopping face down and finally letting the tears fall into my pillow where no one, not even I, can see them.

I spend the rest of the weekend raiding the fridge and finishing up a paper for my Gay and Lesbian Literature class on Sarah Waters's *Tipping the Velvet*. On Sunday I call a taxi, make sure my room looks exactly the way it did when I arrived, and head back to my new life, leaving my old one, which no longer seems to fit, behind. When I come home for winter break a month later, I hug my mom and tell her it's so good to finally be home.

CHAPTER
Ten

THE HOUSE I grew up in—or rather the house I spent my adolescence in after my mom married Randy when I was twelve—sits in a row of identical houses all the same sunburnt shade of pink stucco. When I was growing up, the driveways were always empty, as the elderly residents of our neighborhood rarely used their equally elderly cars unless they were going to weekly doctor's appointments, country club buffet lunches, or games of bridge. Over the years, as they moved on and younger families moved in, those driveways have filled with SUVs and minivans, and now the once-quiet streets ring with the voices of children at play, their skin lit up by the bright Florida sun.

I, for one, preferred when it was all old people. Screaming children give me a headache.

It's evening, and the street is mostly empty save for a few parents calling their kids home for dinner. The light is burnt orange and deep blue and the air is warm and as thick as pudding, even in early November. My mother pulls into the driveway, which is always left wide open for whatever angle she's inventing that day. Randy got sick of replacing his fender, so he parks in the garage.

"Do you need help bringing your things inside?" The question trails off as she opens the car door and walks toward the front of the house.

For some reason just being here, standing in the driveway where I used to sunbathe while the pool was being remodeled, looking out at a street that I could navigate in my sleep, has my chest tight with emotion. Coming back here doesn't always feel good or comfortable, but it always *feels*. For the ten thousandth time, I shake my metaphorical fist at estrogen and how it opened the floodgates of my feelings. Or maybe I'm just grown-up and self-aware. Ugh, gross.

Bags in tow, I stop to smell the gardenia bush on the way in. Randy gifted it to my mom when the twins were conceived, so I'm shocked it hasn't spent the past fifteen years eating people like Audrey II in *Little Shop of Horrors*.

"Hi, Julia." Speak of the devils.

Standing in the doorway are my fourteen-year-old half brothers, identical down to every last mole and freckle, their uncanny resemblance heightened to Kubrickian levels by their matching outfits. My mom stopped dressing them the same when they were toddlers, but they started up again once they were old enough to pick out their clothes for themselves. They dress like mini octogenarians, and for all I know their clothes are fished out of the donation piles left by our dearly departed neighbors. Or possibly stolen directly from their corpses.

"Hey, guys."

"Can we help with your bags?" Not once in their lives have I been able to tell them apart, but I *think* it's Brian who offers.

"Sure," I answer, handing them over, "although I don't have cash for a tip."

They stare, unblinking, and turn away to lead me upstairs.

True to Mom's mercurial tastes, the house is full of new furniture, art, and tchotchkes, but it's still the house I grew up in. We cross through the large open foyer and past the living room, with its gigantic flat screen and overstuffed leather couches, and up the staircase, which was carpeted this time last year but is now paneled in warm wood and leads to scattered accent rugs. When I was twelve, I kicked Aiden down these very stairs and was grounded for a week. Ah, youth.

The house around them has changed, but the photos hung along the wall are the same, and my own face stares back at me from several of them. There I am next to Mickey Mouse at Disney, barely reaching his knee, ice cream melting in my hand. There I am singing my solo in a middle school production of *Annie*, the only boy at Miss Hannigan's orphanage. There I am next to my mom on the day of my bar mitzvah, smiling through a mouthful of braces, though I can remember vividly how itchy and uncomfortable I felt in my Men's Wearhouse suit.

Maybe the discomfort is something only I can see. If anyone else could, these pictures probably wouldn't still be hanging on the wall.

The twins deposit my things in the beige guest bedroom I spent my teen years locked inside, listening to The Smiths, feeling misunderstood.

"Our mouse got loose last week," says one of the demon spawn.

"It died in this room," says the other. "We haven't found it yet."

"Perfect," I sigh, heaving my bags onto the bed and starting to unpack. If my clothes weren't put away within twenty minutes of my arrival, my mother would disown me, and River gave very strict instructions about the care of Hannah G's pilfered couture; when I told them I didn't own a garment bag, I'm pretty sure River popped a few blood vessels in their eye. "I don't smell anything, so we should be fine."

"Do you want to come hang out in our room? We have a PlayStation now," says Thing One.

"And a rotary saw," adds Thing Two.

"Maybe later. I need to lie down for a bit."

They nod in unison and leave the room on silent feet. Creepy little fuckers. I love them.

Later, I find Mom in the kitchen drinking a Diet Coke and watching the news. My mother, for all her Pilates and flowy linen outfits, is not very healthy. She "doesn't drink water," having always claimed to not like the taste. She will only drink Diet Coke, and not even out of the can: every morning, she goes to the McDonald's drive-thru to buy a fountain Diet Coke and slowly sips it for the rest of the day. Thank god she has veneers and a stomach hardened by my grandma's abysmal cooking.

"Are you hungry, sweetie?" She opens the fridge. "We've got hummus, cheese sticks, strawberries, yogurt. There's some brisket from Passover in the freezer I could heat up for you."

"Passover was six months ago. But thanks. Where's Randy?"

"He's at Costco," she says, rolling her eyes.

As far as I know, my stepfather spends thirty percent of his life at Costco. The remaining seventy percent is divided into making googly eyes at my mother, watching CNN, playing golf, and being late to every appointment, dinner reservation, and family function possible. I'm pretty sure the main reason he and my mom fell in love was their mutual love of procrastination. Also, they have sex loudly and always seem to be enjoying themselves.

Mom met Randy just a year after she and Dad got divorced. She was a hot young single mother with two kids and liked to power walk through the neighborhood, and Randy was the lifelong bachelor who lived down the street and would stare through the window to watch her pass by and ogle her spandex-clad ass. They were married within a year, and we all moved into this house, my mom cheerfully sending Randy's black leather couches to Goodwill and sending Aiden and me off to sleepaway camp so the newlyweds could fuck their way across Europe every summer. A few years later the twins were born, and as much as my mom tried to make us a neat little family unit, this always felt like *that* family's house, one I just happened to live in. I'm more comfortable now as a visitor than I ever was as a resident.

I steal a sip of Mom's Diet Coke, which is mostly melted ice at this point. "That's disgusting."

"So are your shoes," she counters, eyes on her phone. "We'll go to the mall tomorrow and get you a new pair. You *cannot* wear those to the club."

"I did bring another pair, you know. It's not like I was planning to wear these to the rehearsal dinner."

"Well, what *are* you wearing to the rehearsal dinner?" I've fallen neatly into her trap. "You've been so cagey."

"It's mostly to avoid prosecution. River helped themselves to a few things from Hannah G's closet and let me borrow them."

Mom gasped. "Oh, I *love* Hannah G. That one song is *always* playing in Publix. What's it called, it's the one with that chorus that goes like, *hm hm hmmm hm hm.*" I've gotta admit, she has good taste. That Hannah G song was one of my most-listened-to songs three years ago, meaning it's just the right time for it to go triple platinum in a Florida grocery chain.

We stand around the kitchen island gossiping for a bit, Mom filling me in on the latest drama with her friend group. This summer they went on a Mediterranean cruise and one of them almost fell off the boat in an incident involving too many margaritas and a broken flip-flop. In turn, I catch her up on work, showing her photos on my phone of Everett's new brownstone, which she oohs and aahs at, insisting that one day I'll have a home just as nice. And the nice thing is, she believes it.

An hour of chatting later, I check my phone.

> I'm home, come by whenever :)

"I'm going out," I say, wondering where I can possibly pretend to go on a Sunday night in Boca Raton. "I forgot to bring toothpaste, I'm going to run to Publix."

She hands over her keys without question. "Can you grab me another Diet Coke while you're out?" Even if she's asleep when I get back, she'll drink it first thing in the morning. I send a text back.

> Same address?

I haven't even pulled out of the driveway when the response comes in, blown up on my mom's navigation system, where I've connected my phone.

Yup, writes Ben Otsuka. **See you soon.**

CHAPTER Eleven

BEN ANSWERS THE door looking far better than someone who voluntarily lives in Florida deserves to.

"Hey, Jules," he drawls with a smirk. "Come on in."

It would be so satisfying if Ben's townhouse were full of framed Quentin Tarantino movie posters and gravity bongs, but it's infuriatingly tasteful. The furniture is a mix of Ikea and West Elm, but it's been carefully selected, maintained, and styled. I do take pleasure in noticing that the candles have only *just* been lit—the sting of sulfur from the matches hangs in the air—but otherwise, the scene is perfectly casual, cool, and undeniably masculine.

And that's Ben Otsuka in a nutshell. He wears his white T-shirt and scruffy jeans like an off-duty model—catalog, not runway—and his hair is just the right amount of tousled. He's barefoot, which I find strangely sexy despite not having a foot fetish. OK, there *was* that six-month period when I was twenty-three and frequenting this one sex party in Washington Heights . . .

Ben leads me to the living room, where vibey electronic music is playing, and saunters off to grab me a sparkling water. There's a book face down on the coffee table, something Kyle had been going on about at dinner two weeks ago that sounded mind-numbingly dull and excruciatingly intellectual. I like to read, but my tastes are far more mainstream—I'm the kind of philistine who considers *Gone Girl* to be peak literature. Thank god I never got that Rosamund Pike bob. I don't have the bone structure for it.

"When did you get in?" Ben hands me my LaCroix—decanted into a glass, can you believe—and settles into an armchair across from the sofa. "A few hours ago," I admit, wishing I'd showered instead of gossiping with my mom about the women in her yoga class.

Ben's face is smug. "That didn't take long. I'd say I'm flattered but I also know your mother."

We work our way through the requisite small talk, updating each other on whatever details Instagram and our gossiping parents haven't covered. Ben is a dentist with a small practice he runs with his dad, who has finally announced he'll be retiring next year. His mother has, for as long as I can remember, worked at Bloomingdale's one day a week "for the discount" and because she'd probably be there one day a week anyway. I tell him about my job, my friends, and my apartment, mentally checking off a list of everything I need to say before we can stop stalling and start getting naked.

The first time I ever wanted to kiss Ben Otsuka, I was fourteen, we were on a trip to Disney World, and he'd told my brother to stop teasing me for listening to Michelle Branch. We'd each gotten to pick a friend to bring, but none of my friends could come.

I'd expected Ben and my brother to spend the entire trip excluding me, but instead, he'd gone out of his way to befriend me. He sat next to me on Splash Mountain and we shared his Mickey Mouse–shaped Rice Krispies Treat after I tragically dropped my Minnie Mouse–shaped ice cream bar. My crush was incendiary, debilitating, and, so I thought, useless. We were merely two slightly weird kids who noticed something similarly *off* in each other. Ben, whose father was Japanese, was the only Asian student at our temple's Hebrew school. I was a lonely goth who everyone assumed was listening to Slipknot when I was really listening to Tori Amos.

The first time I kissed Ben Otsuka was the summer after my freshman year of college. Mom, Randy, and the twins were on a trip Aiden and I hadn't been invited on and we (well, Aiden) decided to throw a party in the empty house. Ben, a year older than my brother, had just graduated and seemed so mature and thoughtful compared to Aiden's other friends. I had just spent my first year in New York and felt happy to be back somewhere I *knew* without a doubt I was the coolest, most interesting person for miles, but also like I'd been shoved back into an ill-fitting suit long outgrown, a metaphor that would become much more appropriate in a few years. We'd left the party to get stoned on the small balcony outside my bedroom, and in the middle of arguing over Britney Spears's shaved head and what it said about the state of celebrity surveillance, Ben leaned over and kissed me.

We spent the rest of that summer hooking up in any empty house, car, or moonlit beach we could find. It was never necessarily a secret: I'd been out since high school, and Ben had told Aiden he didn't care about gender when it came to sex during a game of truth or dare—I think he currently identifies somewhere around pansexual. But we certainly didn't advertise that we were hooking up, mostly because it was just sex and I had absolutely zero desire to talk to my brother about my sex life.

In the years since, when I'm visiting, if we're both single, I'm usually in Ben's bed within twenty-four hours of landing. I thought it would be too weird to keep it up after I transitioned, but on my first trip home as Julia, I'd gotten a text that simply said **very excited re: boobs** and the only thing that changed was now I have longer hair for him to pull.

"You look good," he says, giving me *the look*. You know the one. I set my glass down on the coffee table—where of course there is a coaster waiting for it—cross to his chair, and lower myself into his lap.

His hands grip my hips. "Hi," he says, nuzzling against my nose.

"Hi," I repeat, muffled against his lips. It's easy, so easy to kiss him, an intimacy as well-worn as my oldest pair of jeans. We kiss and grapple and grind against each other. I break away to tear off my shirt, and he trails kisses down my throat and lower, catching a nipple in his teeth. I tug at his hair with one hand, working the other between our bodies to palm at his dick. We've rehearsed this so many times that the choreography is effortless. Together we get our jeans unfastened and the combination of skin and friction and knowing what this man has wanted for years is too good to be believed. It only takes a few minutes to come.

I settle next to him in the chair, smushed against him with one leg still hooked over his waist. He draws little patterns against the skin of my stomach. It's always been this easy with him. There's very little need for small talk. Our bodies have the conversation.

Ben steals one more kiss and pulls back, swiping my bottom lip with his thumb. "It's such a relief to know I won't have to spend Aiden's wedding cruising for someone to take home after."

I nip at his fingers. "Got a hot date lined up?"

"No, but I happen to know the best woman has a dirty mind and truly incredible stamina."

"I hate to break it to you," I say, pulling back to stretch out a kink in my neck, "but though you're correct about my stamina, you'll have to make other plans. I have my sights set on someone even prettier than you."

"No one is prettier than me," he says, and he's charming enough that it isn't obnoxious. It's also kind of true.

"Kim Cameron is."

His eyes widen and he scoffs. "As in newly minted maid of honor Kim Cameron?" He draws back, looking thoughtful. "I suppose it does have a nice symmetry to it. And it's sort of full circle. Didn't you have a thing for her in high school?"

"I guess." There's a part of me that wants to spill my guts and tell Ben everything. He knows me so intimately, in every sense of the word, and we've had fun over the long years of our entanglement, keeping each other up-to-date on our various sexual exploits. There's no jealousy built into our relationship, just a mutual appreciation of pleasure and years of history. He'd understand how much I wanted to get close to Kim, and he knows me well enough that he might even understand the lengths I've gone to in the hopes of making it happen.

But Ben is also, unfortunately, a genuinely good person. He used to bring my mom flowers when she was pregnant with the twins, drove down from school for Aiden's high school graduation even though he was in the middle of finals, and talked me down over the phone when a longtime fuck buddy rejected me post-transition. I can imagine telling him the story I concocted for Kim, and the disappointed look on his face as he realized that not only had I lied to someone to get in their pants, but that I'd used *Aiden* to do it. He knew how close we were, and while he cared about me deeply—maybe more deeply than I sometimes wanted to admit—he loved Aiden like a brother.

I wish, not for the first time and I'm sure not for the last, that I hadn't lied to Kim.

A few minutes later, after some rushed cleanup in the bathroom, I'm on my way out the door.

Ben is used to abrupt exits after a decade of hookups, but he stops me with a hand—the one that was just down my jeans—on my arm.

"Is everything OK?" He knows me too well, he's too perceptive, too *good*. Far too good for me, just like Kim Cameron.

I kiss his cheek, feeling the downy fuzz of his facial hair. I wonder what it would be like to be a simpler girl who could live down here and let Ben Otsuka love me. We'd grocery shop at Trader Joe's and meet Aiden and Rachel every weekend for bagels, which I'd always complain about because you can't get good bagels outside of New York. We'd go to the movies and he'd remind me how much popcorn made my stomach hurt, but I'd eat it anyway and he'd rub my belly in bed, spooned up behind me when we got home. It sounded nice. It sounded boring.

"Everything's great," I tell him.

CHAPTER
Twelve

EVERY DAY AT my grandparents' country club is like a bar mitzvah. This is only a slight exaggeration—my actual bar mitzvah was held here. From the complimentary valet parking to the ice sculpture swans taking flight above giant tureens of tuna salad, this is a place of luxury, comfort, and excess.

I'm not feeling very comfortable *or* luxurious, tapping my foot impatiently as a woman clutching a walker in one hand and a ladle in the other takes her sweet time with the chicken noodle soup.

I'd offer to help, as she looks about two days away from making everyone named in her will *very* happy, but I'm not having a good day.

The house was dark and quiet last night when I got home from Ben's, though I saw lights flickering under the twins' bedroom doors. Everyone but Randy was gone this morning when I woke up, and we made uncomfortable conversation (on my part, at least, as Randy can happily chat with anyone, anywhere, anytime) over coffee before I escaped back to my room to spend a few hours remotely coordinating furniture delivery and a light installation at a client's Hamptons house. Mom picked me up for a girls' lunch out and spent an hour offering unsolicited opinions on my hair, skin, and nails in between calls from various friends and family members. I'd dropped her off at work and taken her car for the rest of the day on the condition that I had to pick Brody and Brian up from school, which had quickly turned into me chauffeuring them and their creepy little friend Eugene to an abandoned Best Buy parking lot, where they presumably mutilated stray cats for the rest of the afternoon. By the time I picked Mom up from work, a migraine had started to throb at my temples, the pain ratcheting up another notch every time she asked me a question about my day or reminded me how excited I should be for the wedding.

I breathe in and out, willing the thunder rumbling in my head to quiet. I keep reminding myself that this week is a marathon, not a sprint, and I can't burn out this early in the game.

Finally, the crone in front of me hobbles off with her soup and I ladle out a bowl, plopping in a gigantic matzoh ball and snagging a packet of oyster crackers. Back at the table, my grandpa is in the middle of a story I've heard roughly sixty times.

"So there I am, on top of the bar at the Hotel Biancamaria in Capri, pants around my ankles, while the accordion player starts playing 'Moon River.'" Grandpa holds court with ease, even though most of the table isn't paying attention. "I'm about to start singing when I notice someone climbing up onto the bar next to me. And do you know who it was?"

Everyone at the table knows their role in this tale. "Who was it?" we ask together.

"Audrey fucking Hepburn." He holds a beat to let that sink in. "She says to me, 'I think I know this one if you'd like to duet.' And I turn to her, and do you know what I say?"

"What did you say?" I ask through a mouthful of matzoh ball. It's too hot and burns my tongue.

"I said, 'My dear, it's rather loud in here, so don't *go lightly.*'" He looks expectantly at Brody and Brian, the two people at the table who have heard this story the least and are therefore most likely to react to it, but they probably think Truman Capote is either a dead U.S. president or a nonbinary YouTube vlogger and don't look up from their phones.

My grandma rubs his hand reassuringly, her silver bracelets clacking. "It was very clever, dear."

When I was growing up, my grandparents seemed shockingly young compared to those of my friends. They were always jetting off on European vacations and African safaris, hosting cocktail parties full of interesting people, and taking Aiden and me to Broadway shows when we visited them in New York. They were true snowbirds, spending summers in the Long Island home they'd lived in since before I was born and winters in Florida. Once they hit their seventies and my mom had the twins, they'd moved down here full time. Since then they'd suddenly been noticeably *old*, finally looking like the grandparents I'd always expected to have, slow and brittle and occasionally cantankerous.

But they certainly put on a good show. My grandma is immaculate—she gets a blowout on the same day every week, and her hair is huge and stiff. Her nails are perfectly manicured and she's wearing her signature Chanel lipstick. Two years ago I asked what shade it was and she'd shaken her head sadly. "Oh, darling, you'd never pull it off."

Grandpa is still wearing a polo shirt from his afternoon golf game but has a cardigan draped over it. He gets cold so easily now, and the indoor temperature in Florida always hovers around frigid, even in early November. His smile is as wide and impish as ever under the huge nose carved sharply down his face. And his voice is still so loud, too loud, especially as he calls across the crowded restaurant. "Over here!" We all turn to look, and Aiden is waving at us from across the room.

My brother is tall and handsome, all wide shoulders and big hands—traits I somewhat regrettably share. His hair is darker, flat, and straight whereas mine tends to wave and frizz. He's got scrunchy little eyes that soften him, making him seem friendly and approachable. He's not as freckly as Mom and me, but with the Florida sun there's always a constellation dotted across his strong nose. When we were little, he had gigantic ears that he's since grown into. The twins have the same, and they'll probably look just like him when they're grown-up.

Everyone stands to welcome the groom-to-be and I wait my turn. Aiden looks at me for a moment before a smile breaks over his face and he reels me in for a tight hug. "Welcome home, Jules."

I'm hit with an almost overwhelming rush of affection. I *like* Aiden. Sure, he's my brother and because of that, I love him by default. We grew up together, endured our parents' divorce and Mom's remarriage, and suddenly had baby siblings as teenagers, feeling like the odd ones out in our own house. We have the type of shared life experiences that means we just get each other, and even if I hated him I'd still understand him. But I don't hate him. Aiden is a genuinely nice guy and, even though we're extremely different people, once we were adults and had to work to understand each other because we no longer ate dinner together every night and argued over how long one of us (me) took in our shared bathroom, we did the work. We made a healthy, functional, loving adult relationship.

"It's the man of the hour," Grandpa crows. "How ya doing, kid? No cold feet, I hope?"

Aiden, playing along, reaches down to rub an ankle. "Nice and toasty, Grandpa."

Mom starts interrogating Aiden on wedding-week updates, and he dutifully answers even her most insane questions ("Yes, the bar will have Diet Coke on tap. Not cans.") before heading to the buffet. I join him, filling him in on my trip and the first day back home as we load our plates with prime rib and mashed potatoes. I'm lingering at the carving station, debating the merits of corned beef, when Aiden plops several bright-green half-sour pickles on my plate. I've already gotten him a bowl full of black olives, which he used to put on his fingers and chase me around the club with when we were children.

We know each other the way only siblings can. So, as he tugs on my hair the way he has our entire lives and heads back to the table, why am I, left holding my overstuffed plate of food, feeling so damn guilty?

Twenty-One
YEARS AGO

MOM AND DAD are fighting again.

It happens almost weekly now. Mom shuts Aiden and me into our room for the night, looking sad and distracted as she kisses our foreheads and turns on the Winnie the Pooh nightlight Aiden can't sleep without. She'll tiptoe out on the soft carpet, shutting the door as lightly as possible. I can usually hear Aiden start snoring by the time the door is closed, his soft whirring barely audible from my spot above him on our bunk bed.

Moments later, the yelling starts. They probably think that with two doors and a living room between our rooms we can't hear them, but they're so loud. Not loud enough to make out all the words—although reliable phrases like "just like your mother" and "how can you say that to me" are now familiar enough to hear clearly—but the feeling behind the argument all but rattles our small house.

I know how this will go. They'll scream for an hour. Mom will cry, Dad will go quiet. Then Mom will start yelling again, and *Dad* will start crying, something I used to think was impossible. The cycle will repeat a few more times until finally they go quiet.

Maybe it's because they're louder than normal tonight, or maybe it's because he's older than he was when this pattern started six months ago, but suddenly Aiden is standing on the ladder beside my bed, big brown eyes wide with tears.

"Can I sleep with you?" he asks.

I nod into the darkness, moving over to make room.

We lie together in silence listening to our parents scream at each other. I wonder if this is the first time they've woken Aiden up, or if it's happened before and he's just lain in silence listening the same way I have. The thought of that makes me sadder than the fighting, which at this point is so familiar I'm becoming numb to it.

"Why are they so angry," Aiden asks, face turned away from me.

"I dunno."

"Do you think . . ." The silence stretches out for a long moment. "Is it our fault?"

Sometimes I do. Sometimes I think they'd be happier without us, if they didn't have to take care of us and worry about having enough money and had more time to spend together. Sometimes I can't understand why they even wanted us if they so clearly hate each other, and how we've made it impossible for them to escape each other.

"No, of course not." I draw an arm around his little body and squeeze him in tight. "It's grown-up stuff. It has nothing to do with us."

"Really?"

"Really," I say, not believing it but hoping desperately that my sweet little brother does. "Now go to sleep, and don't hog the covers."

CHAPTER Thirteen

MOM'S CAR IS full—her, Randy, the twins, and the mountain of leftovers no one will eat—so Aiden offers to drive me home.

Despite his obsessively neat appearance, Aiden is a huge slob, and his car is littered with empty energy drink cans, tissues, stray gym clothes, and reusable shopping bags. I tease him as we pull out of the club. "Is Rachel not allowed in here?" He grins.

"We usually take her car. The last time she was in here she almost called the wedding off."

Rachel's car is probably just as tidy as their little house, where there's a place for everything and everything is in its place. Rachel is the kind of girl who stocks her guest bathroom full of travel-sized toiletries and absolutely notices if you take them with you. What can I say, I was running low on toothpaste the last time I stayed with them.

Aiden turns the car on, and the speakers immediately start blasting a song from Hannah G's last album. I can't help but giggle. "Aiden, are you a Bananah?" As in a Hannah Bananah, the official name for her biggest fans.

He smiles sheepishly. "Rachel and I are kind of obsessed with her. I still can't believe you've met her."

"I did poppers with her a few weeks ago."

"Shut the fuck up," he yells. "That is so cool. You're so cool!"

I'm really not, but I love the way everyone here sees my life. It sounds much more sophisticated and cosmopolitan when I tell my little stories than it felt to live them, but I suppose compared to life here, mine is chic and glamorous. Although I tend to leave out details like sweating on the subway when I'm loaded down with throw pillows or the way I've started to live off take-out Thai food and bodega sandwiches because one of my roommates broke our microwave and I can't cook anything more complicated than hard-boiled eggs.

"Hold on, how do you know what poppers are?"

A smirk. "Rachel is kind of a top."

I retch. "Please don't say another word. I hate you so much." He reaches a hand out to ruffle my hair, laughing as I swat him away. "Watch the road, you little whore!"

He's still laughing. "What can I say, my proximity to queerness has expanded my mind . . . among other things."

"I will grab the steering wheel and kill us both."

"Like you almost did when Mom taught you how to drive?"

He's got a point.

"How *is* Rachel?" I ask, turning the music down. "Excited for the big day? Or is Bridezilla stomping the streets of Boca, terrifying the locals?"

"Oh yeah, she's a total mess." He laughs, shaking his head fondly. "Every day there's some new meltdown. Today it was the band not knowing 'Single Ladies,' yesterday it was her shoes pinching her feet, the day before that it was—"

"Firing her transphobic maid of honor?" I hadn't meant to say it, but we only have a few minutes, so might as well get on with it. Aiden sighs, long-suffering, a sound I've heard at some point during every argument we've had since puberty.

"Look, I know we probably should have talked more, but the past few weeks have been insane."

"No, it's fine, I'm sorry. I shouldn't have brought it up." A sunset of brilliant pink and orange has cracked open the sky. The truck in front of us is carrying demolished trees, their leafy limbs shuddering as it changes lanes. I think of *Final Destination,* of one of those trees coming loose and smashing through our windshield. Aiden might prefer that to having this conversation. Come to think of it, I might too.

Aiden's face is unreadable behind his sunglasses. "I feel bad about dumping that on you and not having a longer conversation about it. Rach does too."

Aiden, flying in the face of every straight-guy stereotype, *loves* to talk about his feelings. After our parents got divorced, we were forced into family therapy and he discovered the joy of processing. It's a testament to how busy he's been with the wedding that we didn't have an hour long video call to work through how this made me feel, possibly with a PowerPoint presentation and a few bell hooks quotes.

"It's OK, we're good," I say, aiming for reassurance. Because the more I see how clearly concerned he is about how this might have affected me, the more I'm haunted by everything I said or insinuated to Kim in that booth at the Cheesecake Factory. She's only miles away right now, fully convinced that my brother is some emotionally constipated, mildly bigoted asshole, and it couldn't be further from the truth.

"After the wedding and the honeymoon and all this craziness dies down, let's do something. Maybe a trip somewhere?"

"I don't know if I can afford that right now," I say sheepishly. "Weddings are expensive for everyone involved. Couldn't you have just gone to Vegas?"

"Why don't I come visit you in New York again? I can finally meet your friends."

"Ah, I see what you're trying to do. You want me to introduce you to Hannah G."

He grins over at me. "It would make one hell of a wedding present."

CHAPTER Fourteen

"BLACK? THIS IS a wedding, not a funeral." The look on my mom's face is sour as she looks down at the nail technician working on my toes. "You couldn't do something a bit happier? Something *pretty*?"

I roll my eyes. "I like black. It's neutral."

"It reminds me of your goth phase. I'm half expecting to look up and see your hair dyed that awful red color."

Ah yes, my Hot Topic era. "Don't worry, I left my spiked collar in New York."

Mom sighs, relaxing back into her spa chair, her chest bouncing alarmingly from the electric massager. "Thank god for that. Do you have everything you need, though? We could stop at Nordstrom and pick up shoes. And I have jewelry you can wear."

"I'm fine, Mom. My friend River, the stylist, lent me some stuff."

"Oh yes, the one with the interesting haircut." She says "interesting" like an insult, or at least an accusation. "She's very cute, have you two ever dated?"

"*They*, Mom, River's pronouns are they and them."

"Right, sorry."

"And no, we've never dated." Hand jobs at a rave in 2014 don't count. "River's only interested in men anyway."

There's an uncomfortable pause. "But it's not like you... I mean you still..."

I know she's not trying to be offensive. She's genuinely curious about the dynamics. It still stings a little. "It's not just about parts, Mom. River is attracted to masculinity. They're always sleeping with these adorable himbos," I explain.

"What's a himbo?"

I snort. "Aiden, if he had bigger shoulders and a lower IQ."

"Ah," she says. "My son is very handsome."

I know she's biased because he's her son, but Aiden *is* kind of a catch. "Remember how awkward he was as a teenager, though? His Eminem phase?"

She snorts. My phone buzzes with a text from Kim, asking if I want a ride to the welcome dinner tonight. We've been texting on and off since the Cheesecake Factory, ostensibly under the guise of our duties. Still, the chatter has gradually expanded to random chatter about our lives—and flirty banter. She's also checked in a few times since I got to Florida to ask how everything is going, *everything* clearly meant to stand in for my supposedly problematic family dynamic. In the few weeks since we'd seen each other, I'd been able to minimize my deceit in my head, assuring myself that it hadn't been as bad as it was. But after last night at Ben's, it all feels so much more insidious.

That doesn't mean I'm going to pass up the chance to live out my teen fantasy of being picked up for a date by Kim Cameron.

I guiltily check my work email, something I haven't been doing enough since I touched down. Technically I took the week off from work for the wedding, but Everett doesn't really understand things like *boundaries* and *out of office*. There are five emails from him with no subject lines, each containing random questions, requests, and reminders.

> start sourcing art for Ira Streit's fire island house, brief is "tasteful phallic"

> what is my social security number again?

> remember to book rental car for hamptons next month!

I add these to my running list of work tasks and open the final email.

> Jules, I'm thinking it's finally time for you to work on your own project. Why don't you do one of the rooms in my new house? Less pressure since it's not for a client, although we'll have to be a bit more strict with the budget than usual. Let's talk more when you're back next week!

Everett initially hired me as an assistant, and I've worked my way up to project manager over the past two years. He's always alluded to wanting to properly start training me as an actual designer, but I figured I was too useful to him as a gopher and it would never really happen. I turn, smiling, to tell my mom about this exciting new career development, but she's busy chatting on the phone. So much for mother-daughter time.

Later, my toes—black polish and all—are squeezed into a pair of Prada boots Hannah G wore to the Billboard Music Awards. The rest of me is squeezed into a black leather cocktail dress Hannah G wore to Kristen Stewart's birthday party, and I'm *attempting* to squeeze my phone into a Gucci clutch Hannah G once chucked at River's head after a night of too many Negronis. From what I can see in the bathroom mirror, I look good. The dress is a bit tight and short, but in a slutty way rather than a desperate one, and I don't mind looking a little slutty tonight. I have a date, after all. Kind of.

Buzz, buzz. **Here.**

Speak of the devil. One last poke at my lashes, which have a tendency to droop, and I'm down the stairs and out the door.

"Are you wearing a bra?" Mom, Randy, and the twins are watching TV on the couch.

"What's a bra?" I ask, rushing out the door. "Don't wait up!"

Kim Cameron watches me through the windshield of her rental. The boots give my hips a swing they don't usually have, and my hair is loose around my shoulders, bangs sleek above my kohl-lined eyes, the dress short enough to show how long and pale my legs are. I'm hoping the look is more Debbie Harry and less Warped Tour.

"Hi," Kim says once I've climbed into her Honda Civic. "You look great."

"So do you." And she does. Kim's style leaned more boho in high school, but always with a masculine edge, something she's leaning much more into these days. She's devastatingly sexy in a fitted gray suit, kept casual by the tank top underneath and what must be pounds of silver jewelry and black eyeliner. If we were an early 2000s couple being splashed on Perez Hilton, she'd be the Samantha Ronson to my Lindsay Lohan. I wonder if she'd be down to role-play . . .

"How was your flight?" I know she just got in a few hours ago and yet is remarkably unrumpled.

"Not bad. You ready for tonight?"

"Ready to chitchat with dozens of people I last saw ten years and one gender ago? Oh, absolutely. Are *you* ready?"

"I've never been great at small talk," she says, eyes on the road but occasionally shooting a look my way. At my legs, specifically. Nice. "And Rachel and I were always the kind of friends who were only friends with each other, never fully integrated into our respective social circles."

"Y'all were roommates in college, right?"

"Yeah, freshman year. We shared a bedroom. I walked in the first day and Rachel was already there. All of her food in the fridge was in color-coordinated Tupperware labeled with her name. I didn't know people did that in real life."

"I'm pretty sure she still does that. Aiden told me he took some leftovers to work for lunch once and she drove to his office to get them back." We both laugh.

"She's a lot, yeah. She knows what she wants and doesn't take no for an answer. She kind of just . . . decided we were going to be best friends and all of a sudden, we were. The first time I brought a girl back to our room, Rachel almost seemed disappointed I wasn't harboring some giant crush on *her*. Then she told the girl *Ugly Betty* was on in forty-five minutes, so she'd better get me off quick."

I guffaw, gleefully horrified. "She did not!"

"What can I say, I've always had a thing for Vanessa Williams."

"Well obviously," I say.

It makes sense, in a way. Rachel was raised with the kind of privilege that leads to exacting standards and zero filter. The first time Aiden brought her over for Hanukkah, she'd thanked my mom for having her and assured her that if she added a bit of matzoh meal to her latkes, they'd be much more crispy. "Don't worry, Dana," she'd reassured her on her way out the door, "in a few years Aiden and I will be hosting and all you'll have to do is bring the wine!"

"What a bitch," Mom said once they were gone. "I give it six months."

Look how that turned out. And honestly, Rachel's latkes *are* superior.

Soon we're parking in front of Boca's closest approximation of a hip bar. "You really do look great," Kim says as I check my lipstick. "Your legs in that dress . . ."

"It's too much, right? I'm wearing a pop star's castoffs and he"—I point toward a man entering the bar—"is wearing those cargo pants that zip off at the knee."

Kim looks up from my legs, which I most certainly don't mind her noticing. She can notice them for as long as she likes. "Nah, you're going to be the hottest girl in there." She says it so casually, but my heart still speeds up.

Pitbull is playing inside the bar, which is pretty much exactly what I expected. We're ushered into a large private room, something that wouldn't be possible in New York, where square footage is in short supply. Kim grabs my hand, our rings clinking together. The moment we cross the threshold, an earsplitting shriek, comparable to the sound the Ringwraiths make in *Lord of the Rings,* rends the air. Poor Pitbull, you'll never overpower a Jewish bride days out from her wedding.

Rachel rushes over, wearing an honest-to-god Hervé Léger bandage dress as if it's 2012 and she's the bottle girl. Her normally curly hair is blown straight, whipping behind her like the flag of some country where the national flower is Daisy by Marc Jacobs and the currency is Lululemon gift cards. She's startlingly pretty, a natural beauty enhanced by expertly applied makeup and, I'm fairly certain, a nose job. She's in fantastic shape and has no problem sprinting across a crowded room in six-inch heels, and even at a distance, you can tell that this is *her* night, her week, her wedding. She's as gorgeous as she is terrifying, and then she's right there in front of us, pulling Kim close and shrieking her name. She'd probably cry if it wouldn't ruin her eyeliner, but she also may have had her tear ducts removed in high school when she did her nose.

"Oh my fucking god," she whines, clutching Kim tight. "It feels so real now that you're here. My maid of fucking honor!"

Kim pulls back and, for all her bluster in the car and over the past few weeks, she looks genuinely happy to see my soon-to-be sister-in-law. "I can't believe you're getting *married* this weekend. Holy shit."

Rachel grips Kim's (extremely toned) arms, staring ferociously into her eyes. "We have so much to talk about. Every day there's a new disaster, I just found out from the caterers that there's a cream cheese shortage and they won't be able to do the mini bagels with lox during the cocktail hour. Is that not apocalyptic?"

"Florida has shit bagels anyway," I cut in. "Hi, Rachel."

Rachel lets out another squeal and pulls me into a hug. "Jules, you're here!" I was right: she is wearing Daisy by Marc Jacobs. She pulls back to take in my outfit. "Oh my god, is that the dress

Hannah G wore to Kristen Stewart's birthday party?" Wow, she really is a Bananah.

"Hey, guys," Aiden says, sliding into our little circle and slipping an arm around Rachel's waist. "I mean, sorry, *hey, y'all*. Or should I say *hey, folks?*" Rachel, Kim, and I simultaneously roll our eyes, although I'm sure each of us for very different reasons. I know Aiden is probably earnestly trying to phase gendered language out of his vocabulary, but considering what I've told Kim, it's easy to mistake his comment as rude and dismissive, maybe even aggressive. She certainly doesn't give him a warm welcome and presses her shoulder against mine supportively. It makes me feel excited and icky all at once.

I sweep my gaze around the room as they chitchat, taking in the crowd for tonight's event, the official wedding kickoff for the under-forty wedding guests and any of Aiden and Rachel's friends who didn't secure an invite to the actual reception. It's a lot of unfamiliar faces, but I smile at a few extended family members, already anticipating a night of stilted, awkward conversations. And of course, there's Ben, looking far too handsome in a tight blue button-down that hugs his shoulders and black slacks that cling to his butt. I love his butt.

He looks up and waves hello, and the satisfaction of his eyes widening as he takes in the way Kim Cameron is pressed against me was honestly worth the price of my plane ticket.

I zone back into the conversation, which has moved on to Aiden and Rachel's favorite date night activities. "One of those places where you can paint and drink wine just opened up in Delray and it's like, so incredible to be doing something creative." Rachel smiles at Aiden. "Right, honey?"

"Yeah, I can't wait to pass some shitty art down to our kids as heirlooms. They'll break out some sort of futuristic black-light technology and see that *Vase with Dandelions* started as just *Boobs*."

"You two are going to look so great walking down the aisle together," Rachel says, smiling at Kim and me. "Things worked out perfectly."

"I don't know about perfect," Aiden says, a pained look on his face.

"Yeah, it's too bad about Jenna," Kim says, her tone firm, maybe even combative.

Aiden doesn't notice, shooting me a guilty look. I know it's because he feels bad for how long it took to figure out how serious Jenna's hostility toward me was, but from the way Kim's eyes narrow, she must read something else into it. With the foundation I've given her, it must be so easy to interpret how uncomfortable he is as directed toward me rather than on my behalf.

Kim wraps her arm around my waist, mirroring Aiden and Rachel, and squeezes me in a way that would be delightful in literally any other context. Aiden looks surprised, but it quickly melts into the face I remember from childhood, the one he'd get before my stuffed animals went missing. Devious little shithead.

"I'm sure Jules is much happier walking down the aisle with you," he says, grinning.

"Well, I do have not being an asshole going for me," says Kim.

"No, I just mean, well," he laughs, "she had *such* a crush on you in high school."

My brother loves me, but he loves to torture me even more. And now he's potentially blowing my cover. I expect Kim to shrink away from me, but instead, she smirks. "I know."

I snort some champagne out my nose. "Excuse me?"

She laughs, and actually *tightens* her arm around my waist. "You weren't very subtle. There was this one time I gave you a ride home from school, I don't know if you remember, I think it was when we did *A Midsummer Night's Dream*." She'd played Titania, of course.

"*Into the Woods*," I say without thinking. Her smile gets even bigger.

"So you *do* remember."

"Maybe."

"This is incredible," Aiden says.

"You're so annoying," I say, hoping to shift the attention away from my adolescent yearning. "Rachel, are you sure you want to marry him? He's such a douche."

"But he's *my* douche." She smiles widely as the rest of us laugh.

The happy couple must return to their duties and mingle with the rest of their guests. Kim keeps a hand on my waist as we move through the crush of bodies to get to the bar—there's no way I'm making it through this night with champagne alone—and the heat of her hand through my dress feels so good. I just have to make sure not to burn myself on it.

CHAPTER Fifteen

"I'M SOOOO HAPPY you went with the Balenciaga," River squeals.

"The black is a bit . . . witches of Eastwick," Daytona rebuts. "Or Bushwick, I guess."

"Can we *please* not mention Bushwick," Kyle moans. "I'm still recovering from last week's K-hole."

I'm locked inside a single-stall bathroom on an emergency emotional support four-way FaceTime. I'm not feeling especially supported. "Can we please focus? I'm in the midst of a crisis."

They all roll their eyes simultaneously. "When are you *not* in the midst of a crisis?" asks Daytona.

"I don't know, I think I had a good week sometime in April. But seriously," I grip the sink for support and also so I can push my boobs together for optimum cleavage in case anyone decides to take a screenshot. "Aiden just revealed my very real teenage crush to the girl I've duped into paying attention to me. She's going to realize I concocted this whole charade as an excuse to perv on her!"

"Can we make this quick?" Daytona says, across a small, messy room from her phone. I believe she's staying in a punk squat in Atlanta. "I'm off testosterone blockers again and I've been *extremely* preoccupied since I got here. Last night I spent about six hours inside the sweetest little twink."

"I thought you were in your daddy phase," River says.

"I was, but then it turned into my mommy phase."

"Focus!" I clap my hands like a kindergarten teacher at the end of recess. "I'm dealing with my actual, biological family members and their repeated attempts to ruin my life."

"I don't know, babe, Aiden telling your pseudo-girlfriend that you used to write her name in bubble letters on your binder doesn't sound all that diabolical," Kyle muses. "Considering the circumstances it's almost, like, supportive."

That's perfectly rational, but after a glass of champagne and two cocktails, *I* am not. "He's not being supportive, he's trying to embarrass me. And now Kim keeps giving me these *looks*."

"Are they sexy looks? Also, does anyone know how long I'm supposed to leave this on for?" River is painting bleach onto their eyebrows, a look I tried during my club kid phase and could never pull off. I'm sure they'll look infuriatingly cool.

"No more than twenty minutes," I caution. "And I wouldn't call them *sexy*, per se. Although Kim is always sexy, so I wouldn't be able to spot the difference."

"You may have to accept that your embarrassing crush is not as embarrassing as you think, and this girl could be into you. Anyway, I need to get ready, I'm running late for a sex party," says Kyle. He's shrugging into a leather harness, silver glitter dusted on his high cheekbones. It hits me deeply how much I miss all of them, how much I wish they were here, and also how strange it would be if they were. My life in New York and the person I've become there feel light-years away from this bathroom stall in this lame bar in this claustrophobic little town.

River perks up. "Oh, is it the one in that dungeon in Park Slope?"

"No, it's in the secret back room inside that fried chicken spot in Bed-Stuy. Wanna come?"

River squeals and they start discussing outfit options. I mumble out a goodbye and hang up. So much for moral support. I reapply my lipstick, sniff under my arms to make sure my nervous flop sweat isn't too noticeable, and open the door. Rachel is standing on the other side. "Oh, thank god," she moans, pushing her way into the bathroom and locking the door behind her with me still inside. "I have to pee *so* bad and I had no idea how I was going to get this dress off. Can you help?"

It takes a minute, but between the two of us—me yanking up the stiff fabric of her dress, her wiggling down as hard as she can—we get her bottom half free and she squats over the toilet, sighing in ecstasy, but the relief is short-lived. "I want to know what you're doing with Kim," she says, eyes sharpened to a point.

Fuck, is the jig up that quickly? "I don't know what you mean."

She raises an eyebrow. "Come on, Julia, I know you're very smart, and despite what you might think, I am too." She is still peeing. Loudly.

She's not wrong. Rachel is an attorney and by all accounts a very competent one. She might be a bit silly, a bit dramatic, and she has a distinct lack of tact that only comes from a life of extreme privilege, but she's sharp. Those big Bambi eyes see everything, and right now they're seeing far more of me than I'd like. And she's *still* peeing. "She's the maid of honor, I'm the best woman. We're just . . . getting to know each other."

"So you weren't making bedroom eyes at Ben Otsuka across the bar ten minutes ago?"

Well, that's not where I was expecting this to go. "First of all, who uses the term *bedroom eyes*? Did we time travel to the eighties without my realizing it? Is this *Mannequin,* starring erstwhile *Sex and the City* actress Kim Cattrall?" I heave in a breath and count to ten. She's still peeing. "No, Rachel, I was not giving him eyes associated with any kind of room. Those are just . . . my eyes."

"You guys have had a thing on and off for a while, even though we all like to pretend you don't. I know for a fact that when he stopped by last Thanksgiving to return Aiden's electric carver, the turkey wasn't the only thing getting stuffed."

"Oh my god."

"Kim is my *best friend,* and she might come off all tough and independent, but she's a highly sensitive person and she's been through some shit. I don't think it's appropriate for you to be wooing the maid of honor *and* hooking up with a groomsman."

She's. Still. Peeing.

Turning away from her, because it's very hard not to stare directly at her vagina, I grip the sink for support that has nothing to do with my cleavage. "Rachel, this might be hard for you to conceptualize, since you and Aiden have been together for years and are literally getting *married* this week, but Kim and Ben and I are all adults. *Queer* adults at that, and it's pretty presumptuous of you to assume that we have the same ideas about monogamy as you."

"I'm not some basic straight girl you need to educate about queer relationship dynamics. My best friend is a lesbian. I know all about polygamy."

"Might you mean polyamory?"

"Whatever!"

"I'm also not some chaotic bisexual stereotype who just wants to fuck anything that moves, Rachel. Just because I *have* hooked up with Ben doesn't mean I'm going to again." Even though I did so not twenty-four hours ago and, depending on how things go with Kim, I likely will again at some point this week. And even if I *was* in a relationship with Kim—the thought of which causes my heart to beat a little faster—I don't know that I even believe in monogamy.

"Just don't fuck with my maid of honor, especially during the most important week of my life. If you're gonna hook up with Ben, be honest with her about it. There's nothing Kim hates more than a liar."

"I wouldn't lie to her." Again. Hopefully.

I hear her finally stop peeing and tear off some toilet paper. "By the way, you're coming to my bachelorette party on Thursday."

I whirl around, shocked. "I am?"

"Of course. You're about to be my sister-in-law." She stands, dress still scrunched up around her torso, panties around her ankles. "A little help, please?"

I help her back into her dress and zip it up for her. "You don't have to worry about me and Kim. We're two consenting adults."

One of whom has lied to the other in a bid for sexy sympathy. "Sure, I had a major crush on her in high school, but that was over a decade ago." And yet every time she looks at me, I feel sixteen again, sweaty palms and all.

Speaking of palms, Rachel grasps my hands, despite having not washed hers yet. Gross. "OK. I trust you." That should be reassuring, but my heart sinks. She shouldn't. "Julia, I think part of the reason why Kim and I got so close in college—"

"—is that you were secretly in love with her and now you're going to leave Aiden for her?" I can't help but tease, trying to break the tension.

"—is that I've always wanted a sister. And after this weekend, I'm finally going to have one." She smiles at me, moves to wash her hands, and fixes her makeup. I'm gobsmacked and shocked to find my eyes stinging with tears. She catches my eye in the mirror and wiggles her eyebrows. "Should we do a little coke? It usually gives me the shits, but I can't eat until Saturday if I want to fit into my wedding gown."

Sisters, amirite?

CHAPTER
Sixteen

SOMEHOW I MAKE it through the rest of the evening without another incident quite as dramatic as my bathroom tête-à-tête with Rachel.

Kim and I mingle, chatting with people she knew from college and people I knew from high school. All night I catch interested glances from across the room, people who knew who I was and everything that entailed. It's such a different experience from what I'm used to in New York, where I regularly run into people I haven't seen in a few years and have to update them on my presentation and pronouns. Maybe it's because I'm so insulated, or perhaps New Yorkers are just that much more cosmopolitan and unflappable. It's not like Boca Raton is some backwater hick town—the entirety of Palm Beach County is rather progressive—but context is everything, and Florida is such an unbelievably weird and shitty state.

But tonight feels more than anything like wading in, a preview of what the next few days will be like. Because Aiden's friends who half remember an old version of me from ten years ago might not approach me with inappropriate and uncomfortable questions, but my extended family would certainly have no problem doing exactly that. I'm already exhausted and on edge in anticipation, which is how Kim and I have ended up here.

. . .

Here is the Publix bakery.

Founded in 1930 by George Jenkins, Publix is a chain of grocery stores covering the south: Florida, Georgia, both Carolinas, Virginia, Alabama, Kentucky, and Tennessee. You might think your local grocery store chain is the best in the game, but you'd be wrong. Publix has an unmatched deli—their chicken tender subs are divine. The air of Southern charm extends to the friendly staff, who will walk you to your car and load your groceries into the trunk without expecting or accepting gratuity. But best of all is their cake.

I am basic and boring and never as happy and blissed-out as when I'm eating, from a pan larger than my torso, yellow sheet cake covered in buttercream so thick and sweet I should schedule a dentist appointment after the first bite. The cake is so moist and spongy, with colorful frosted flowers piped lovingly along the sides. Honestly, if I had a cake-sitting fetish, there is no cake I'd rather sit on. But I'd prefer to just eat it.

There are fewer cake slices than there were last night when I stopped in for a postcoital sugar rush—I've never been shy about eating my feelings. Standing under the fluorescent lights in the empty bakery department, I hold up two options for Kim. "Chocolate or vanilla?"

"Neither," she answers. "I'm not really into sweets."

I clutch my heart in mock horror. "How can anyone resist Publix cake? I don't care if you're not *into sweets*, Publix cake is like, transcendent. I think there's heroin in it."

She grabs the slices from me and starts toward checkout. "I had more than enough growing up. My mom always brought a huge cake to school on my birthday to share with the class. I will forever associate the taste with unwanted attention."

"See, I had the opposite problem. I'm a summer baby, so I never got the school birthday experience."

"Summer baby . . . wait, what's your sign? I can't believe we haven't done this yet."

I laugh. It's true, though. I don't think I've met a queer person since college and not known their zodiac sign within the first twenty minutes of conversation. "I'm a Cancer. July fifth. You?"

"Sagittarius. December fifth." She stops to peruse beverage options at a large display case.

"Interesting. Water sign"—I point to myself—"and fire sign"—I point at her. "We're . . . steamy." That came out much flirtier and more suggestive than I'd intended.

Kim turns and gives me that same look she did in the car earlier, one far too dark and searching for Publix at 10 P.M. All I can do is give her a bland smile and duck my head.

There's only one register open, and the person behind it has hair so shockingly pink it looks like a MySpace background circa 2005. Their face is studded with piercings, covered with the kind of pubescent acne that looks like it hurts, and smudged with eyeliner that clearly started in one place at the beginning of their shift and has since migrated. They are painfully young and have perfected an aura of ambivalence thicker than Axe body spray.

Oh god, it's me at fifteen. The horror.

Kim drops our loot onto the conveyor belt and the cashier looks up at her, eyes widening a little bit in a way I'm coming to realize *everyone* does when faced with Kim Cameron in her full glory, before finding me standing next to her. They snort. "Wow, two nights in a row? You know this stuff is like, pure lard, right?" Oh, they must have checked me out last night when I was too deep in my self-flagellating spiral to notice. They scan our purchases.

I cross my arms, aiming for haughty rather than defensive. "I happen to have a very fast metabolism." Not quite the sickening comeback I was aiming for, but I lean into Kim to show off a bit. She takes it in stride, even paying for the cake she won't be eating. I could swoon. She grabs our bag and heads out the door, and it takes me a moment to get my body moving again.

The surly nonbinary teen rolls their eyes. "Um, hello, *follow her*."

So I do.

There's nowhere to sit outside, so Kim and I take our (my) snack to her rental car. Despite my repeated offers to share my cake, she's untempted. A pity, as it would be very romantic to feed it to her and fulfill some weirdly specific adolescent fantasies.

Kim shifts her body to lean against the door and turns to look at me. "Tonight wasn't so bad, right?"

I do the same on my side. "No, it was mostly fine," I answer.

"I totally got what you meant about your brother, though," she says, wincing as if in pain. "That *folks* joke. And the way he reacted to me bringing up Jenna. What a dick."

For a moment I'm pissed and want to jump to my brother's

defense, but I can't. She's only following the breadcrumbs I left for her, interpreting everything through the lens of my lies. I chew my cake slowly, giving myself a moment to think. This is my chance to come clean. I don't even need to tell her the full scope of my fibbing. I could just minimize everything I'd said, or tell her that Aiden and I have cleared everything up over the past few weeks.

But then her hand comes down on my thigh, and she looks at me so sweetly, sincere and sympathetic and lovely. I think of myself at sixteen, as awkward as the cashier who just checked us out, in this very same position. Sitting in a car next to Kim Cameron, wanting her but knowing she'd never want me back. I don't want to be that kid again.

So I swallow my cake and nod. "I don't really wanna talk about it," I say, because the least I can do is not dig myself in deeper. She nods, so understanding I could die from shame. I have to change the subject.

"You know, Rachel kind of accosted me in the bathroom to ask about my intentions with you."

Kim's face is surprised, and also perhaps a bit pleased. "She did not! What did she say?"

"That you're a perfect lesbian saint and she will personally have me banned from every coffee shop in Greenpoint if I break your heart." She laughs. Delighted at the sound, I shovel more cake into my mouth. I decide to be a little brave. "I can't believe you remembered driving me home that time. And here we are again, sitting in your car. It's bringing up a lot for me. All we need is Ani DiFranco."

"How could I forget? You looked so lonely sitting outside all by yourself."

"I was pretty lonely, yeah. I think it was partially self-imposed, teen angst and all. But I don't think I let anyone in, because if I did they might . . . you know, actually *see* me."

"Would that be so bad? Being seen?"

"Back then? Definitely." I shiver. It's because of the AC, I tell myself. "Now . . . I'd like to think I let people in a little bit more. The people who count, at least. But I still feel so, I don't know, passive all the time. Like my life isn't something I'm participating in, but something that's just happening to me."

"I think that's bullshit."

I choke on a piece of cake and Kim magnanimously offers a sip of water from a reusable bottle in the cup holder. "Care to elaborate on that?" I ask once I've recovered.

"I won't presume to know *that* much about you, but I don't think a passive person would be living the life you're living. You fucking *transitioned* in a world where that's still a pretty radical thing to do. The world told you that you were one thing, but you said fuck that, *you're wrong*. That's fucking badass."

"I know all that intellectually, I guess, but I can't always *feel* it. When I came out, it mostly felt like . . . a lie I just couldn't keep telling anymore. That's what no one here seems to get. At first, everyone saw me as this impulsive weirdo who woke up one day and decided poof, I'm a woman! And I couldn't judge them *too* harshly for that, because I have always been impulsive."

There's nothing Kim hates more than a liar, Rachel whispers in my head. But I'm not lying. I'm just . . . curating the truth.

"That doesn't give them a pass to be shitty. You don't have to apologize or make excuses for them. It sucks that they think that."

And I let myself do the thing I shouldn't do, in fact just promised myself I wouldn't do: I dredge up all the old hurt and paranoia of four years ago, the fears my family disproved almost immediately after I came out. "It sucks to know that they think this is something I'm going to change my mind about in a few years."

"Damn," Kim says, sucking a breath in through her teeth. "That's brutal."

"One of the most—and believe me I'd love to *not* use this word—*affirming* moments when I first started transitioning was telling my grandparents. I was terrified, so sure that they wouldn't get it, that they'd just have no way to even conceptualize what I was talking about. But when I told them, my grandma said, 'When you were little, you used to always tell us you were a girl.'"

The story is spilling out of me in a way I can't control.

"And that was great, because they got it, and they've been supportive even if they get a pronoun wrong or slip with my name now and then. But like, if I *told* them"—and I hate so deeply that I can feel my throat getting tight, my eyes burning—"why didn't they just *listen*? I know, I know, it was a different time and there wasn't the fucking *visibility* and *resources* there are now, but it's what makes me furious because you're right, Kim." I lift my head up to look into her eyes, which are wide and unblinking. "Deciding to transition was one of the first times in my life I took real agency, where I made a big scary decision about who I was and how I was going to show up in the world, and I worry sometimes that they think twenty years from now we'll be sitting around Aiden's perfect house while his perfect children and their golden retriever run around the backyard, laughing about that time I decided to be a girl for a couple years."

For a moment there's just the sounds of the AC blasting, the faint hum of the radio playing Fleetwood Mac. I did it again, took something real but made it uglier than it was, made myself the victim, all so Kim would look at me with that same frank, open expression on her face, no pity or sympathy or unease at my extreme overshare. Just letting me vent, letting me dig myself into a deeper hole of lies and drag her down with me, all so I can prove something to my sad little inner child. I have to salvage this, somehow.

"I'm sorry, that was a lot. Too much."

"It wasn't," Kim says. "And I can't say that I get all of it, because I'm not you, but I think I get a little bit of it." There's a moment where she seems to teeter on the edge of a decision, searching my face for . . . something. It looks like she finds it. "Do you remember Emily Sullivan?"

"Oh god," I groan. "I haven't thought about her in years." Emily Sullivan was every high school archetype come to life: perfect, pretty, popular, and mean enough to make you cry if you crossed her. She'd been in Kim's year and so far away from my subterranean social status that we'd never even interacted, but every school had an Emily, someone who shone with their own self-importance, making everyone around them that much duller in comparison.

"We . . . dated isn't even really the right word for it. We hooked up all through senior year. I was totally, ass over tits in love with her. And the crazy thing is, I think she loved me too. At least a little bit."

I'm shocked, but not that much. I distinctly remember hearing at some point that Emily had come out after college. "She wouldn't tell anyone about us," Kim continues, "especially her parents. It wasn't because of the gay stuff, or at least not just because of it. She said her parents might be able to handle her having a girlfriend. But not a Black girlfriend."

"Fuck."

Kim shakes her head with a haunted look in her eyes. "I haven't always been as self-possessed as I appear."

I snort. "That can't possibly be true. I bet you came out of the womb cool, calm, collected and flirted with the doctor."

"Something like that, yeah." She's smiling again, so there's that. "I let Emily keep me her dirty little secret for far too long because at that point I . . . maybe I didn't agree with her, but I loved her enough to hurt myself for her. So yeah, I know a little bit about not fitting into someone's idea of what their life should look like. I know what it's like to watch someone say one thing and do another, and how much that hurts."

I am a monster. I am the worst person who ever lived. Not only because I'm another girl who has used Kim, but because I'm not going to stop.

"I'm sorry that happened to you," I say, grasping her hand where it's still resting on my thigh. "Thank you for sharing that and . . . for everything."

We gaze at each other for what feels like an eternity, but is only long enough for the Fleetwood Mac song to end, giving way to Kate Bush.

". . . *you had a temper like my jealousy, too hot, too greedy . . .*"

"I'm really glad to be here with you," Kim says.

She shouldn't be. I know that now more than ever. But I'll take it.

CHAPTER
Seventeen

DECIDING WE'VE SPENT far too long around straight people tonight, Kim makes the executive decision that we need to find the closest gay bar and "recharge." The closest gay bar happens to be a spot I know rather well, as it was where I used to cruise the summer between high school and college when I realized I was about to move to New York City and had no idea *how* to cruise. Hudson's didn't exactly prepare me well, because I was young and cute enough that all I needed to do was walk in to have my pick of the patrons—not that the selection was huge.

As we enter, I realize not much has changed. Same weathered vinyl booths, same stale smokey air, same peeling Tom of Finland posters dotting the walls. The jukebox in the corner is playing Donna Summer but no one is grooving on what could only generously be called the dance floor. There are only a few patrons scattered around, but they all swivel toward the door when we enter and immediately dismiss us when they see we're women. Some things never change.

"Ladies," drawls the old queen behind the bar—a loving moniker I'm sure he'd appreciate. "What can I get you?" We order beers and walk them over to a faded pool table where, at Kim's insistence, we start setting up a game.

"I have to warn you," I tell her, "I'm fucking terrible at pool. I'm pretty sure the last time I played was at Nowhere Bar in 2016, and even then it was only so I could bend over and catch the eye of a very sexy veterinarian."

"Why do you think I suggested it? Bend away, Rosenberg."

It doesn't take long for her to realize I wasn't joking. "You are fucking terrible at pool," she says as I scratch for the third time.

"I have dismal hand-eye coordination. Also"—I do a Beyoncé voice—"*I been drinking.*"

We chat about our plans for the next day as we continue our game. Kim has a few maid of honor duties to attend to, while I'll be spending my evening at Aiden's bachelor party. Before that, I'll be seeing my dad.

Dad hasn't been in the best of health the past few years and needs help locating his wedding suit, which is trapped in the detritus of his house, which would not be out of place on an episode of *Hoarders*. He's somehow roped Aiden and me into helping, insisting that he needs some quality time with us while I'm in town. I exhausted every plausible excuse to get out of it before finally admitting defeat. Also, the prospect of unearthing some of my favorite childhood books from the depths of his garage is enticing.

Kim sinks one of her balls into the corner pocket. I wish she'd sink *me,* but I shake it off. That's not what we're doing here, despite how increasingly date-like this whole evening is starting to feel.

"Tonight was chill, right?" Kim asks. "Using the buddy system seemed to help."

"It did. Having a buffer between me and people I barely remember from high school was great." Having Kim less than a foot away all night had been far better, but I don't want to admit that. It would be too thirsty, too overeager. It's clear at this point that there's something between us—besides a whole bunch of lies—but I think now the proverbial ball is in her corner. Pocket, I guess, since we're playing pool.

"Good, I'm glad. I saw you talking to Otsuka. You guys have a thing going?" Her tone is casual, but there's a real question in those words.

"Yeah, we're kind of . . . fuck buddies, I guess?" Ugh, that's such a disgusting term. "Friends with benefits?" That sounds super gay. But then again, sex with Ben Otsuka is kind of gay. There's a certain freedom in having sex with a man, as a man, that I no longer get to participate in anymore post-transition, this *we're all dudes here* vibe that is hard to put my finger on—in. But with Ben, maybe because he's one of the few people I've had sex with before and after transitioning, that feeling of pure sexual camaraderie never faded.

"He's cool," I say, lamely. "And seeing him is one of the parts of all this that doesn't suck."

"You deserve for this to not suck." Kim's so sincere, and so sexy, I keep catching myself staring at her for too long. I remind myself that's why she's here. She is being kind, showing me the kind of solidarity that was rare growing up down here as a queer kid. She doesn't even care about my casual hometown hookup! That reads friend zone . . . or maybe it's because we're both gay sluts who like sex and aren't shy about it. From the bits and pieces I've gathered, Kim leaves a trail of obsessed women in her wake, so it makes sense that she wouldn't be judgmental.

But if I want to be one of those obsessed women, I'm going to need to step my proverbial pussy up. Kim knew me when I was a pimply teenage *boy*, and I'm using every weapon in my arsenal to have her look at me and see a woman she could date.

Some of this must show on my face because Kim's brows crease. "Everything good?"

"Yeah," I lie, lining up to flub another shot. "Just peachy."

"Are y'all almost done?" asks one of the other patrons, a sour-faced man with enough gold rings on his fingers to make Gianni Versace jealous. "As fun as it's been to watch your match, we'd love a turn." Behind him, a twink barely old enough to be here nervously clutches their drinks, sweating through his polo shirt.

"We're still playing, but I'm sure she'll beat me into submission *very* soon, and then the table's all yours," I say through a tight smile.

"Or not," Kim adds as she bends over to line up a shot. "I might want a rematch."

Versace rolls his eyes. "Honey, I've never seen you here before, but generally we all take turns. Maybe the girl bars have different rules."

Kim snorts. "Which bars, exactly? There are less than thirty lesbian bars left in this country and the closest is in Orlando." She fixes her cold stare at him. "Do I look like I spend a lot of time in Orlando?"

She doesn't.

Our new friend sighs, long-suffering. "That's not my problem."

"Of course it's not," says Kim. "Why should you care if there are spaces for queer women to congregate, as long as you have somewhere to check Grindr."

"I don't think that's a very fair stereotype," the twink adds haughtily. "I prefer Scruff."

"Clearly," I mutter, shooting a glance at his date.

"We have as much right to be here as you do." Kim still hasn't looked up from our game, but she doesn't need to. The interlopers, along with everyone else in a five-foot radius (it's not that many people, the bar is depressingly desolate) are giving her their full attention. "This entitlement you have, because you're some old white guy who thinks gay marriage was the pinnacle of queer political achievement, it's not cute. If we want to go best of three, we will. And when she loses," she adds, nodding toward me, "if I want to make her feel better by dragging her off to the men's room, because why should there even *be* another bathroom in a place like this, and have my way with her while y'all line up outside and piss yourselves, I will. Now will you kindly *fuck off* and let my girl and me finish our game?" She punctuates the question by sinking the maroon ball, number seven.

I have never been so turned on. *My girl.*

"Whatever," sniffs Versace. He grabs his twink and they retreat to a booth on the other side of the bar where they grumble and glare at us as we finish our game.

A few more beers and one embarrassing and anticipated loss later, Kim drives me home. I'm climbing out of her rental when she stops me with a hand on my arm. "I had a really good time with you tonight," she says, and my stomach twists so hard, wanting this to be real.

"Me too," I croak out. "The way you eviscerated that dude was . . ."—hot, so *hot*—". . . impressive."

"Oof, I kinda lost it for a minute there." She looks chagrined, but also clearly pleased. "I'm just so sick of feeling unwelcome in places that are ostensibly for all of us when really, they're just for cis gay men."

I nod. "It sucks. I've never felt super comfortable in gay bars, even when people just assumed I *was* a cis gay man. But like . . . where else are we supposed to go? *Straight* bars?"

We groan in unison, laugh, and say our goodbyes. There's a moment, before I close the door and she's still looking at me, when I let myself think *what if,* what if Kim grabbed my hand and pulled me back into the car and we made out like teenagers and she tucked my hair behind my ear and told me I'm a good girl or a bad girl or anything, *anything,* so long as I'm *hers,* wouldn't that be wonderful.

But she doesn't do any of those things, just gives me a little wave and watches me through the windshield as I walk inside.

The house is dark, but my mom's keys are right by the door in the same place they've been for almost twenty years, so it's easy to grab them and squeeze my palm around them so they don't make a sound. I wait a few moments to be sure Kim has gone before I let myself out the door I just came in, unlocking my mom's car and texting Ben to let him know I'll be there in fifteen.

I make it in ten.

We don't bother with pretense this time. I'm pulling my shirt off as Ben locks the door behind me. Ben's house—or perhaps just any space Ben inhabits—has always been one of the only places in Boca I've ever felt truly comfortable. There's an understanding between us born out of our familiarity with each other's bodies combined with a life lived going to the same schools, eating at the same restaurants, talking to the same people, but always feeling slightly outside. Ben's just always been able to . . . pass better than me, and when we're close like this—

his hands in my hair, his mouth on my neck, how hot he is inside

—some of that ease and self-assurance bleeds into me, if only for a little while.

"You good?" he asks later, stroking a hand down my back. I'm not much of a cuddler, but it feels nice to lie curled up beside him, allowing that one point of gentle contact. I wish, fiercely, that I could scoot back and press my back to Ben's chest and let him hold me all night, let him love me. I wonder if I'd let Kim hold me.

"I'm fine." I turn my head to give him a smile over my shoulder, then I get up and pull my clothes on.

CHAPTER Eighteen

"WELL IF IT isn't my two favorite children," my dad crows from the doorway.

"We're your two *only* children," I mutter, moving into an awkward hug. Even in sneakers, I'm half a foot taller than my father.

"What's up, Pops?" asks Aiden, swooping in for his own much more genuine embrace, complete with manly back-patting.

The house is as cluttered as I remember from the last time I was here two years ago. Every surface is covered in unopened junk mail, deflated Publix shopping bags, mugs of old coffee, half-read books with cracked spines, empty take-out containers, and, of course, a metric fuck ton of cat hair. When my parents separated and my dad moved into a new apartment, the first thing he did was adopt a cat. My mom was incredibly allergic, so it was the perfect symbol of his new life away from her.

The fact that *I* was also incredibly allergic to cats didn't seem to factor into his decision. Most of my memories of weekends spent at my dad's are clouded by a haze of Benadryl. I would take library books out to the community pool behind his apartment building and read all day while Dad and Aiden watched sports, coming inside only when I had to pee or was so hungry I thought I'd faint. As soon as Dad dropped us back off at Mom's I'd strip off my clothes and throw them in the wash, but I'd still be sneezing, bleary-eyed, and drowsy for days afterward. When I turned fourteen, I stopped going altogether, filling my weekends with rehearsals and trips to the mall. Dad never seemed to miss me.

"Good to see you, kid," he says. He's always careful to call me things like *kid* so there's a lesser chance of him forgetting to call me Julia. It hasn't happened in years, but I still feel anxious around him, waiting for the other shoe to drop.

"How's the Big Apple?" he asks after we've cleared off enough of the couch to sit on. One of his three cats winds its way around my ankles, so these jeans are definitely getting washed later, or possibly burned.

"Good." There's a beat of silence before I realize I should probably expand on that. "Yeah, everything's fine, same old same old."

"Job's good?"

"Yeah."

"How much money are you making now?"

"I don't really feel comfortable answering that."

"Aw, come on, you're my . . . kid. What's the big deal?"

Aiden joins us on the sofa, handing out cans of Diet Mountain Dew—which Dad drinks instead of water—and rescues me. "Come on, Dad, not everyone feels comfortable talking about money like that."

"How am I supposed to know anything about your life," he asks me, "if you won't tell me?"

You're not supposed to know anything about my life, I'd like to say. "So you need us to find your suit, right?"

Aiden and I leave Dad on the couch watching a game (I'm not sure what sport it is and I'd never ask) and head to the garage. If the house is messy, the garage is postapocalyptic. There are boxes everywhere, bikes that likely haven't been ridden since the nineties, broken furniture, and a lingering smell of what can only be described as *hopelessness*. If we're able to unearth a suit from this, there's no way it can be worn to a wedding this week.

Nevertheless, we persist.

"Do you remember this?" Aiden asks twenty minutes later, holding up a stuffed Kermit the Frog. Something sharp twists inside my chest and I let out a little "Oh!" of shock, rushing over to grab it from him, but he's too fast, snatching Kermit away and holding him above me, a haughty smile on his face. "You were *obsessed* with this thing."

I stand on tiptoes, trying to snatch it away. "I've always had excellent taste in men."

He yanks up an eyebrow. "Women too. Rach told me she talked to you about Kim."

Ah, so this is why he's holding Kermit hostage. I step back and cross my arms over my chest and watch him do the same. Inside, I'm sure our father is sitting on the couch with arms crossed exactly the same way. The thought is sobering enough that I yank my hands free until my arms hang at my sides, hands clenched. "Yes, we had a lovely little chat while your future wife peed for so long I was worried she'd lose a kidney."

He laughs. "Rach has a very large bladder."

"I really don't need to know how you know that."

"You excited for my bachelor party?" he asks, starting to stack boxes in a worryingly wobbly tower. After we leave here, we're headed straight to Boomers, a hybrid arcade and mini amusement park where we used to have our birthday parties as kids. Aiden couldn't resist the lure of their frozen pizza and go-karts, so we're going to spend the afternoon reliving our childhood, only this time with beer. I'm half excited, half anxious. It'll be the first time all the grooms*people* are gathered together, and I'll be the odd woman out.

"Excited to kick your ass at laser tag," I say, searching a shelf full of dusty lamps for anything that might resemble a garment bag.

"It's gonna be an epic stag do."

"You're not British."

"Bollocks," he says in a terrible accent. "And I'm going to kick *your* ass at air hockey. Cheerio, pip-pip."

"Not if I lock you in this garage with one of the cats." Aiden might not be allergic, but he had an irrational childhood fear that the cats wanted to eat him. I watch him shiver with a smirk.

We continue searching and sorting in silence, the only sound the hum of the second refrigerator as it keeps cases of Diet Mountain Dew at the perfect temperature.

"Sorry if I embarrassed you in front of Kim last night," he says after a few minutes. "You looked so cute together, I couldn't help myself."

"It's fine," I say. Guilt, my constant companion, floods back. I grab Kermit from where Aiden left him, press my face against his felt chest, and sneeze from the years of dust.

"I have to say, she looked pretty into you. Maybe all your teenage dreams are about to come true," Aiden says. His earnestness hurts worse than if he were teasing me.

"Maybe," I reply. Thankfully, I spy the garment bag wedged under a crate of vinyl records and call off the search, bringing an end to the conversation I'm dying not to have. Aiden knows me too well, will see through me too easily.

Back in the house, Dad is sitting on the couch, arms folded against his chest, asleep. He looks so small and frail, and I'm hit with a wave of affection for him. I don't always like him, but I do love him. I'm pretty sure the feeling is mutual.

He stirs as I sit down next to him, eyes cracking open and taking me in. "Hey," he says. "Find anything good out there?"

I hold up Kermit, and he chuckles softly. "You used to carry that thing everywhere. God, you were such a cute kid." His eyes get that faraway look that tells me he's lost in memories of a time when I loved him wholly and completely with the uncomplicated affection of a child.

The moment is broken when I look behind him, to where a photo of him and me at my high school graduation is hanging on the wall.

"Can't you take that down?" I ask, pointing at the offending proof of my pre-Julianess. "I'm sure we have a more recent photo together that could go there."

I expect him to get defensive, but instead he just looks sad.

"We don't," he says. I don't have a response, so I just dig my fingers into Kermit's threadbare green belly and let the sound of the TV fill the silence.

· · ·

Three hours later, I'm taking a sharp corner around a racetrack in a go-kart that sounds like it should have been retired around when I went through puberty—the first time. The entire bachelor party zooms around me in singles and pairs. Brody and Brian, who are honorary groomsmen, have lapped us twice.

There was a little awkwardness when we all said hello. Ben was the only one of Aiden's friends I'd ever spent real time with, and I hadn't seen the rest of them in years. But they'd all clearly been primed and were perfectly nice. Any lingering tension faded sometime between the second pitcher of beer and the first round of laser tag.

The twins win the go-kart race easily and request a beer each as their prize.

"No way," says Aiden, slurring a bit. "Mom would kill me."

When he's distracted by some kind of zombie shooting game, I slip Brody and Brian sips of my beer as we munch on leftover pizza. We're the only ones at the table, and I'm reminded of the countless birthdays I spent seated at this same table with this same red-checkered tablecloth. I always managed to end up sitting by myself while the other kids played, even at my own parties.

"Just pour us our own," one of the twins begs.

"It's not as illegal if you sip from mine," I shoot back, watching Aiden pump his fist in victory across the room. He proceeds to give David, one of the groomsmen, a noogie.

"Come *on*," pleads the other. "Aiden is so lame, you're our *cool* sibling."

"You really think I'm that easy?" I shoot back, shaking my head. Kids today. "Besides, we're in Florida. I don't need some concerned mother looking over here and seeing me getting you drunk." As I say it, I'm struck by how real that statement is.

While Boca Raton is a little bubble of quasi liberalism, this state is about as regressively conservative as it's possible to be. It's always in the back of my mind, the need to be more careful here than I would be in New York. But now I can't help looking around, making sure no one is watching me corrupting my teenage siblings. The best woman getting arrested would put quite a damper on the wedding festivities.

Satisfied we're not being surveilled, I look back at the twins, surprised to find them looking at me with more thoughtfulness and, dare I say it, concern than I've ever seen.

"You don't have to worry, Jules, we'd never let anything happen to you," one of them says, rather fiercely.

"We could easily cause a distraction and get you out of here," says the other. "I'm pretty sure a small-scale explosion would do it."

"Aw, you'd commit arson for me?" I joke, even though it doesn't feel very funny. I'm touched.

"It's so stupid how people are here about stuff like that," says a twin.

"Property damage?"

"No, the whole trans thing. Like, who even cares. It's not like you were ever really a boy."

"Right," chimes in the other. "You were just pretending."

"You were always Julia," says Brian, and for some reason, I can finally tell that it's him. One of his eyebrows arches a little higher than Brody's. And Brody's freckles are a little more dense around his nose. I know them, in some deep, intrinsic way. And they know me too.

"Fuck it," I say, pouring them each a glass of beer. "Don't tell Mom."

Leaving Brody and Brian to get tipsy and wreak havoc, I leave the table in search of my other brother. I hear shouting in the distance and know immediately where I'll find him.

Steps away from the giant glass display case full of prizes, Aiden is locked in a heated air hockey battle. There are two empty pitchers of beer next to him and the rest of the groomsmen are cheering him on as he whacks his puck in the direction of his opponent: a tween girl in overalls who grins cruelly at my brother through a mouth full of braces. I check the electronic scoreboard over their heads and confirm my suspicion that she's winning.

"You know what rhymes with puck?" she shouts at my brother, her hand a blur as she defends her goal. "Suck. Which is what you do at this game."

Not quite a devastating read, but when you're getting your ass kicked at an arcade game by a pimply teenager, it probably cuts deep. Across the table my brother's face twists into a grimace. His usually perfectly polished exterior is gone: hair a mess, red-faced, and sweating. He's always been competitive, and alcohol only exacerbates the problem. It doesn't help that the groomsmen are egging him on.

"You can take her, man," Derek yells, punching Aiden's shoulder.

"Victory is yours," shouts Martin, a friend from Aiden's job. He was very buttoned-up when we arrived, but now he looks positively prehistoric. The energy feels distinctly locker-room, and I'd feel bad for the girl if she wasn't kicking Aiden's ass so masterfully and looking unruffled while doing it. She even pauses for a fake yawn, as if the game is boring her, tossing a long braid over her shoulder. She can't be older than thirteen. She's terrifying.

"You've got this," I say, patting Aiden's shoulder, even though I'm sure he doesn't. I'm the best woman and it's my role to be supportive—literally supportive, in fact, because Aiden slumps against me.

"Jules, I'm soooooooo drunk," he groans into my hair. Aiden is such a lightweight. "You've got to take over for me." He pulls away and grips my shoulders with his hands, more for support than emphasis. "Our family's honor is on the line."

"Are we finishing this or not?" asks his opponent, inspecting the chunky glitter polish on her nails.

I nudge Aiden aside and take his disc, squaring my shoulders and facing my new nemesis. Underneath her overalls, she's wearing a tie-dye T-shirt featuring a galloping horse that I'm kind of jealous of. I must destroy her.

The room dims around me as we start to play. My arm moves without conscious thought, blocking off my goal and knocking the puck across the table toward hers. As if from a great distance I can hear our party chanting my name. The girl no longer looks bored, she's almost feral, hunched over the table with her face twisted into a snarling grimace. My face is probably doing the same.

"Your boyfriend is gonna cry when I beat you," she says, whipping the puck toward me and scoring a goal.

"Gross, he's my brother." I score a goal back.

"I guess being ass at air hockey runs in the family." She's a blur of speed, blocking my shots and sending them back at me with the furious energy of youth. My arm is starting to get tired and my back hurts from leaning over the table. I check the scoreboard; after picking up Aiden's slack, we're now tied. Whoever scores the next point wins the game.

I decide to beat her at her own game. Not air hockey: being an annoying little cunt.

"No friends to cheer you on?" I sneer at her, channeling every girl who ever bullied me. There are lots to choose from. "What're you gonna do after you lose, Rollerblade home and watch *Frozen*?" Sounds fun, if I'm being honest.

"What are *you* gonna do after *you* lose? Untuck your dick from between your ass cheeks and write about it on your blog?"

I'm horrified. "I don't have a *blog*, you little bitch."

We're in a tense standoff for the next five minutes, neither of us scoring the final goal. At one point my hand slips on the disk and the puck whacks my middle finger, shattering the polish and, possibly, bone. *You already ruined your manicure!* my mother's phantom voice wails in my head. I'm losing steam quickly, and conscious of the audience gathered around us. I flash back to my conversation with the twins and nervously scan the crowd, worried I'm going to see this little shit stain's mother leading security to come apprehend me.

That one moment of distraction is all she needs, and the game is over. The boys pat my back while Ben leads Aiden toward the bathroom, presumably so he can puke. Horse girl comes around the table and eyes me evenly, all malice vanished.

"Good game." She raises her hand and I'm too stunned to do anything more than shake it and watch her flounce away toward Dance Dance Revolution, where a group of kids her age, all as pimpled and gangly, cheer as she blushes and gives a shy little smile.

Whatever, at least *I* don't have algebra homework to do.

Aiden is resting his head on our table when I finally make my way back, while Ben insists he drink a glass of water.

"I don't wanna." Aiden's voice is muffled by the vinyl tablecloth. He sounds as petulant as he did when ordered to clean his room at age eleven.

"Just think of how dry your skin will be tomorrow if you don't hydrate." Ben rubs Aiden's back, using the kind of tone you use with children and small animals. Aiden shoots up and chugs the entire glass in one go.

Twenty-Two
YEARS AGO

"OW!"

I'm seven years old, in the back seat of our dad's Honda in a Publix parking lot. Aiden is five, and he's just bitten me. Dad has been inside for the past twenty minutes buying the ingredients for tuna salad. Dad makes it with celery and raw onions, which I hate.

Aiden's teeth are sharper than they have any right to be, nearly piercing my skin through the sleeve of my blue cotton summer camp sweatshirt. I roll up the sleeve and see the shape of his little bite imprinted on my skin.

We've been fighting over who gets to choose the radio station. Dad left the car on with the basketball game he and Aiden had been avidly listening to still playing, and as soon as he was gone I switched it to a station playing Stevie Nicks, a song I recognized from hazy Saturday mornings when my mother would light candles and clean the small house that seemed so much bigger now that dad had moved out.

My arm throbs and I start to cry. Aiden looks at me with his huge green eyes and starts to cry as well. "I'm sorry," he shouts. "I didn't mean to but you were being so *mean*." I sob harder because I *was* being mean, but I hate being stuck with Dad and Aiden. They like all the same things, or rather Aiden likes everything Dad likes on principle, and I never feel as alone as I do when I'm with them.

"Here," Aiden says, thrusting his arm in my face. "Get me back so we're even." I don't know how to tell him that it doesn't work that way, that hurting him won't make me hurt any less. But, with fat tears still rolling down my face, I open my jaw wide to take a bite.

By the time Dad gets back to the car, we're happily singing along to Whitney Houston.

CHAPTER Nineteen

"DAYTONA, YOU KNOW I can fully see your asshole, right?" I'm a little hungover from last night and five o'clock seems way too early to be looking up my friend's sphincter. I haven't even had a cocktail yet.

"You're welcome," she says, shimmying above her phone, which is resting on the floor, her leg stretched over it to rest on the edge of her bathtub as she shaves. Daytona's legs are so fantastic they should be insured: she shaves twice a week and obsessively slathers them in coconut oil, body butter, and other lotions and potions. As far as I know, she does not own a single pair of pants and has her stems displayed in dresses and miniskirts 365 days a year. Last winter, she legitimately almost got frostbite wearing open-toed shoes in a blizzard. "Worth it," she'd assured me from beneath one of those foil shock blankets.

That's why I've enlisted her help directly rather than calling for a confab to pick my bachelorette party outfit. Kyle is very opinionated and sexy but knows nothing about women's fashion. River is really only interested in women aesthetically and their advice would be more about showing off *their* taste than *my* body. Daytona will make sure I achieve my goal tonight, which is very simple: looking hot. Hot enough to blend in with a group of cis women drinking out of penis straws, hot enough to catch Kim's attention . . . and maybe, just maybe, hot enough to keep her arm tight around my waist and her eyes on me all night.

"What do we think of these boots? They're . . . interesting." The boots in question are Margiela, with a tabi split-toe.

Daytona peers down at me between her legs. "You'd better leave those hoof shoes in Florida where they belong. Didn't River pack you a good pair of fuck-me pumps?"

I drop to my knees and search through my suitcase, pulling out Agent Provocateur lingerie (aspirational), Spanx (practical), and granny panties (realistic). "It seems like River packed me enough underwear for the wedding *and* my brother's honeymoon, which I'm definitely not invited on."

"You have to miss out on whatever Sandals Resort they're going to? Tragic."

"They're spending a week in Italy. Positano, I think. It was a gift from her parents. What about these?" I ask, holding up a pair of Gucci sneakers. "I could do a whole hypebeast moment."

"Absolutely not."

"Aha!" I yell, unearthing a pair of Balenciaga knife heels from underneath a pair of leather pants River insisted would be good for "lounging around." I hold them up to the phone, which is propped up against a lamp on the nightstand. Daytona is gliding a razor up one buttery leg. "Do these work?" She peers at me between her thighs, purses her lips, and gives the barest Miranda

Priestly nod of sartorial approval. "Yes. Wear the leather pants, you have the thighs for them." It's one of the nicest things she's ever said to me.

"What's on the agenda for tonight?" she asks. "Are you girls popping Molly and getting lap dances from gay dudes? Kind of right up your alley."

"It's somehow sadder than that," I counter, wriggling into the pants one leg at a time, wishing I'd thought to bring my own coconut oil, or maybe a tub of Crisco. "We're going to one of those pottery studios where they get you so drunk on cabernet you think adult pottery is actually fun, followed by a private midnight screening of *The Wedding Singer* to satisfy Rachel's childhood crush on Adam Sandler."

"Is she gonna be like, fingering herself in the theater?"

"Please never talk about my future sister-in-law's vagina again. It's been haunting me all week." I'd been keeping the group updated with blow-by-blow recaps, including my audition to be Rachel's new gynecologist. "How's Atlanta?"

"Same old. The show last night was good. I did a Barbra suite and cleaned up in tips, although someone spilled poppers on them. I got high trying to count earlier."

"Does someone mean you?"

"I refuse to dignify that with a response. Unrelatedly, when we're both back in New York let's swing by the Leather Man so I can pick up a new bottle."

"Why are their poppers so fucking good?"

"They're probably organic. Farm-to-table alkyl nitrites." Daytona moves on to the next leg. "Or maybe there's a little meth in them. How're things going with your big lesbo crush?"

"Oh god, I'm like in *love* with her. It's worse than when I was fourteen and obsessed with our rabbi. I got really into Judaism for the summer so I could come to his house and ask questions about the Torah, but I just ended up hooking up with his daughter and never going to temple again because it was so awkward." I pause, trying to figure out which side of my shiny Chloé top is the front. "Oh god, what if Esther is at the wedding?"

"Esther is kind of a sickening name. So it's going well?"

"As well as can be expected, I guess. But who knows, it could all go ass over tits tonight. I mean, I'm preparing to spend an evening with a bunch of cis women who are probably going to go completely silent when I join them in the bathroom to touch up my makeup and check under the stall door to see if I still piss standing up."

"At least you were fucking *invited*, girl. At least your family wants you around. At least they aren't chasing you into the town square with pitchforks like you're fucking Frankenstein." There's a current of anger and resentment in her voice, and I remember that not all of us have families we can go home to.

"You're right," I murmur, feeling awkward and uncomfortable in my bra and my stupid leather pants, complaining about my family drama to someone whose only real family is . . . well, Kyle, River, and me. My heart clenches in my chest again, and I miss Daytona fiercely, wishing I could bury my face in her long mane of hair and breathe in its summery strawberry scent. I always ask what shampoo she uses to get it to smell like that and every time she smirks and shakes her head. "Women need their secrets, honey." Daytona is a woman built of secrets, fashioned out of pain and fury and an unbridled hunger for life on her own terms.

"It's OK," she tells me, unusually tender. "Everything's gonna be OK, honey."

"I love you," I tell her, because I do, and you should tell the people you love that you love them as often as you can.

"I know," she says, smiling. "Take off the bra, it's doing *nothing* for you."

Mom comes home from work right after I hang up with Daytona, and we have a quiet dinner with Randy and Brody—Brian is at an oboe lesson. I didn't even know he played.

"Interesting outfit," Mom says as I'm checking my lipstick in the mirror by the front door. The guard gate had just called—Kim would be here any minute to pick me up, which she offered after Rachel extended the last-minute invitation. Obviously, I said yes.

"Thanks." My bangs aren't doing what I want them to, and I try running my fingers through them a few times before sighing in defeat.

"Let me," Mom says, turning me toward her and licking her hand, bringing it to my cowlick.

"Mom, gross." But in reality, I'm preening under her attention. I let her fuss with my hair for a moment before drawing back to admire her handiwork.

"Perfect." Her eyes move down to my chest. Her lips purse, but she's learned her lesson.

A car honks from outside.

"Have fun. Bring me home a vase for the collection." Mom has a display case dedicated to her children's artistic endeavors, which includes some of Brody and Brian's most terrifyingly bloody early work—we went through red crayons quickly when they were little—and a teapot I painted to look like Mrs. Potts from *Beauty and the Beast* who could make it to the final four on *Drag Race*.

A few minutes later, I'm buckled into the front seat of Kim's rental, admiring the way her legs look wrapped in perfectly faded vintage Levi's and imagining how much better they'd look wrapped around *me*. Her hand rests between us and it would be so easy to lace my fingers through hers, but I won't, despite the look she gave me when she saw my leather pants, which I'll generously call *smoldering*. I didn't know people could smolder outside of Gothic literature and the Xena/Gabrielle fan fiction I wrote in middle school, but Kim Cameron somehow manages it.

"Do you know a lot of the other bridesmaids?" I ask over the Portishead playing from Kim's phone—hot *and* great taste in music.

"A few, from college. But Rachel and I were never really part of the same group of friends, just friends with each other. They're all nice, but . . . intense."

"Rachel does seem to have a type when it comes to friends," I acknowledge, "and it's . . . more Rachels."

She shoots me a look. "Are you calling *me* a Rachel?"

"You're about as far from a Rachel as it's possible to be. You're"—I wave my hands, hoping the perfect descriptor will magically appear—"a Kim Cameron."

A laugh. "I'll take it."

That makes two of us.

In no time at all, Kim is opening my door in yet another strip mall parking lot as a burning-ozone sunset lights up the palm trees across the horizon. She walks behind me and, when I turn to make some joke about the name of our destination—Kiln Me Softly—her guilty eyes snap up from where they have been, dare I say it, ogling my leather-clad ass. I somehow manage not to punch the air in triumph and settle for a knowing smirk. But this is Kim Cameron, so all she does is gaze back at me, unbothered, and place a hand at my back to guide me through the door. The touch lights something up inside me, and I can feel the static electricity crackling between us.

Oh, it's on.

"Kimmy!" shrieks a gorgeous blonde surrounded by five nearly identical white women, all looking like they just finished a round of pumpkin spice lattes.

"Kimmy?" I mutter into Kim's ear.

"She will be dealt with."

Hugs are exchanged alongside names, none of which I have any plan to keep track of. Instead, I decide to give them numbers: Rachel 2, in the miniskirt, greeted us. Rachel 3 is wearing a hat so wide brimmed that no one can get closer than two feet from her. Rachel 4 has lips so freshly filled with Juvéderm the bruises are peeking through her matte lipstick. Rachel 5 has glasses and really *is* also named Rachel and seems nice, greeting Kim with a long, sweet hug. Rachel 6 looks like a real bitch, if I'm being honest, giving me a smile so forced she looks constipated.

"And this is Aiden's sister, Julia," Kim says, her hand still warm at my back.

"Ohmygod, *Julia,*" says Rachel 4, gripping my arms tight enough to hurt. "We've heard *so* much about you."

"Your shoes are *incredible,*" gushes Rachel 2.

"You're so brave," gasps Rachel 3, wide-eyed.

"I am?" I ask. Cis people *love* calling trans people brave, usually concerning our incredible *journeys.*

"Yes! I'd be so worried about getting clay on those amazing pants!"

Oh. Am I being an asshole assuming *they're* going to be assholes? Am I such a jaded New Yorker, so insulated in my bubble of coastal elites that I just assume anyone who's chosen to live in Florida must be some well-meaning yet still subtly transphobic hick? Maybe I should be a little kinder, less judgmental, and give these girls a chance to prove me wrong.

Rachel 6 looks me up and down as if assessing a threat. "We thought it would be just us . . . bridesmaids tonight," she says, and the emphasis on bridesmaids feels loaded. "But it's so . . . *fun* that you're here."

Or perhaps they'll prove me right.

The tension is swiftly broken by the *actual* Rachel arriving with Rachel 7, a curvy childhood friend I've met before who was narrowly beat out by Kim for replacement maid of honor and still looks a bit salty about it. She overcompensates by making it clear she was the one who organized the evening's festivities, greeting the woman behind the counter by name. Stephanie has dark-brown skin and an adorable gap between her two front teeth and is far too beautiful to be working at a tipsy pottery studio in South Florida, but she's friendly and patient as she uncorks our first bottle of the night, an orangey skin contact wine. We all sip and murmur appreciatively as she leads us to a large table toward the back of the warmly lit studio. Mazzy Star's "Fade Into You" is playing softly from well-hidden speakers, and the whole vibe is extremely cozy. If this place were a coffee shop, I'd want to spend all day here reading . . . or playing a game on my phone while my book sat untouched.

There are big lumps of clay waiting for each of us at the large farmhouse table, and Stephanie walks us through dividing them and measuring out balls that will become the base of our vases. The idea is that each bridesmaid will save a single bud from their wedding bouquet and keep it in the vase as a treasured keepsake from the special day. I have to admit, it's a thoughtful little memento. Hopefully my mom enjoys it.

"Now you'll be able to save your boutonniere, Julia." Rachel 6 looks wide-eyed and earnest, but I'm not buying that for a second.

"I'm wearing a corsage, actually." I will not sink to her level. "I haven't had a facial in forever, maybe I can use this as a face mask." I turn to Stephanie, whose own clay ball is so perfectly spherical it looks 3D-printed, and raise my clay-covered hands to my face. "Is this stuff good for your pores? Or am I going to wind up with lead poisoning?"

She laughs, somewhat generously considering the obvious tension and the fact that my joke wasn't funny enough to break it. "You might want to stick with something from Sephora."

Rachel Prime shoots her wily bridesmaid a cautioning look before giving me a little smile. "I'll make sure to save you a bud from my bouquet, Jules."

"You can have one from mine too," Kim says from next to me. I've been very emphatically *not* looking at the way her strong hands are working at the clay, and have to bite back a whimper as I sneak a glance and imagine how they might look flexed around something much more skin-like. My skin, to be precise.

"I'm so excited for Saturday, Rach. Your parents' country club is gorgeous." Rachel 3's hat keeps slipping off and is already caked in clay from her repeated attempts to secure it. "Which ballroom is it in?"

"The main one," Rachel answers, looking somewhat sheepish. If I remember correctly from the year I turned thirteen and attended a bar or bat mitzvah every single weekend, that ballroom is the kind reserved for New Year's Eve parties and presidential visits.

Rachel 4 looks impressed. "That must have been *expensive*."

"Only the best for his only daughter," says Number 6, "and it's not like he can't afford it. What are they shelling out for this wedding, a hundred grand? A hundred fifty?"

"I don't think that's an appropriate question to ask." Number 5 seems scandalized that we'd do something so crass as to talk about the gross capitalism of the wedding industrial complex over wine and DIY crafts.

"Really, though, it's *so* generous of your parents," says Number 6, steamrolling right through the awkwardness. We're all two glasses in at this point, but I don't think this is a girl who needs alcohol in her system to say things she shouldn't. "Especially considering Aiden's family and their . . . limitations." She eyes me with faux sympathy plastered over obvious scorn, as if those limitations encompass everything from my family's lack of staggering wealth to, you know, *me*.

"Aiden's family has been very involved and *very* supportive," Rachel says through gritted teeth, hands squeezing her clay a little tighter than they probably need to be.

"Oh, of course," Number 6 says with wide, innocent eyes. "But still, I know it must be difficult, considering how many more resources your parents have." That's a very diplomatic way of saying *You're rich and he's solidly middle class at best,* but we all hear her real meaning nonetheless.

Aiden and I grew up with basically everything we wanted, all of our needs met, clothes, books, and vacations. But the recession hit my mom's real estate business hard, meaning the big house and its constant renovations are more about the *appearance* of affluence. Dad taught middle school English for exactly as long as it took to retire and live off his 401(k). By the standards of most of the world, Aiden and I are extremely lucky. By Boca standards, we're approaching Oliver Twist territory.

"I'm sure Aiden is excited about marrying into a family with . . . well, a more *elevated* lifestyle," Rachel 6 barrels on. Her gaze alights on me again, and she really can't hide the condescension this time. I can feel myself shrinking under her gaze, twisting inward in an attempt to disappear. "You must be *so* proud of him, Julia."

The table has gone very quiet, and everyone is very focused on their clay. "I am," I tell her.

"Although I'm sure all this is a bit uncomfortable for you, considering the circumstances." Her smile is feline, predatory. I suppose that makes me the mouse. "It's so sad that Jenna couldn't be here."

I feel very small.

"That's enough, Danielle," says Rachel. So that's her name. Rachel doesn't look at me, just gazes into her wineglass and picks at the clay stuck to her nails, wiping them furiously on a rag like some kind of Etsy Lady Macbeth.

"I'll be right back," I say, standing up. "Just gonna run to the bathroom."

"The ladies' room is just behind the kiln, on the right," Stephanie says. Rachel 6 huffs. Loudly.

In the bathroom I run my hands under the cold tap, press

them to my flushed cheeks, and lift my hair to fan the back of my neck. I haven't met this kind of open hostility in a while. I'm used to the occasional knowing look back in New York—I can't help but recall Lorraine at Born to Bride eyeing me in the dressing room—and an incorrect pronoun from a waiter or salesperson. But the antagonism simmering in Rachel 6's eyes is more obvious and downright *nastier* than anything I've experienced in ages. On the one hand, it's refreshing to know where I stand with her. On the other hand, it makes me want to get out of here as fast as I can. And there's also the dark rabbit hole looming, that just because *she* is the only one being so forthright with her nastiness doesn't mean the rest of them aren't thinking it.

"It's fine," I tell my reflection in the mirror. She's upset her sorority sister got axed and wants to make sure I know it. "It's fine," I repeat, wishing it didn't sound like a lie.

When I'm done, Kim is waiting outside the ladies' room. She holds up a joint, wiggles her eyebrows at me, and points to the back door, through which I can see an employee parking lot behind the shop. I almost sag with relief.

Outside, Kim lights her joint for us and takes a long drag. "Danielle is a cunt," she says on an exhale, smoke curling around her face. She passes the joint.

"I honestly can't remember any of their names, but I assume you're talking about the one who made it *very* clear she was ready to fight me on Jenna's behalf?" She nods, but there's no patronizing look of empathy or outrage on my behalf, which is honestly a relief.

"If it makes you feel better, she went to school with Rachel and me, and I have it on good authority that she once did so much coke she shit her pants at a Halloween party while wearing an extremely culturally insensitive costume and spent three semesters known as Diaper Genie."

I snort so hard I start choking on the hit I've just taken, and Kim starts laughing too, and soon we're both doubled over next to a dumpster full of vases, mugs, and ashtrays that were never picked up by their creators. We pass the joint back and forth in comfortable silence for a few minutes, inching closer and closer together against the concrete wall every time our hands brush. Soon we're shoulder to shoulder, and it feels like I can taste every breath Kim takes. She turns to look at me and her face is so close our eyelashes almost brush. She has really long eyelashes. Or perhaps I'm just really stoned. Her gaze flickers down to my mouth.

She's looking at me *like that* again, and at least this time I didn't have to lie to make it happen.

"This is really good weed," I tell her, and then she leans forward and *bites my lip.*

Kim bites my lip between her teeth and sucks it into her mouth, which is a little dry from the weed and a little sour from the wine, but it still feels *so* good. It takes a moment for me to realize this is really happening but then I *do* and I kiss her back, moving my lips against hers until between us there is only slick wet heat. For a moment we're just standing there, close together but not as close as I'd like, kissing lazily with an inch of space between our bodies. But then I let my tongue drift lazily into her mouth and she *sucks* on it, and whoever was holding the joint drops it and we grab for each other, my hands around her waist and hers tangled in my hair. We kiss and kiss and kiss, pressing our bodies into each other. Kim turns so she's against the wall and works her hands down to grab at my ass, and something embarrassingly like a whimper steals out of my mouth when she *lifts* me up *by my ass* so that I'm straddling one of her long, lean legs.

I feel feverish, manic, and out of control. Kim kisses like it's last call and she's convincing me to take her home, and I kiss back like someone who does *not* need to be convinced. I run my hands up and down her arms, rejoicing in every new inch of skin and wishing desperately there was more to touch. Our teeth clash and she pulls my hair back, angling my neck so that she can move her lips to my ear, tug the lobe between her teeth, and *bite*.

Another embarrassing, humiliating whimper. "Fuck," I gasp out.

"God," she whispers in my ear, tongue following the breath of her words, "you taste even better than you look."

Whimper. "You too, shit." More kissing, more groping. Another turn so my back is against the wall. Her hand reaches inside the waistband of my leather pants to squeeze my ass.

"And you feel so fucking good," she groans against my neck. Is this *real*? How is this *happening*? Getting stoned and making out with Kim Cameron behind a strip mall is one of my most tried-and-true teenage fantasies. A younger, more acne-ridden me used to masturbate to the very thought of this *exact* scenario not five miles from where we're standing. Leaning. My legs are not working very well at the moment, to be honest.

"All I want to do," she whispers in my ear, tongue flicking out to tease it on every syllable, "is take you back to my hotel room and peel these *insane* pants off of you."

"It'll probably be, uh, pretty hard to get them off," I huff out.

"It's kinda humid and they're like, stuck on *really* tight." What the fuck am I saying? Shut up! Shut *up*, you idiot. "I'd be all, like, sweaty."

"Just how I want you," she says and kisses me again. There's no more talking for quite some time.

Eventually—and regretfully—I pull away. "We have to go back inside," I tell her, ducking my head at the sight of her dark eyes, and her swollen lips. "Rachel is probably wondering where we are."

She laughs, nuzzling her nose into my throat. "I'm sure Rachel knows exactly where we are and what we're getting up to. We used to live together, remember? She knows what I like to do with girls like you."

"Girls like me?"

She makes an affirmative noise against my collarbone. "Hot, long legs, *easy*." It's said with a curving smile against my skin but still comes out a little mean, just the way I like it. "Quiet, but in that way where you know you can make them scream if you try hard enough." She raises her eyes to look into mine. "I can try *very* hard."

That is . . . information. Information I am not equipped to process. "Our clay is probably dry by now," I say dumbly. She leans back, looking for the first time uncertain. "It's not that I don't want to keep doing . . . this." I'm pretty sure it's obvious from how close we are just how much I want to keep doing *this*, every part of my body feels like it's vibrating, straining toward her. "But we are at a bachelorette party for which you are the maid of honor."

She pouts. "But I don't *wanna*." A hand traces up my side

and lingers against one of my breasts. "I'd much rather have my hands on you than some overpriced organic clay."

And I'd like to agree, and let her mold me into whatever she wants, something or someone new, indelibly marked by her. I'd like her to carve her initials into me and get me hot enough that they'd fix and never fade. But she knows I'm right, so she pulls away and helps me fix the hair she'd put so much effort into mussing. She opens the door for me, and just before we walk back inside she kisses the corner of my jaw. "Later," she promises. And I let myself believe her.

CHAPTER Twenty

"WAKE UP, WE'RE going to the mall!"

"Five more minutes," I mumble out.

It takes me a long moment to realize I am not, in fact, sixteen years old. Yes, I'm in my old room at my mother's house and that very same mother is shouting at me through the door. Yes, I fell asleep thinking about Kim Cameron. Yes, I've somehow managed to displace the duvet, sheets, and pillows while sleeping and am lying in a bare bed with sunlight pouring in the window like a personal attack.

But I also have a throbbing headache from all the wine I drank last night, and I detested wine as a teenager, much more likely to get a buzz from a few Smirnoff Ices. Also, I'm wearing a set of silky pajamas pilfered from a pop star's PR pile that I would never have allowed myself to covet when I lived here. And most important, Kim Cameron kissed me last night. Not in a fantasy, but in real life. In a smelly, muggy parking lot behind a novelty pottery studio while my future sister-in-law and her clones got drunk on rosé and made commemorative vases.

"Julia, are you up?" my mother asks through the closed door, despite knowing from years of experience that I'm still horizontal, if not unconscious. Thank god I locked the door when I came home last night, otherwise, she'd be dragging me out of bed by my feet. That's not an exaggeration: it's how she woke me up through most of middle school.

"Yes, Mother." She hates when I call her that. "Give me half an hour."

"Twenty minutes," she shouts back, voice fading. "I need a Diet Coke ASAP."

Groaning, I roll out of bed and into the bathroom, wincing at my reflection. Despite how often my mother has drilled into me over the past few years that you should *never* go to bed without washing your makeup off, I look like I've just come out of the pool at the end of *Rocky Horror*. I switch on the shower, thankful for the giant suburban water heater downstairs when it instantly turns scorching hot. As I rinse off my makeup and, hopefully, some of the hangover, I puzzle out the rest of last night.

After our still-shocking encounter behind Kiln Me Softly, Kim and I rejoined the group to knowing looks from Rachels 1–5 and an apology from a chastised Rachel 6. I never managed to transform my lump of clay into anything more than, well, a lump of clay, but everyone else was so wasted by the time the eponymous kiln was fired up that it didn't matter. The midnight movie screening was torturous, both because I had to listen as a group of drunk women talked about how bad they wanted to fuck Adam Sandler *and* because Kim kept her leg pressed tightly against mine in the dark theater for the entire movie, occasionally tracing her fingers along my leather-clad thigh. We'd both been sloppy and exhausted by the time the movie ended, but had made plans to "hang out" this evening after the rehearsal dinner. The dinner was at a restaurant conveniently located in the very hotel where Kim was staying, and she'd suggested we get a drink at the bar afterward. "Or just hang out in my room," she'd said, uncharacteristically bashful. I'm cautiously optimistic that means what I think it means, and hope the dress I'm wearing tonight is easy to get quickly in and out of.

An hour and a quick stop at the McDonald's drive-thru later, Mom and I are marching through Bloomingdale's toward the shoe department because she's decided she simply *must* have a new pair of shoes for tonight despite owning a collection that would rival Carrie Bradshaw's—if Carrie Bradshaw were really into Tory Burch. I think she's also realized that we haven't had much mother-daughter time this week.

"You could use something like this," she says, pointing at a pair of hideous Michael Kors wedges. "A nice, feminine, everyday shoe. Those"—she looks toward my beat-up black boots (the only pair of my own shoes River let me pack), nose scrunched in disdain—"have got to go."

"As I have no plans to visit a yacht club or a white nationalist rally anytime soon, I'll pass."

"I have them in beige."

"Of course you do."

Thankfully, a smiling sales associate interrupts us. "Can I help you?" She's an older woman, around my mom's age, and already looks tired at 11 A.M. I can relate.

"Yes," says my mother, "my *daughter* and I are looking for

shoes for an event tonight. My son's rehearsal dinner. He's getting *married* tomorrow."

She does this a lot when we're out together, emphasizing the *daughter*, and telling nail technicians we're having a *girl's day*. I'm sure she does it unconsciously, but a small, nasty part of me worries it's because she's sure something about me—my low voice or my wide shoulders—will give me away.

And if that's true, if she believes that's how other people will see me . . . is that how *she* sees me?

I squash the doubt down, and make it as small as possible. *I've always wanted a daughter,* I remind myself. *That's what she said when you told her.* That *is what matters. That's real.*

"Congratulations," the sales associate says, managing a smile that looks roughly forty percent sincere. "Were you looking for anything in particular?"

"Something strappy," says Mom. "And beige. And she'll"—she points at me—"probably want something in black."

"You know me *so* well," I say, "but I don't need shoes. I'm all set for tonight."

Mom gives me a look. "Sweetie, it's my treat. And while I'm sure what you brought is . . . nice, this is your brother's rehearsal dinner. Let's get you something *elegant*." She turns back to the sales associate. "Do you carry larger sizes?"

The headache that's been rumbling around on a low simmer all morning starts to throb. "Seriously, Mom, I'm good. Remember, River lent me some shoes."

"I'm sure whatever *they* let you borrow is lovely," she says, making sure to emphasize the pronoun, "but wouldn't you like a nice pair of heels you don't have to give back? Every woman should have a good pair of black pumps. Right?" she asks the associate, who nods, clearly wanting to be involved in this conversation as little as possible. That makes two of us.

"I'm more of a combat boot girl," I tell the associate, trying to make the whole thing funny rather than awkward. The pained look on her face says I'm not succeeding.

"You've been wearing the same pair of boots since you were fourteen," says Mom, clearly exasperated. The *when you were a boy* goes unsaid, but I hear it all the same. It's like she's asking me what's the point, why did I transition if I'm going to leave the house with chipped black nail polish and no bra? How am I a woman if I don't get a blowout every week and own a pair of pumps?

So I give in. "OK, yeah, fine." I smile at the sales associate. "I wear an eleven." Mom's smile is victorious.

It doesn't stop at the pumps. I let her buy me a pair of ballet flats I'll never wear, a bra I can't fill out, some perfume that has no hope of making it on the flight back to New York with me. I let myself be dragged out of Bloomingdale's and around the mall, becoming more sullen with every new store we visit. I feel ten years old again, forced into a Sears changing room to try on a suit for my cousin's bat mitzvah. When I ask if we can stop at the bookstore so I can grab something to read on the flight home, she insists we don't have time, then steers us into Sephora where we spend thirty minutes finding me the perfect shade of concealer. I think it makes me look jaundiced, but whatever, she's paying.

"It's just for touch-ups, of course," she says. "I booked someone to come do our hair and makeup tomorrow."

"Oh." I'm pleasantly surprised. "That's nice."

"Hopefully she can do something about *this*," she says, tugging at the hasty bun I'd managed to wrangle my hair into that morning, ruffling my messy bangs. Aaaaand we're back.

I do manage to sneak in a few things I want, like a cherry red lip gloss that I hope will look sophisticated with my cocktail dress tonight—and I get a little thrill when I imagine it smeared on Kim's mouth or leaving a sticky trail up her thighs. Mom spends ages plucking new variations of the same products she already owns off the shelves, talking to every employee she sees, and asking my opinion only to immediately disagree with it.

Finally, we're done, and all I want to do is go home and crash for another few hours, maybe spend some time daydreaming about what might happen with Kim tonight. But Mom decrees that we're getting lunch, and so I find myself once again wedged into a booth at a mall chain restaurant that is just barely a nicer version of the Cheesecake Factory.

"I'm starving," Mom says as she peruses the menu. "But I didn't eat breakfast."

"You don't need to justify being hungry." Thanks to Grandma, who spent a year of my childhood eating rice pudding for every meal, Mom has always had a complicated relationship with food. "You can just, you know, *be hungry*."

"I know that," she says, acid in her voice, brows lifted high at the criticism. She can dish it out but has never been able to take it. This is the woman who still ends our arguments by insisting, "I'm right because I'm your mother." I sigh, and when the waiter comes to take our order, I try to ignore the look in her eyes when I ask for a cheeseburger.

As we wait for our food, I look out the windows next to our booth and let my mind drift, staring at the tall palm trees ubiquitous to Floridian landscaping swaying gently in the breeze. Even though it's a weekday, the mall is packed, little knots of shoppers hurrying through the parking lot to reach the air-conditioning and escape the muggy heat. A mother and daughter walk past the window, talking animatedly with their shoulders brushing, hair swinging in identical ponytails.

Would days like this be easier if I'd had them growing up? Mother-daughter shopping trips where I was carefully instructed in the ways of womanhood, welcome to it as my birthright rather than something I'd claimed and conquered for myself? *I always wanted a daughter* . . .

Or would our relationship be just as thorny and complicated, just as comfortable and combative as it is now? Would raising a girl have softened my mother in some fundamental way, made her feel like she had an ally in a house full of boys?

I wish we had the kind of relationship where I could ask these questions and, more important, get honest answers.

My phone buzzes with a text from Everett, and I feel a shock of panic realizing I haven't checked any of his emails for days. I'm about to open it when Mom says my name, with an emphasis that makes me realize it isn't the first time.

"Sorry, what?"

"Have you written your speech yet?"

"Kind of." I snag a breadstick from the basket between us, snapping it in half and chewing with my mouth open just to annoy her. "It's a work in progress."

"The wedding is *tomorrow*, Julia. You're always leaving everything to the last minute."

"Is *your* speech ready?" I ask.

"I'm going to speak from the heart," she says, tossing golden hair over one shoulder. I guess one of us should.

Eighteen
YEARS AGO

MY MOM LOOKS so beautiful on the day of her wedding to Randy. Her hair is huge and curly, and her dress as poofy as the Disney princesses I won't admit I still love. Even as a child, I understand that the wedding has happened rather fast. Dad only moved out two years ago, but Mom had been sad for so long.

We get our cheeks pinched all day by relatives we barely know, telling us how handsome we look in our little tuxedos. We carry the rings down the aisle, and part of me likes the attention. The other part of me is so jealous of my cousin Alyssa and her sparkly pink dress as she scatters rose petals down the aisle.

Someone gives me my first sip of champagne, and my head is all fuzzy. My bow tie is tight enough to feel like it's choking me, and the music is so loud. There are some other children here, cousins and second cousins and Mom's friends' kids, but I'm not in the mood to play with any of them. Aiden is, though, and despite our promise to stick together tonight I haven't seen him in hours. "Sweetheart," my mom coos as she drops into the chair next to me, her dress knocking a glass of water off the table. "Are you having a good time?"

"Yeah," I lie. "Are you?"

She smiles, the kind of real smile I never saw when Dad still lived with us. "So happy, baby. This is the happiest day of my life." She catches herself, giggles a bit. "Except for the days you and Aiden were born, of course."

"Happier than the day you married Dad?"

"Different," she says. Throughout the divorce and the months of family counseling, Mom always tried to be honest, to talk to Aiden and me like adults. "It's different, baby. But it was a wonderful day, and I will always love your father because he gave me you." This has been a constant refrain since they sat Aiden and me down two years ago and told us Dad was going to live somewhere new, one Mom has maintained while Dad has never said it again.

"I love you, Mommy." It's not something I call her anymore, feeling far too old at eleven to call my mother something so childish. But I like the way it softens her, makes her pull me into the cloud of her skirts and her sweet gardenia scent.

"I love you too, baby. You'll always be my first, my perfect little boy."

It feels wrong, and I won't know why for a long, long time.

CHAPTER
Twenty-One

THE OLDER I get, the faster time moves. Every year seems to fly by, but there are days when an hour can feel like a decade, and today is one of those days. Maybe it's because of how torn I am this evening: part of me is anxious about seeing my entire extended family and being seen by them for the first time in years, all at once. The other part is just as nervous, but it's a hot flush of anticipation and desire, wondering what might happen with Kim after the rehearsal dinner. A drink, a few more kisses . . . something more?

wyd after dinner tonight? texts Ben with stunning timing as I'm lying face down in bed, procrastinating getting ready. I think about it for a second: finally getting my hands on Kim Cameron—and more important, getting *her* hands on *me*—after dinner, and winding down with an entirely predictable fuck at Ben's as a nightcap. There have been many nights in my life where I've done something similar. I like sex. I'm not ashamed of liking sex. Maybe fucking two partners of two different genders on the same day would make me a bit of a stereotypically wanton bisexual, but if the size-eleven shoe fits . . .

It's not that, though. Over the past few years, it's gotten harder and harder for me to have random sex with people who don't care if I live or die, and Ben knows me, not just my body but *me*. There is intimacy there, and Ben offers it easily without expecting anything more than what I can give.

The difference is that I feel like I finally have something to give, and I'd like to give it to Kim.

hopefully tiring myself out with the maid of honor ;) I write back.

nice!!!!! suppose i'll try my luck with that sexy cousin of yours

the accountant

with the arms

If you fuck jeffrey you MUST tell me everything, it's ALWAYS the quiet ones I reply, smiling in relief.

ok perv ;) see u tonight

Well that's sorted, thank god. Kim already knows that Ben and I have our recurring casual encounters, but I want it to be clear tonight that I'm hers for the taking. (I would very much like to be took. Taken?) I'm pretty confident Kim wouldn't mind knowing I've hooked up with Ben this week, and if she did I'd be more disappointed in *her* than anything. But thankfully that's one interpersonal snafu I don't have to concern me tonight, which is good because I have *so many others* to fret about.

My phone vibrates with a FaceTime call from Kyle, who has an uncanny ability to know when I'm freaking out. "Thank god," I say, answering the call.

"That bad, huh?" He's behind the bar at Tony's, restocking wine in a Hannah G concert T-shirt and tight jeans. I miss him and New York and *my life* with a sudden, fierce pang. I groan, flopping back on the bed and propping my phone up against my folded knees. "You have no idea." That's not exactly true—I've already filled the group chat in on the bachelorette party and the kiss with Kim, but they're only getting the highlights, not all the uncomfortable little moments buzzing around me like gnats in August.

"I hate who I am here," I tell him. "The moment the plane touched down I turned into this whole other person."

"Aw, but you're so good at that," he says with a grin. I narrow my eyes. "Haha," I return, wooden.

He cracks open a bottle of rosé, perspiration clear on the glass even through our phones.

"Going home sucks, I don't know what to tell you. And weddings make everyone crazy. You're dealing with fucked-up family dynamics dialed up to twelve right now, but this too shall pass."

"Speaking of passing, I have to shave. My mother was eyeing my chin over lunch earlier."

"Ah yes, how's Dana?" Kyle and Mom have a long-distance love affair established two years ago when she was in town to visit our relatives and came into the city—begrudgingly—and took us out to dinner. They got on like a house on fire and now every time Mom calls and Kyle is there, one of them will insist I put the other on the phone so they can talk about reality TV.

"Oh, she's drunk on power knowing she gets to be mother of the groom all weekend. It's put her in a great mood. She only criticized my wardrobe, hair, and skin today, didn't even make it to my career."

"I'm sorry, babe." He's sipping wine and I wish I were there, having this conversation from my usual perch at the bar, a thousand miles away from anyone I'm related to.

"No, it's whatever, at least I got a few hideous pairs of shoes and a slice of Godiva chocolate cheesecake out of it. How are you?"

He fills me in on Tony's, his various sexual conquests, the party River dragged him to last night—though Kyle is rarely *dragged* anywhere. He likes to roll his eyes and complain, but he is far too exacting to ever do something he doesn't want to do. When we first met and slept together, he'd turned to me afterward and said, "You're cute, but we're not doing that again. Want to help me move this weekend?" I'd helped carry his antique dresser up four flights of stairs, bitching at each other all the way, and knew almost prophetically we were going to be friends forever.

Kyle took me to my first loft party in Flatbush and showed me how to find the rhythm in a house beat, introduced me to Daytona at a Disney-themed drag show at which she'd performed Scar's "Be Prepared" from *The Lion King*. If River is my fashionable fairy godmother—godthemer?—and Daytona my ice queen sister à la *Frozen,* Kyle is the Timon to my Pumbaa, the Lilo to my Stitch, the fox to my hound.

Fuck, am I becoming a Disney adult? I need to get out of Florida. Quickly.

I try to chime in, ask him questions, and engage in the conversation because I feel like all my friendships have been focused in one direction (mine) recently, but it's hard with the big question mark of tonight looming over me. Kyle can tell.

"Cheer up, Charlie."

"Don't deadname me." Charlie is not my deadname.

"You are much too glum for someone about to scissor their high school crush," he chides.

"I think you need two vaginas for that."

"All right, you'll staple. Or paperclip. Or three-hole punch. There's a whole world of office supplies out there."

I'm laughing, and for the first time today not thinking about tonight, which is exactly why I needed to talk to Kyle. It doesn't last, though, and the doubts creep back in. "What if it's bad?" I can't help but ask. "Like, maybe she's bad at sex."

"Does she kiss like she's bad at sex?"

"Very much no. What if *I'm* bad at sex?"

"You're not. You're very . . . eager, which is why we only had sex once." He takes a snooty sip from his glass. "I require a more aloof lover."

"If you want to be *technical* about it, we had sex twice." He looks confused. "Remember? That foursome on Fire Island?"

"Oh that barely counts, my balls were in your mouth for like, thirty seconds *max*. I will be generous and say we've had sex 1.5 times."

We fall into a well-worn argument we've been having for years, and the easy bickering carries us through another few minutes before Kyle is dragged away by a customer who, it turns out, has been sitting quietly waiting to be served throughout our entire conversation. He makes me promise to keep him updated on tonight's events, and I end the call feeling a bit more centered, a bit more *me*. I can do this. I don't really have a choice, but I can do it anyway.

CHAPTER
Twenty-Two

MOM AND RANDY are explaining to the twins why they are not allowed to bring their pet snake inside the synagogue, so I leave them in the car and make my way inside alone. The parking lot is nearly empty—Mom wanted to stop for a Diet Coke so we left early and arrived twenty minutes before the wedding rehearsal was due to start. When I attended Hebrew school here the parking lot was always packed to the brim with Audis and Lexuses that clashed with Randy's huge, hulking white Suburban.

The sanctuary doors are closed when I step inside the lobby, and I consider waiting out here for the rest of the wedding party to arrive, but I haven't been here in so long and can't resist the opportunity to take a look inside while it's empty and quiet. I might not be religious, but I've always appreciated the sheer aesthetic beauty of the sanctuary: the stained glass windows and red velvet auditorium seats, the heavy silence that comes with being somewhere you know is meant to be connected to the divine.

The dark carpet masks the sound of my feet as I approach the bimah. I experience a weird sense of doubling as I remember taking these steps dozens of times as a teenager before I decided Hebrew school wasn't really for me. To be bar or bat mitzvahed, you had to attend fifty hours of services. We were never a very religious family, so Mom would drop me off alone on Friday nights. The other kids in my year would sit together in the mezzanine, whispering and laughing together during the service, but I always sat below at the back of the room, hiding my Game Boy in my siddur and gazing longingly at Rabbi Hoffman during his sermons.

I stop at the bimah and gaze out at the empty pews. I remember, vaguely, my mother's concerned face as I ascended to this very spot the August after I turned thirteen. I was a summer baby, so everyone in my year had already had their bar or bat mitzvah. I'd attended one of them almost every weekend that year, invited not because they were my friends, but because my mother knew their parents and it was expected I'd be invited. They'd all seemed to handle it so easily, but I'd struggled to learn my haftarah portion, which required additional time with my tutor that my mother paid for not necessarily because she was concerned that I didn't learn quickly enough, but because it wouldn't be good if I embarrassed her. She'd still been worried about me embarrassing her that morning, it was clear on her face from where I now stood. But I'd leaned over the Torah and recited the Hebrew words I'd memorized over long, frustrating afternoons, words I realize with a jolt I still half remember. And yet I need three separate phone alarms to remind me to inject estrogen every other week.

I turn to look at the ark behind me, its huge wooden doors protecting the collected teachings of *my people,* passed down through generations. What would they think of me standing here, in my mascara and thong gaff and spiritual apathy?

"Shalom."

I whip around and forget all about my ancestors because Kim is walking toward me, looking sleek and sexy in a dark suit. Watching her walk down the aisle my future sister-in-law would be walking down tomorrow to get married makes me feel kind of psycho, but in a good way.

"I like your dress," she says. "Didn't Hannah G wear that in *Vogue* last month?"

How River hasn't been fired yet is beyond me. "I really don't like that you know that," I say, preening a bit.

The dress is a deep red so vivid I immediately vetoed it when River pulled it out—I have a very pink undertone!—but once they'd bullied me into trying it on, I couldn't deny the color was striking. It's skintight, with exaggerated boning making me very hesitant to eat anything at dinner. The bodice is so snug it's difficult to breathe, but my breasts have never looked better and the silhouette makes me longer and leaner than I actually am, as do the pointy platform heels I'm wearing, which weigh about ten pounds each.

I won't deny it: I look hot. I'm not sure I've ever looked hotter, including the summer I got strep throat and lost fifteen pounds. I might hate myself, but I'd also hate fuck myself.

Kim joins me at the bimah, lays her hand on my shoulder,

and kisses me. It's not as hungry as our kisses last night, but still pointed. Claiming.

"Don't," I whine. "We're in a *temple*."

She slides her hand around to squeeze my ass.

"My mother could walk in any second."

"Is that supposed to dissuade me? She's kind of a MILF." She shakes her head as if remembering something. "Has it been OK with her this week?"

Goose bumps erupt on my arms and I can't blame it on the air-conditioning. In this sacred space, standing on the very spot where I'd once become a man in the eyes of God, I feel the real weight of my deception, which I've been rationalizing as a white lie, a harmless twisting of the truth to endear myself to a hot girl I'd wanted to make out with for over a decade. But I now see it as the gross manipulation it really is, and I hate myself for it.

But it hadn't gone too far yet. I could come clean right now and atone. Every year on Yom Kippur I'd stood at the man-made pond behind this very building, stomach clenching in hunger as I shredded challah into small pieces and tossed them into the water, one for each of my sins. Here is the chance to do that for real, to clear the air and maybe see if this thing between us could be more than just a wedding fling.

"Julia!" It was my mother, walking through the now-open doors of the sanctuary flanked by the twins, Randy trailing behind. "You couldn't have waited for us?"

Kim's lip twists in a sneer, and her arm moves around my waist to pull me close, almost behind her. I think about the fleeting references she'd made to her own mother, the way she'd softened toward me over the past few weeks, the teenager I'd once been who never stood a chance with a girl who liked other girls.

"It's fine," I muttered in Kim's ear. "It'll be over soon." Even in six-inch heels, I'd never felt so small.

. . .

Rabbi Hoffman is somehow even more handsome than I remember, tall and tan and solid with a salt-and-pepper beard, curly grown-out hair pushed out of his kind eyes, and hands I used to fantasize about spanking me as punishment for getting the Mourner's Kaddish wrong.

"Hello, Julia," he says with a big, friendly smile. This man has been, without fail, the most reliable tool in my orgasm arsenal for most of my life, waiting patiently in my spank bank until I needed him to help make it through a lackluster sexual encounter or lonely night with nothing but my Hitachi Magic Wand. Seeing him in the flesh and having him look so good and be so nice is *excruciating*.

Kim gives me a wicked smile from her place opposite me, clearly reading my mind. We're standing where the chuppah will be tomorrow—they're getting it out of some storage closet right now—Aiden and Rachel between us, ready for what I've been assured will be a quick run-through.

I'd like to be run through, I think, gazing at Rabbi Hoffman's hairy forearms.

"Most of what happens tomorrow will be just like what you've seen in the movies," Rabbi Hoffman tells the wedding party. "Aiden will wait here with his groomspeople"—no awkward pause, damn he's good—"and Rachel will be escorted down the aisle by her father."

"It's gonna be so hard to give my baby away," says Rachel's dad, a mousy little man I've spoken to only a handful of times.

"We don't like to think of it as *giving away*," says Rabbi Hoffman, soft but stern. "This is a union, not an exchange."

I get it, Kim mouths at me, nodding at the rabbi. Having the biggest crushes of my formative years—aside from my AP world history teacher and Gina Gershon in *Bound*—in one room is dizzying.

We move quickly through the ceremony, and at the end Aiden and Rachel make out disgustingly enough to have me worried about what the real thing will look like tomorrow. Everyone is in their finery for tonight's rehearsal dinner. Rachel's dress is black and surprisingly chic, Aiden's navy suit fits him perfectly. This is really happening.

"How am I gonna survive a night without you, baby," Rachel whines, loud enough for most of us to hear it and groan.

After the actual rehearsal, we mingle outside the synagogue. The rehearsal dinner won't start for another forty minutes and is only ten minutes away—Boca problems!—so everyone is taking their time.

Kim and I are loitering by the water fountain. I want to bend over and take a sip but my dress is so tight I'm not sure it's worth it.

"You look really good, if I didn't already say it," she says.

"You didn't really," I say, shuffling closer. "But I could kinda tell."

She laughs, surprised. Kim has such a beautiful smile, a little crooked on one side, big and broad with perfect white teeth. I want to lean in and just *sniff* her so bad, shove my face into her armpit and slobber all over it. That's probably not appropriate in public, let alone a place of worship with my entire nuclear family ten feet away.

And getting closer.

"Hello, *ladies*," Mom says, drawing close to us. Kim's suspicious look returns at the emphasis on *ladies*, which I know is my mom trying to be cute, or to do the annoying supportive cis woman thing and constantly reaffirm a trans person's gender, but to Kim's ears I'm sure it sounds mocking, downright hostile. "I don't think we've had a chance to be properly introduced, I'm Aiden's mother."

"And Julia's," Kim says, hostility clear in her tone. Mom, usually blithely unaware of social cues, seems to hear it nonetheless.

"Well yes, of course." She laughs awkwardly. "And you're the maid of honor?"

"Kim," she says, nodding. "Nice to meet you." Nice is not the word I'd use. My palms start to sweat. I've led us here. Kim is about to verbally bitch-slap my mother in a temple and it's all my fault.

"You two are going to be quite a sight standing next to Aiden and Rachel tomorrow," Mom continues, confused but clearly trying to be complimentary, but *god*, her choice of words is digging the hole deeper. Do I say something? But if I say something now it's going to cause a scene, *both* of them will be furious and then Aiden will be furious and Rachel will probably bludgeon me to death with a prayer book for ruining her wedding before it could really start.

"I'm sure no one will be looking at us next to the happy couple," I say, attempting to redirect the conversation. Kim squeezes my hand and I see my mom catch it, her eyes lighting up. She opens her mouth to say something else meant to be nice that will only cause some kind of interpersonal supernova when, for the first time in my life, my father saves the day.

"Does anyone know where the bathroom is? They've remodeled this place at least twice since I was last here and I've got to piss like a racehorse."

Mom rolls her eyes and stalks off as I direct Dad to the bathroom, but not before he gives Kim a once-over and shoots me the world's least subtle wink.

"God, your mom," Kim says once he's gone. "I'm so sorry, Jules."

"No, really, it's not—" And then my phone starts buzzing in my hand, and I see Everett's name flashing on the screen. "Fuck, I have to take this, it's my boss."

"Of course." She nods, so sweet and understanding. I creep miserably outside and swipe to answer. "Hel—"

"Julia, why did I just receive a very angry call from Rosalind Schwartz about a bulldozer turning up at her house this morning?"

Fuck fuck fuck fuck fuck fuck fuck fuck fuck fuck fuck fuck.

"Oh my god," I gasp. "I forgot to reschedule it. Everett, I'm *so* sorry, I can call the construction company now and—"

"I've already done that," he says, "after I spent half an hour talking her down, a half an hour she spent naming no less than fifteen other designers who would be more than happy to take over the project if I was no longer *up to the task.*"

Fuck fuck fuck fuck fuck fuck fuck fuck fuck fuck fuck fuck.

"Everett, I can't even begin to—"

"No, you really can't." He takes a deep sigh. "Look, I know you're technically out of office this week, but I told you to let me know if you needed me to handle this while you were away and you didn't, then you just dropped the ball—almost literally, because there was an *actual fucking wrecking ball* involved!"

"I know, I screwed up, I've been so busy and overwhelmed. Do you want me to email Mrs. Schwartz?"

"What I want you to do is take the weekend to assess if you really want to be doing this work."

"Everett, of course I do!"

"Because it isn't just this, Julia. It's one thing for you to roll your eyes when I ask you to pick up my new harness from Purple Passion, but you *told me* you wanted more responsibility, that you wanted to be a real designer, but I'm just not seeing it."

Hot tears spring into my eyes and I fight to hold them back. Through the glass doors Mom gives me an annoyed look, gesturing for me to come back inside. Beside her, Kim glares, looking back at me with sympathy.

"I'm sorry," I say again, though this time I'm not sure who I'm apologizing to, or what for.

Everett sighs again. "Look, I don't want to ruin your weekend. Have fun at the wedding, and we'll talk when you're back."

"Everything OK?" Kim asks when I'm back inside.

"It's fine," I say. She looks like she wants to say more, but instead squeezes my hand in one of hers and shoots another glare at my mom. I should say something, but my stomach hurts and my heart is pounding and my feet are aching in Hannah G's stupid fucking shoes.

In the back seat of Randy's car on the way to the rehearsal dinner I compose an email for Everett and an explanation for

Kim, swiping back and forth between the two. It's always been easier for me to write down what I want to say in a stressful situation, helps me get my thoughts in order. It's not working, so I open my speech for the reception tomorrow, which is more of a bulleted list of childhood stories carefully selected to embarrass Aiden on his big day, my duty as the older sister.

But the closer we get to the dinner, the more dread chokes me. Every second is bringing me closer to walking into a room full of people who have known me my entire life. People who were there when I was born and graduated from high school, people who had my Little League pictures stuck on their refrigerators with magnets. People who sent me checks for my bar mitzvah made out to a name that's not mine and never was.

And they know, of course, what my name is now, and what pronouns they should be using. Some of them have seen me over dinner when they were visiting New York, or just a few nights ago at the bar where I saw more of Rachel's vagina than anyone but Aiden and her gynecologist should ever see. Many of them received the email I sent out three and a half years ago, in which I explained that I was a woman whose name was Julia and linked out to several helpful resources for families of trans people. I received many sweet responses to that email and even some surprising ones. (My cousin David told me his best friend from college had transitioned a few years ago—although he *also* assumed we *knew* each other, as if all trans people are part of some secret underground network through which we share hormones and talk shit about how problematic and dangerous *Silence of the Lambs* is.) (I fucking love *Silence of the Lambs*!) (I also love *Mrs. Doubtfire*.)

But there is a difference between knowing and *seeing*, and especially seeing in *context*. My close friends have been with me through my transition, but the way my life has worked out over the past couple of years is that for the most part, the people I engage with on a day-to-day basis are people who have only ever known me as Julia. They might have been there for that horrible first year when I was still growing out my hair and figuring out how to use makeup, how often I needed to shave, and the right way to keep my head down on the train so no one bothered me, but they implicitly understand that I am . . . this. Me. Even my New York friends who knew me *before* had only known me for a few years, and in those few years, I was a slutty bisexual demon who spent my weekends dancing with almost no rhythm in dive bars and abandoned warehouses with glitter on my cheeks and clothing that grew increasingly androgynous.

But the people at this rehearsal dinner tonight knew me when I was a little boy, or at least when I thought I was supposed to be one, when I was *told* I was supposed to be one, and I can't help but be terrified that's all they're going to see, a little boy playing dress-up in someone else's clothing. Because, if I'm being honest, there are still plenty of days when I look in the mirror and that's all *I* see.

I could blame that on the obvious things, like my fivehead or my shoulders or the fact that I have to shave my face every few days and my breasts are still kind of pointy rather than full and rounded—I'll never have the dirty pillows Carrie White's mom murdered her over. But those things are the most boring things to feel bad about as a trans woman, and after a few years of living in this cyborg body, I'm kind of sick of being bothered by them. More than anything, I just fundamentally still feel like the same person I was *before* I worried about them, and I'm terrified at how quickly I became a quieter, angrier, *lesser* version of myself as soon as my plane touched down on Floridian soil. Or, the ultimate horror, I've been that version of myself all along.

That's the lie of transition, of congestible politics and born-in-the-wrong-body rhetoric: there is not a *before* and an *after*. I came here hoping to make some triumphant debut to my family, floating in like a butterfly and banishing any memory of the awkward little boy who used to race around their houses trying to find the afikomen at Passover. But to have that experience, I'd have to believe that in transitioning I have *transformed* . . . and I don't. I was not a boy who felt wrong his whole life and then, through a combination of hormones and hair removal, became a girl. I am a girl who was told she was a boy and didn't have any way to dispute that, tried her best to make that work for a couple of decades, was *really* bad at it, and decided to stop pretending. I'm just a person who used to show up in the world in one way that didn't work for me and made me fucking depressed and checked out of my own life but couldn't figure out or didn't want to admit why, and once I finally did, there was no going back. So I transitioned.

And now I'm still that person, only I have pointy little boobs and long hair and a closet full of, let's admit it, *stolen* designer dresses and a different name, and all those things might seem trivial to someone else, but they make me feel like I can exist in this world in a way that's not necessarily easier, but at least more fucking honest.

My whole childhood was spent wearing a Halloween costume I wasn't allowed to take off. But I wasn't *miserable*. I didn't grow up wishing I'd been born with different chromosomes because for the most part, I didn't understand how to put what I was feeling into words. Just call me Julia and keep it pushing!

None of this makes sense, even in my head. Or maybe it makes too much sense. Transness is nothing if not a series of contradictions, bending oneself into a living question mark, a riddle, your very own puzzle that no one—least of all yourself—knows how to solve.

I watch my mom in the front seat, my beautiful mother with her immaculate manicure and long golden hair, and despite how annoyed I was at her earlier today a rush of gratitude fills me now. She might make me want to scream and sulk when she tells me I should never leave the house without a bra, but I know it's her way of acknowledging my womanhood. She's relating to me as a woman the only way she knows how, by being an annoying mother telling her daughter to sit up straight and wear some mascara, the same way *her* mom did with her.

I am so incredibly lucky to have a family that's listened to me, learned with me, tried to do right by me and the choices I've made about my life. That's why I feel so guilty for the lies I've told Kim—and I can't keep writing them off as omission or manipulation, I've had plenty of chances to course correct and haven't done it. If I'm being honest, this has long since gone past some stupid scheme to fuck my dream girl. I like her, I *really* like her, and I'm too deep into my lies to be honest with her without creating the kind of scene that would make this week even more about me and my insecurities than it already is.

Because that's the reality I have to get through my thick skull with its prominent, *masculine* forehead ridge: this wedding isn't about me. No one is out to make me uncomfortable or unwelcome or embarrassed. This is my family, who accepted me with open, if somewhat limp, arms. *I* am the one expecting a deadname around every corner, I am the one who has created this entire romantic drama as a way to distract myself from how nervous I was that the moment was here at last. My namesake, Julia Roberts, would be proud.

I've come this far and I have to see it through. I'm going to walk downstairs on wobbly heels and a dress that is technically *at large* from a Kids' Choice Award–winning singer, smile until my gums hurt, and be extremely grateful about the insanely hot girl I never thought would want me, whose clear interest is the final proof that despite all this crippling insecurity I *am* a woman, so who gives a shit what my second cousin the accountant with a wonky eye and two failed marriages thinks?

A woman who is opening my door for me, her rental parked next to the spot Randy has just pulled into.

"Done freaking out?" she asks, taking my arm to lead me inside. She knows me so well already.

"Fuck no." I catch her eyes in the mirror and raise an eyebrow, hopefully in a sexy way and not a deranged one. "Let's go make this rehearsal dinner our bitch."

CHAPTER
Twenty-Three

"OH MY GOD, I *love* your dress!" Rachel 3 grips my shoulders, which she hasn't let go of since the hug she yanked me into when Kim and I entered the bar. "Amazon?" she asks.

"Vivienne Westwood."

Her eyes widen. "Wow. Did you get it at the mall?"

"No." I don't have the bandwidth for the Rachels right now. I have to escape. Quickly. "Oh, there's my Aunt Harriet." Aunt Harriet died during the Bush administration. The second one. "Good to see you!"

I hurtle myself away from her and straight into Uncle Aaron and his wife Brooke, whose house I used to stay at for a few weeks every summer before sleepaway camp. Aaron gives me the kind of back-slapping half hug he's been doing since I went through puberty (the first time) but Brooke wraps me up in a proper embrace, pulling back to give me a thorough scan. "Sweetie, you look incredible!" Their kids, a pair of boys a few years older than Brody and Brian, give me awkward hellos. I went to their house on Long Island for Rosh Hashanah two years ago, and while our catch-up chitchat is a bit stilted, it's mostly because we don't see each other that often and run out of pleasantries quickly.

Kim's at the bar getting us drinks, and I attempt to weave through the crowd to her but am stopped by Randy's mother Alice. "Oh my lord," she says. "Look at you." Her red hair is teased and blown out larger than hair has any right to be, her eye shadow a shocking blue, lipstick bleeding into the wrinkles around her mouth. I haven't seen her in five years and could have gone for another five. Here we go.

"Hi, Alice," I say, leaning in to kiss her cheek. "It's lovely to see you."

"My word," she says, clutching a martini to her chest. She has the kind of Southern twang that could deep-fry a chicken in seconds. "I'd heard all about *you*, of course, but my Lord!" Randy is only Jewish on his father's side, and Alice has clung stubbornly to her good Christian gentility. "You know," she says, assessing, "you're actually very pretty like this."

"Um. Thank you."

"And of course you were always . . . different." It sounds like a dirty word in her mouth. She sips her drink. I wonder how many she's had already. "I suppose we know why now, don't we?"

"Oh, I don't know," I say, looking back toward the bar but not spotting Kim. "I'm sure I'll have some new shocking revelation to share with everyone before long."

She clucks her tongue. "Bless your heart." Another gulp. I'm pretty sure she just swallowed an olive whole. "That's quite an outfit." She rakes her eyes down my body. "I hope tomorrow you'll be wearing something a bit more tasteful."

Fuck it, I probably won't have to see this woman again until Brody and Brian graduate, and they could be in prison or attempting world domination by then. "I'm picking my gimp suit up from the dry cleaners in the morning. Have a great night!"

Across the room I see my mom standing beside Rachel and Aiden as they welcome guests, Rachel's parents flanking their other side. Mom is, of course, wearing beige. When she waved me off earlier, on my way to the hotel, her eyes went straight to my feet, noticing the absence of the heels she'd paid for this morning. Her gaze was all the reproach I needed, but I reminded myself that these shoes have walked a red carpet and the ones she bought me at Bloomingdale's were thirty percent off. She can return them for all I care.

"There you are," Kim says, easing effortlessly through the crowd to hand me a glass of champagne. We clink our glasses and she moves beside me, wrapping one of those strong arms around my waist. If the bodice of my dress wasn't so tight my nipples would probably get hard.

"Hello, ladies." Ben looks dashing in a navy blue suit, dark hair slicked back. His gaze flicks to where Kim is wrapped around me and he smiles. "You both look fantastic."

"Uh." How exactly does one handle casual conversation with a person they've fucked in the past forty-eight hours and one they'd *like* to fuck in the next . . . three, tops? It's not the first time I've encountered the circumstances—Fire Island, again—but the context is wildly different. "Thanks."

"You look pretty good yourself, Otsuka." Kim, where she's

pressed against me, is as relaxed as ever. "I think you might have your pick of the bridesmaids."

He shrugs, a small smile on his lips. "One or two of the groomsmen too. But I've set my sights a little higher. Toward the heavens, one might say." He nods his head over toward the door, where Aiden and Rachel are greeting Rabbi Hoffman, the object of my preteen lust.

"Ben, if you fuck Rabbi Hoffman at my little brother's wedding I'm going to be *so* jealous." Adolescent fantasies centered around the private lessons for my haftarah portion come rushing back. "He was an extremely integral part of my bisexual awakening!"

"Imagine what we could use the tallit for."

Laughing, we wish him luck and watch him stalk toward his prey. I'm relieved, even though I'd known neither Kim nor Ben would make the situation uncomfortable. Thank god that I can share my body with people who don't feel some implicit ownership of it just *because* I've shared it with them. Even if this thing with Kim and me becomes something more—a possibility that's hot to the touch, too bright to look at closely—who's to say Ben and I won't fall back into each other the next time I visit? Kim doesn't seem possessive, and I have little desire to be possessed—outside of sex, at least. Although who knows, Rabbi Hoffman might be the jealous type.

And of course that's when my grandparents arrive.

"Hiya, doll," says Grandpa, pulling me into a hug. Grandma accepts a kiss to the cheek with the dignity of a monarch, eyes me up and down with pursed lips. "That's some dress," she says. I'm not sure what "some" is supposed to mean, but I doubt it's good.

"And who might you be, my dear?"

"Kim," she says. "Julia's friend. And Rachel's maid of honor."

Wow, I rank before maid of honor. That shouldn't feel as good as it does. It does anyway.

Eyeing her suit, Grandpa reaches forward to shake her hand and gives an overexaggerated wince.

"What a grip!" He shakes his hand out as if he's playing to the cheap seats. "Careful, I'm a very frail old man. At least, that's what my wife keeps telling me."

"Well, you were much handsomer when I married you," Grandma says, extending her own hand to Kim for a limp little shake.

"When was that again?" I ask them. "Sometime around the fall of Rome?"

"Romulus and Remus attended the ceremony," Grandpa fires back, not missing a beat. "You be nice to me, doll, or I'll write you out of the will."

I give a mock shudder. "Oh no, how will I *ever* hope to survive without your stamp collection?"

"Stamps are actually a smart investment," says Kim. "Better than the stock market."

Grandpa smiles. "I like this girl," he tells me, sotto voce, though we all can hear.

"Me too," I say, more to her than my grandpa. Kim squeezes my waist.

My grandparents soon abandon us for the bar—Grandma sternly reminding Grandpa that he can have *two martinis and that's it*—and I'm hopeful we might make it to dinner, where I'll be seated at the center table while Kim dines with the bridal party, without further interruption. I know I should get through all my awkward family interactions now, before the emotional shitshow I'm sure tomorrow will be, but all I want to do is stay tucked into Kim in this little corner, trading snarky comments about people's outfits and heated glances heavy with the promise of what might happen after dinner.

Alas, I have never been that lucky.

"Parental unit incoming," Kim warns.

"Ah, yes, the boss of this level. Hi, Dad." He's wearing the suit I unearthed from the depths of the garage, which looks like he took it out of the garment bag and put it straight on without even considering an iron or, god forbid, dry-cleaning. My father has likely never had an item of clothing dry-cleaned in his life. For the thousandth time in my life, I wonder how my mother—a woman so obsessed with order that it borders on OCD—ever married this man.

"Julie," he crows.

"I have asked you repeatedly not to call me that."

He rolls his eyes. "Right, *another* thing I'm not supposed to call you." He holds his hand out for Kim, and winces at her grip. Unlike my grandpa, I don't think he's exaggerating. Then she winces, and I follow her gaze to where Rachel is clearly summoning her. "A maid of honor's duty never ends," she tells my father apologetically, giving me a final squeeze before leaving to deal with whatever Rachel-shaped emergency had emerged.

"Nice girl," Dad says. "Pretty, if you like that type."

"What *type* is that, exactly?" I say, bristling.

"You know—butch. I guess that was always kind of your thing with girls," he says, chuckling. "You watched *Alien* every day when you were thirteen and wouldn't shut up about Sigourney Weaver."

"I can't believe you remember that," I say.

He shakes his head, a little sad. "You're my kid, I remember a lot of things about you."

This is true, but doesn't mean what he thinks it means. One of the reasons I barely talk to my dad is because it never takes long for him to start reminiscing about my childhood, how close we were, that I was his *little buddy*, following him everywhere. He misses that version of me, the one who loved him in a way that was uncomplicated, who *was* uncomplicated. A child he understood.

"Really, though," he says, "she seems great. And I can tell you like her. You look at her the way you used to look at a box of crayons when you were a kid." He reaches out to lay a hand on my shoulder. "I'm happy that you're happy."

My throat feels tight. "Thanks, Dad."

"Bit out of your league, though," he says.

"Thanks, Dad."

A bell rings. We move toward the private event space and find our seats in the cavernous dining room of the snooty Italian restaurant housed in the hotel most of the out-of-town guests are staying at. All around me are cousins and sleepaway camp friends and my mother's clique of female friends, who are essentially postmenopausal Rachels, each double fisting a cocktail in one hand and a Diet Coke in the other. Kim is across the room, walking toward the bridal table with the actual Rachels, sipping from a newly procured scotch like some *Mad Men* lesbian AU fantasy. I need this thing to move *quickly* so I can ask to see her hotel room.

The meal passes in a haze of polite conversation, overcooked pasta, and undercooked chicken. There are speeches from minor players—my own won't take place until tomorrow night. A photographer floats around capturing the revelry, and I pose with the twins, who flank me on either side.

Later, when I'm sipping espresso and avoiding the cheesecake so my dress fits tomorrow, I suddenly feel hot breath against my ear.

"I'm in room 902," Kim says. "Be there in twenty." It's not phrased even remotely like a question, so I nod my assent like a good girl. Across the table, Aiden rolls his eyes.

. . .

The carpeted hallways aren't easy to navigate in my shoes, but every step leads me closer to, I'm pretty sure, a sexual encounter I've been fantasizing about for half my life. I'm not sure if that's fair, if Kim will be able to live up to the ideal of her I've been nurturing since I was a hormonal teenager failing algebra, but the woman I've spent the past few weeks getting to know is so much different and so much more vivid than the one I'd caught glimpses of when we were both growing up and outgrowing this place day by day.

I reach her door. I knock. Everything is very quiet in the hallway, and I'm breathing so loudly she must hear me from inside. The door opens and Kim is standing there, framed by light from the heavy autumn moon shining through the windows behind her. She's taken off her suit jacket and wears only those crisp trousers and a plain white tank top so sheer I can see her nipples through it. Her braids are unbound, her neck is long, her eyes are wide.

"Hi," I say.

"Get in here," she grunts, reaching forward to wrap an arm around my waist and yank me forward, closing the door behind me and pushing me back against it.

"Take it off," she grinds out.

"Huh?"

"That dress looks expensive so please *take it off*"—she pulls a hanger from the closet to her left—"and hang it up before I *tear* it off of you."

"You can't *tear it off*," I manage, head spinning. "This dress belongs to Hannah G."

She laughs, disbelieving, with wild eyes. "I love 'Bonnie and Clyde.'" It's a single from Hannah G's debut album that still gets played almost hourly on the radio.

"I'm more partial to 'Diet Dr. Pepper,'" I respond in a daze. It's kind of a deep cut. "The bridge really goes off."

And then she's on me.

I'm grateful the evening's festivities are over, because there's no way my makeup will survive Kim's brutal kisses. Together we manage to unzip my dress and peel it off. She steps back, slides couture worth more than my mother's car onto a hanger, and shoves it into the closet, pushing me back against the door. My purse hits the ground.

Her hands are in my loose hair, gripping tightly, but don't stay there long. She touches my neck, shoulders, my naked breasts—no bra, sorry Mom—and thumbs my nipples into aching stiffness. Those hands skim my sides and reach down to cup my ass and press me firmer against her. I want to raise my legs up to wrap around her but my shoes are too heavy.

"My shoes," I pant out against her lips. "I need to take off my shoes."

She flicks her eyes down, then back up to mine. "No." Kim pulls me toward the bed and tosses me down onto it. It's unmade, as though she spent the afternoon tossing and turning enough to disrupt the pristine military precision housekeeping left behind, and I feel unbearably tender at the thought of lying somewhere Kim has slept. She stands at the foot of the bed, looking down at me, and her mouth pulls up into a wolfish grin. Her teeth look very sharp and I want her to tear me apart with them.

"What are you waiting for?" I lift my arms above my head, stretching every inch of me in the golden light of the reading lamp on the nightstand. I'm just a girl, lying in a hotel bed in front of another girl, asking her to fuck me.

"Just enjoying the view," she says, and yanks off her tank top. Her breasts are fuller than mine, curving against her ribs so softly, with wide mauve nipples. I need her to lie on top of me so bad I can't breathe, which must show on my face, because she shucks off her trousers—no briefs, sorry Mom—and pounces.

I have so much skin and all of it is pressed against hers. We kiss hard and fast, devouring each other as our hands roam. The weight of her on top of me feels so good I want to cry, but that might kill the mood. I've cried during sex before and unless you're into some very specific kink, it's not really fun for everyone. She nudges my legs open to fit between them, and again I want to wrap my legs around her but these damn shoes are still too heavy. "You know," I gasp out between kisses, "fucking with high heels on might look hot in porn, but I'm definitely going to lodge a stiletto up your ass if I don't get these off."

"Who says I'd mind?" she asks against my throat, and I have to bite back a whimper. But she nods and pulls away, sliding down my front, trailing kisses as she goes, and lifts first one leg, then another, to her chest. The shoes pinch, and the relief of having them off must show on my face, because she turns and presses a tender kiss against the arch of each foot.

Embarrassingly, that urge to cry returns. With anyone else it could be silly, or worryingly close to a *foot thing* I'm not quite sure I'm into, but with Kim it just feels . . . caring. Intimate. *Something* that's been burning hot in my belly rises up to my chest and goes tight at the way she's taking care of me.

Then her eyes snap back to mine, burning so hot I feel ready to melt, and anything careful or tender is forgotten and that molten heat is back in my belly, spreading outward and burning through every inch of my veins. She kisses her way back up my leg, nipping at the skin every few inches, and finally reaches my stupidly expensive underwear. I'm afraid for a second she's going to do something dramatic like pull them off with her teeth, which might really send me over the edge in the wrong direction, but she just hooks a finger into the strap against my hip and tugs off my thong.

Then we're in bed together, naked. No matter how horny I am or whose parts have already been where, this moment is the one that always feels the scariest with someone new. My body is bare for her to see, and tucked inside me is the lingering fear that, no matter what's happened between us so far, she might look at me, at all the flesh I have to offer, and decide it's too much or not enough. I've had partners leave after getting me naked, or caught them in that moment of resignation, of *Well, I'm already here, might as well.* But Kim's eyes are, if anything, hungrier.

"I want," she says, "to eat you alive."

Gulp. "Bon appétit."

The next few minutes are a haze of wet sucking kisses, hot skin twisting and chafing, teeth grazing sensitive flesh. Kim's head is buried between my legs, then we switch so she's straddling my face. I bite each of her nipples and she worms a finger down into my body. I nuzzle my face into her armpit and sniff deeply, committing the musk of her to memory. She smacks a hand against my ass and rubs soothingly at the mark her hand leaves behind. I lick and suck and burrow into the very center of her, trying my best to crawl inside. She wraps me tightly in her arms, only ever bringing me closer, harder, faster, *more*.

It's so hot, some of the hottest sex I've ever had. But it's also *fun*. At one point I accidentally blow a raspberry against her stomach and we both giggle madly, and she gets me back with an even louder blow moments later. If we had time, I'd lay her out and catalog every inch of her, learn every crease and mole and divot. She comes, not loudly because Kim Cameron is cool as a cucumber even when you've got three fingers and a tongue in her, and soon after I come, louder.

Despite my usual aversion to cuddling, I let Kim tuck me close against her as our sweat cools and dries in the overly air-conditioned room. The moonlight is streaming in through the blinds, and the quiet dark of the room is so still and peaceful I could fall asleep.

Kim props herself up on an elbow and looks down at me.

"Hi," I say, which is dumb.

"I hope you brought something for your hair, otherwise everyone in the lobby is going to know what we've been up here doing."

I did. There's oil and bobby pins in my bag.

"I wouldn't mind," I say. "If they could tell."

She smiles, soft and secret. It's not a smile I've seen before, and I think—hope—it might be just for me. "I wouldn't either," she says and kisses me again.

CHAPTER
Twenty-Four

IT RAINS THE morning of Aiden's wedding, but it's that particular kind of Florida rain where the sun shines through the clouds while it drizzles for fifteen minutes, leaving it just as hot and twice as muggy when the downpour ends. I feel remarkably well rested after a night of amazing sex and late-night room service with Kim, watching sitcom reruns on her hotel TV between rounds. Mom was still awake when I got home around one, eyeing me knowingly as she vacuumed the spotless floors in a burst of night-before jitters I remember well from every big family trip we took growing up.

I'm not due at the temple with the rest of the groomsmen until an hour before the ceremony starts—I gracefully bowed out of "groom golfing," citing my scheduled primp-and-polish session with my mother this afternoon. I spend the morning catching up on all the work I'd been putting off, shooting Everett a series of apology texts with no reply. Anxious and at a loss for what to do, I randomly decide to swing by my dad's. He is as shocked to see me when I open the door as I am to be standing there, but he covers it quickly, ushers me inside, and offers me a Diet Mountain Dew.

We sit in silence on his couch, watching CNN and sipping our sodas. I look around at his little house, full of random objects he's held on to since before I was a child of divorce. Dad always insists he'll need them someday. It isn't as bad out here as the garage was, but it isn't great.

"You know, I could help you organize things in here, maybe decorate a bit more . . . intentionally. It's kind of what I do." If we moved the bookshelves into the corner, turned the couch so that it faced the sliding glass doors, and replaced the tattered old desk chair with one of the extra dining chairs I'd seen in the garage . . . this place could be nice. I could think about my dad here all alone and know that at least his home was warm and comfortable and that I'd been able to help make that happen.

"Sure," he says. "But you'd have to spend more than an hour here to do that."

I duck my head, chastised, with burning cheeks. It wasn't that I didn't love him, but every time we were together there was a ticking clock counting down to one of us saying something that would piss off the other one.

"I don't leave until Monday, I could come back after the brunch thing tomorrow."

"Sure," he says again. "We'll see."

CHAPTER
Twenty-Five

"SO, WHAT ARE we thinking? Updo?" In the mirror, I can see the hairstylist Mom hired to get us ready for the wedding eyeing me critically. I'm seated at the vanity in Mom and Randy's giant marble bathroom while Mom lounges on a chaise in the bedroom, preferring to have her makeup applied while she naps. I'm supposed to check every five minutes to ensure the makeup artist isn't taking any creative liberties with her face.

"Uh, maybe we could do something more simple. A nice blowout?" I'm worried about what a Boca hairstylist's idea of a sophisticated updo will look like, imagining something halfway between pageant and politician's wife. "Some beachy waves?" Jessica deflates behind me but dutifully pulls out a spray bottle and a blow-dryer, looking resigned.

As she gets to work, Daytona replies to my text asking how her trip to Atlanta's going, explaining that she's decided to spend an extra week down south. A new text arrives as I'm responding, and I swipe back to my inbox, delighted to find it's from Kim.

> I'm gonna look so stupid in this dress. What color even is this?

> > burnt sienna, duh

> Oh, of course, how could I forget. You're so lucky you get to wear black.

> > idk i kinda liked branching out last night, that dress was fab

> I certainly enjoyed taking it off of you.

> BTW, I have this work thing next week, a launch party for some new celebrity fragrance. Could be lame, could be fun. Want to come with?

Is she asking me on a date?

> > r u asking me on a date?

> Are you saying yes?

My cheeks hurt from smiling.

> > Yes!!!!

Mom appears, makeup flawless, saying something I can't hear over the blow-dryer and the butterflies flapping around my stomach. She's holding a Nordstrom shopping bag, which she hands me with a hopeful look.

There's a lacy black bra inside.

Please, she mouths.

I roll my eyes but nod.

"PLEASE KEEP YOUR HEAD STILL," the stylist shouts behind me.

Four
YEARS AGO

"HELLO, MY DARLING!"

"Hi, Mom."

"How are you doing, sweetie? I miss you."

"I'm OK. Do you have a few minutes to talk?"

"What do you mean? We're talking right now."

"No, I mean, like . . . have an actual conversation. I'd like to talk to you about something."

"I don't know what you mean, honey, we are having a conversation right now."

"Yes, but I can hear the TV on in the background."

"Oh, well I just have Bravo on. Don't worry, I'm listening."

"Yeah, but—"

"You will not believe what Ramona just said to Luann!"

"I don't know who those people are. Can you turn the TV off?"

"It's on the lowest setting! I can't even hear it."

"Well, *I* can hear it and I'm a thousand miles away. Can you please just turn it off and like, give me your undivided attention?"

"Fine, it's off. God, you are so *moody*. Is everything OK? Oh no, is it about that boy, what was his name? David? Daniel?"

"It was a girl. Named Diana. And no, not really. We broke up a few weeks ago."

"Oh honey, I'm sorry. Well, that's her loss. She'll never find another boy as sweet as you."

"So that's . . . actually what I want to talk about."

CHAPTER
Twenty-Six

REMARKABLY, AIDEN IS the first person I run into. He's outside the tall, ornately carved doors of the sanctuary, filling a wicker basket with black yarmulkes. I pick one up and look inside, where Aiden and Rachel's names and the date are stitched in gold.

"I'm so glad I don't have to wear one of these," I say. "It would ruin my hair."

Aiden throws his arms around me. "Oh my god, I'm getting *married* today."

"I know," I say, squeezing him back, letting it sink in for real. My little brother is getting married. Fuck.

I pull back and smile at my brother, who is getting married today. Fuck. "You look great."

He does, in his dark suit, hair combed back, though he is a little pale, with dark circles under his eyes.

"Can I zhuzh you up a little?" I ask.

He nods frantically. "Please. This week has been so stressful and on top of it I ran out of my hyaluronic acid serum. Do you have any concealer?"

"Of course. I knew you'd need a touch-up."

Aiden leads me to the groom's appointed dressing area, and a bolt of déjà vu hits me as I remember standing in this very room sixteen years ago, fiddling with the tallit my grandmother had made me, going over my haftarah portion one last time. I stumble around giving everyone hugs and complimenting their identical suits. Ben looks especially handsome in his, with his hair tucked behind his ears. He looks very grown-up, but also exactly like the boy I've been kissing for the past decade.

"You look amazing," he says after giving me a tight, warm hug.

"Thanks. You too."

"Do you guys want the room for a bit?" asks Derek, one of the groomsmen. "We can go find something to do for, hmm, how long do you need, Ben? Six minutes?"

"*I'd* need at least nine," I shoot back.

"Please, everyone, it's my wedding day. Can we not?" Aiden says.

"You're the boss," Derek says.

"But *only* today," I say, searching through my bag—Hannah G, American Music Awards, last year—for the concealer Mom purchased the other day. "Tomorrow you are back to being mine to torment."

"Did you guys know that Julia once shot a staple gun at me?" Aiden asks the group. "I was seven."

"Shut up," I fire back. "You were nine. You're lucky this is a little too yellow for me. You need to wear more sunscreen."

"Fuck off, I wear SPF fifty! I've just been playing a lot more golf than usual," Aiden says, leaning back in his chair with his eyes closed like a model being prepped for fashion week. "I got a hole-in-one today!"

"Your life is my hell." I start dabbing a light layer of makeup under his eyes.

"I moved the ball while he wasn't looking," Ben whispers into my ear as he leans against the table next to us. "I'm dying to sit down but I don't want to crease," he says at normal volume, shifting uncomfortably in his dress shoes. It's nice to know that his level of perfection isn't easy for him to maintain.

I roll my eyes. "OK, diva."

"You look amazing," he says, bumping my hip with his. "Sure you don't want to take the guys up on that offer to clear the room?"

"Not really," I say, tapping the concealer under Aiden's eyes. "But maybe before the reception?"

"Ugh," Aiden says below us.

Eventually the testosterone starts to become overwhelming, so I escape for a moment of quiet out the side doors of the temple building, where a large courtyard connects the synagogue with the four-story building where I attended Hebrew school until I was fifteen. The courtyard is empty and blissfully quiet, so I walk in a slow circle around the mosaic laid into the ground depicting colorful scenes from the Torah: Moses posed in front of the Red Sea, waves parted to allow the Jews passage.

Passover has always been my favorite Jewish holiday. Hanukkah is lame primarily because it isn't Christmas, Purim is overwhelming. Sukkot is nice enough, but Passover is so rich with ritual, tradition, and food. There is something about sitting around and telling a story, acting out its dramas in the same way they'd been acted out for generations, dipping the parsley in the salt water, hiding and hunting for the afikomen. I always feel connected to something bigger than myself, sitting around that table with the people I love, people who are as familiar to me as the traditions we share.

That's what today is about. As nerve-racking as this week has been, with emotional land mines at every turn, it isn't about me. It's about celebrating life and love and history and the future. I don't believe in a lot of it, can't ever see myself doing it, but I understand why Aiden wants to, and I'm happy that he's getting what he wants. I can do that for him today, and let everything else wait until tomorrow.

I rejoin Aiden and the groomsmen just in time for Aiden and Rachel's first look and an ensuing photo session. We pack into a small but well-appointed room so the happy couple can sign the ketubah. It's packed and noisy in the antechamber. I feel sticky under my dress and we haven't even gotten to the *ceremony*. The bra my mom forced on me is uncomfortable, the underwire digging into my chest, although I have to admit it's doing wonders for my boobs.

Rachel looks gorgeous in a silky, lacy gown I would never have expected she'd wear. It's very vintage and glamorous and sexy while still being modest and traditional. I'd always thought she was pretty, but now I see what Aiden sees. She is gorgeous and glowing, and she smiles every time she looks at my brother. Today is the happiest day of her life, and that's all I want it to be for her.

Before I know it, we're back in the groom's quarters, and I can hear the sanctuary filling up through the thin walls. The groomsmen are passing a bottle around, one I wave off as Derek offers me a swig. I cross to where Aiden stands checking himself in the mirror.

"Don't name your kids something embarrassing," I say. "And don't get a minivan. Go on lots of vacations but only to *interesting* places, like Copenhagen or Tokyo or Mexico City. Do not wear *Just Married* T-shirts at Disney." His eyes meet mine in the mirror. "Don't lie. Don't cheat. Don't vacation exclusively on cruises. Don't go to bed angry. Don't be one of those married couples who only hang out with other married people." I draw closer behind him, fixing and fiddling with the back of his hair. "Tell her how you feel, even if it scares you. Tell her you love her all the time. Mean it."

"I will," he says. "But we already have the T-shirts."

CHAPTER Twenty-Seven

SOMEHOW, I'D FORGOTTEN that Kim and I would be walking down the aisle together.

She meets my eyes warmly, devastatingly beautiful in her burnt sienna slip dress, with her braids pouring down the open back, skin shimmering in the synagogue's warm lights and rich tones. I think about how she'd felt over me, under me, inside me yesterday, how close we'd been. We wait as the couples make their way, one by one, toward the chuppah. When we are the last pair left, she holds out her arm so I can take it and leads me down the aisle. It's exactly as I'd imagined: two beautiful women in gorgeous gowns surrounded by a crowd of family and friends. This is the image I want my family to have of me. To replace the little boy and awkward teenager of their memories and leave me forever as this: a woman, the *best* woman.

I've won. So why doesn't victory feel like I thought it would?

Because with every step toward the bimah, I alternate between memories of last night in Kim's bed and everything I let her assume all those weeks ago. The righteous anger she's deployed on my behalf toward Aiden and my mother, the judgment she's made of my entire family. Victory feels hollow when I've lied for it, when I hadn't really needed it to begin with. In every way that matters I have the life I want. It isn't always easy and has in fact often sucked, but I had said *This is what I want my life to be,* and I had made it happen through sheer force of will. And everyone in this room had said, for the most part, "Cool. Got it. You do you, babe." Why wasn't that enough?

Kim squeezes my arm as we part, and in that moment I resolve to tell her everything tonight, after the wedding. I can't sleep with her again without her knowing the truth, and if I'm able to really explain things to her, maybe she'll understand and I can salvage this thing between us that already feels like something I can't live without. I just have to get through the ceremony and the reception, make sure my brother has the best night of his life, and then we'll see.

Aiden enters with my mother and father on either side of him, and I feel a massive tidal wave of love for all three of them. It is messy and intense but undeniable. My parents are beaming with pride for their son, and a smile breaks my face open. I laugh, just a little. My little brother is getting married.

Rachel makes her entrance, luminous and lovely, and Aiden has the nerve to cry a single, manly tear. I resist the urge to make a barfing noise. He is so *whipped*.

Their vows are handwritten and elaborate. Rachel, who has grown up with boats, talks about Aiden being her captain, which seems a bit misogynistic, and her North Star, which is sweet.

"You will always be the Han to my Leia," she says. Next to me, Ben groans.

"You will always be the Phantom to my Christine," Aiden says at the end of his vows.

"Why do *you* get to be Christine," Rachel whines, but she's smiling so wide I'm worried she'll crack a tooth.

"Because you're the one who likes to stand behind a mirror and watch me sleep, baby."

"You've got me there," Rachel concedes.

"You may kiss the bride," Rabbi Hoffman says, and Aiden does.

CHAPTER
Twenty-Eight

AFTER A BRIEF nosh on wine and rugelach, everyone departs to Rachel's parents' country club for the reception. I mill around during the cocktail hour, saying hello to relatives I haven't seen in years, accepting the congratulations and cheek pinches and the odd awkward moment with a third cousin or family friend who doesn't know if it's still appropriate to offer a handshake, which I always respond to with a quick kiss on the cheek before moving on quickly to the next relation.

An hour and a half later I'm sitting at the nuclear family table, once again flanked by Brody and Brian. They've both got video game consoles in hand and are playing something where they murder people—a bit on the nose if you ask me. Aiden and Rachel are directly across from me doing disgustingly sappy shit, like feeding each other bites of endive salad and accepting envelopes likely stuffed with checks from their guests.

should we get married? seems lucrative I text Kyle, attaching a photo of the envelope pile.

fine but daytona is officiating and I want cheating written into the pre-nup he fires back.

Speaking of speeches, it's almost time for them to begin. I open the note in my phone to run through my bullet list of embarrassing childhood stories, remembering Aiden's note to keep it PG-13, and start frantically googling *how many times are you allowed to say fuck in pg-13 movies* as well as *synonyms for love*.

Grandpa says the hamotzi and the kiddush in flawless Hebrew, but can't give up the spotlight without a joke in English. "I hope you'll be very happy, my darling," he tells Aiden. "And if you aren't, I know a good lawyer."

The meal is welcome after all the champagne I've had, as well as a chance to slip my shoes off under the table, something I'll *never* tell Daytona. As we eat, Brody, Brian, and I chat about things we could do in New York. Across the table, Rachel's brother and his wife try to get their son to eat, with dismal results. Derek ends up with ketchup on his shirt, and I pass him the Tide pen from my bag. Brian scoffs and rolls his eyes.

"You're so *Mom*."

Brody shoots him a look and Brian turns sheepish.

"No, you're right. Just be glad I haven't asked one of you to run out and get me a Diet Coke from McDonald's."

"I think that's where Dad is right now," Brian says, looking over at the space beside Mom at the next table. Come to think of it, I haven't seen Randy in a while.

Kim is two tables away with the rest of the bridesmaids. We make burning eye contact as she licks a spoon. I want to die but in a sexy way. Then the wedding planner approaches our table with a microphone in hand and I want to die in a very *unsexy* way. Aiden takes it and he and Rachel stand to address everyone with some rehearsed banter I'm sure has been sitting in a shared Google doc since the week they got engaged. Rachel makes several jokes about tying Aiden down, which gives me another unfortunate insight into their sex life.

"We're so lucky to be surrounded by so many people we love on the most important day of our lives," Aiden says.

"Not counting the last time the Yankees won the World Series!" my dad heckles. Aiden laughs, but I can see the frustration on Rachel's face at the deviation. She nudges Aiden to continue.

"Some of those people have graciously decided they'd like to share a few words with everyone, and I'm sure there will be absolutely *zero* embarrassing stories," Aiden says with an exaggerated warning look tossed my way.

"Wouldn't dream of it," I say, loud enough to be heard over the crowd's polite laughter.

"My big sister, Julia, everyone," says Aiden, and everyone applauds as I reach across the table to take the microphone.

Fuck fuck fuck fuck fuck fuck fuck fuck fuck.

"Um," I say. "Hi."

The only sound in the room is a burst of static and the scraping of silverware against china.

"Despite his warning, I know how this goes. I've seen basically every romantic comedy set at a wedding ever made. I know I'm supposed to stand here and bring up a bunch of embarrassing shit my brother would kill me over revealing, like the way I used to make him pretend to be the Flounder to my Ariel when we were kids and he got *way* too into it, or that time he killed my turtle by feeding it paint. But I'm not going to do that. Oh whoops, guess I just did." Pause for polite laughter.

"Only, Aiden has never really needed my help when it comes to embarrassing himself. I mean"—I turn to face the room—"who here who knows my brother, *really* knows him, hasn't seen what a doofus he is?"

"*Huge* doofus," Ben calls out dutifully from Kim's table.

"Exactly," I say. "I mean, Aiden spent our entire childhood doing stupid shit like sticking a pencil in his leg so he wouldn't have to go to the dentist, or collecting a bunch of tadpoles from the canal behind our house only to put them in the fridge and freeze them to death. It was traumatizing!" Some more laughter.

Oh no, I can feel my cynicism eroding, the magic of the wedding and true love or whatever the fuck washing it away until all that's left is honest affection. My brother might be ridiculous and nerdy, have horrible taste in music, and care more about his beauty regime than I care about mine, but I love him. I've loved him our whole lives, and I'm happy that he's happy. Like my dad is for me. And sitting beside Rachel, their hands linked together, he's *so fucking happy*.

"Despite all that, my little shithead brother managed to grow up to be a pretty great guy, which I know because he's sitting next to an amazing woman who is now my sister." Aiden is smiling at me, a real smile, the kind he used to give me when we were little and I was his hero. Humiliatingly, my throat gets a bit tight and my eyes burn with tears. I shake it off with a laugh. "So I guess I can forgive him for the turtle."

I raise my glass.

"Congratulations, Aiden and Rachel. I'm so happy you found each other. Cheers!" The room fills with applause and I can't help but seek out the person I wish were sitting next to me holding my hand the way Rachel is holding Aiden's. Kim is sipping her champagne and looking right at me, soft and serious.

Rachel's dad is next, and he grunts out some well-meaning words about how beautiful his daughter is and how Aiden better treat her right or he'll wind up in the Everglades being mauled by alligators. I'm pretty zoned out, still struck by the depth of my own emotion. I've been dreading this wedding for months, *years,* and now that I'm here, despite how uncomfortable certain parts of it have been, I'm starting to feel like . . . maybe it will be fine? I'm surrounded by people who love me, however imperfectly, and Kim is across the room looking so sexy I could cry, and I know that when this is over she'll take me back to her hotel and peel me out of this dress and do wonderful, evil things to my body. Maybe I don't even need to tell her about my little white lie. She and Rachel aren't *actually* close, so there's little worry she'll learn the truth there. We'll go back to our real lives in New York and leave Florida behind us, go to her dumb party next week and have our first real date, for once not surrounded by people related to me. She'll spend the night at my apartment, I'll make her coffee in the morning and take her out for bagels. She'll meet my friends and probably develop a huge crush on at least one of them. We'll keep dating, and I can start dropping hints that the wedding was so healing that, miracle of miracles, my family has started to be totally cool about my womanhood. By the time we visit again for Passover next year, there will be no lie left between us. Kim will still judge my mom a little, sure, but *Rachel* judges my mom too, and she's her mother-in-law!

Maybe, one day, Mom could be *Kim's* mother-in-law too . . .

The crowd is applauding again as Rachel's dad hands my mother the microphone.

"Thank you all so much for being here," she says. "And please bear with me if I get emotional. It's not every day a mother gets to see her son get married." I can count the times I've seen Mom cry on one hand, but sure. "I won't take up too much of your time, because even though I was assured there would be Diet Coke on tap, they only have canned and that always goes right through me."

I giggle, because my mother is very silly but in a totally predictable and endearing way.

"As much as I love my son, I wanted to take a moment today to talk about Rachel." She looks down at the woman in question, who has a confused little smile on her face. "Sweetie, the first time Aiden brought you home to meet me, I pulled him aside and told him, 'You better marry that girl one day or you are the stupidest man on the planet.'" This is *hilariously* untrue because Mom *loathed* Rachel for almost a year after she and Aiden started dating. "And here we are! My son has a beautiful, intelligent, driven, supportive wife who I know is going to take care of him, stand beside him, and"—she dabs at her eyes, although I don't see any tears—"be a wonderful mother to his children."

Across the room, Kim rolls her eyes at me. I hide a laugh behind my champagne.

"Rachel, you are an amazing woman, and I'm so proud to welcome you into our family." She reaches across the table to lay a hand on Rachel's. "I've always wanted a daughter, and now I finally have one."

There's a strange moment of quiet, like the entire room is hesitating. It stretches longer than it should, and that's what clues me in and makes me realize what's just happened. Because that was obviously the end of Mom's speech, the moment where there should have been *awwws* and applause. But there's only quiet, and the rustling sound of heads turning.

Turning toward me.

CHAPTER
Twenty-Nine

ACROSS THE TABLE, Rachel's eyes are wide. Mom is still gripping her hand, clearly waiting for some reciprocation for the tender sentiment she just shared with 150 of our friends and family and perfect strangers. But Rachel just turns to look at me, and in her wake, so does everyone else.

I always thought it was bullshit in books when the main character said they could feel someone's eyes on them. That's not a *thing*, you can't *feel* someone looking at you unless maybe the book you're in is *Lord of the Rings* and the eye belongs to Sauron.

I guess that makes me fucking Frodo because I can feel every single eye in this room boring into me.

I'm shutting down, locking up. I'm a computer that has been left idle for too long and my screen saver is loading, a warning that in a few moments, the screen will go fully blank.

"Oh." Mom looks at me, and then very quickly away. "*Another* daughter. I . . . uh. Well." She lifts her champagne glass, and I see sweat beading on her brow. Since she started menopause any minor shift in temperature can bring on a hot flash, and the room is buzzing with the kind of energy that makes heat rise. "To Aiden and Rachel," she says, plastering on a smile. The crowd echoes her, though with less enthusiasm than they'd given Rachel's dad and me.

It's taking everything I have not to stand up and flee the room because honestly, that would only make things worse. Then this would go from being an uncomfortable slipup for people to gossip about back in their hotel rooms later to the kind of scene we'll still be talking about at the bris for Aiden and Rachel's firstborn son. Although I'm pretty sure I'm morally opposed to ritualized religious genital mutilation.

I know things are bad if I'm imagining a hypothetical circumcision rather than dealing with what just happened.

"Sweetie," Mom says from across the table, but I ignore her. Grandpa has the mic now and has launched into a story about a safari he and Grandma went on in the eighties—it's getting fewer laughs than it did at my bar mitzvah, that's cancel culture for you. But he's a good storyteller, and the room seems to have moved on. They *want* to move on, no one wants to dwell on my mother making it clear that in her mind, she doesn't have a daughter.

Because that's what happened. Caught up in the moment, Mom forgot to pretend. In that one moment of thoughtless honesty, she revealed the truth: no matter what she's said, no matter how supportive she's been, no matter how many times she's called me Julia or reminded me to wear a bra, I'm not her daughter. She might understand that I've decided I'm a woman, but in her eyes, I'll never really *be* one.

"Jules," Aiden says. He looks as horrified as Rachel, as shocked and upset as I know I should feel. But instead, I'm calm, because if I'm going to be honest, I'm not surprised. I've been waiting for this moment for four years. It was all too good to be true. The other shoe has finally dropped and it's one of those beige heels Mom forced on me at Bloomingdale's, one of the few they even carried in *such a large size*. Mom has spent four years pleading with me to wear lipstick and perfume and get blowouts because, to her, *that* is the closest I'll come to being her daughter, at least on the surface, in a way she can understand. If I look the part, it'll be easier for her to pretend, to say the right things, to placate me.

Now Grandpa has the audience laughing, but our table is still silent. Mom looks mortified, but I know that won't last. She's never been able to admit she's wrong, and somehow she'll find a way to make this someone else's fault, *my* fault for misunderstanding, for making something out of nothing. *Of course I didn't mean it like that,* she'll say, *how could you even think that?*

My jaw is clenched so hard I'm going to crack a tooth. I have to get out of here.

"Julia," my mom says, exasperated, whatever shame she might have felt already starting to turn. I ignore her and stand on stiff legs, ducking my head to avoid the heads that swivel my way. I wish I wasn't wearing such an obnoxious dress, wish I was in jeans and combat boots with greasy hair so eyes would slide off me. Rachel starts to stand but I shake my head, sharp enough to make the headache building behind my eyes throb. I weave through the tables, head down, watching my stupid expensive shoes clomp awkwardly across the marble floor, the heels far too loud. I know I'm making a scene, I should have just stayed at the table and pretended everything was fine. But I can't be here right now, and I don't understand how I ever thought I could be here at all. These people have known me for too long, known a version of me I never really wanted to be and they're never going to let me fucking forget it.

There's a patio behind the ballroom that looks out on the country club's golf course and it's blessedly empty, and even the muggy Florida heat is a relief after the way what my mother said sucked all the air out of that room, punched it right out of my lungs. I suck in a deep gasping breath and am horrified when it comes back out as a sob. My eyes are burning with tears. I'm going to ruin my makeup—Daytona would be furious. And *that's* what I need, to talk to someone who knows me, who knows *Julia,* but then I realize I've left my bag and phone back at the table and I almost scream.

"Julia?"

It's Kim.

"Please don't ask me if I'm OK," I say, forcing the words out through clenched teeth.

"I wasn't going to," she says from behind me. "You're not. You shouldn't be."

She's right, but it doesn't feel good to hear her say it. Her saying it makes it real. The idea that she witnessed my utter humiliation burns inside me like kerosene.

"It's fine," I say. My hands are clenched tight enough that my nails, the nails my mother paid to have painted, might break the skin. "I just need a minute to cool off."

Hands settle on my arms, light enough that it's clear Kim is afraid to spook me. "Julia," she says, soft and firm. "It's not fine. It doesn't have to *be* fine."

It does, though, because I can't make this about me. There's no space in this wedding for me to have a meltdown, to cause a scene. Storming out here was bad enough. There's nothing else to do but pull myself together, walk back inside, smile like nothing happened, and bury this down in the unmarked grave inside me. It will haunt me forever, but there are enough restless ghosts there that at least this one won't be lonely.

I lock the tomb of myself tight and turn around to face Kim. Her brows are knit in concern, her mouth drawn down into a frown. I want to collapse into her, fall apart, and let her pick up the pieces. I will never, ever let myself.

"It's fine," I say again, firmer this time. "It sucks, it really fucking sucks, but it is what it is. I just needed a minute, but it's OK. Let's go back inside, I don't want to make a whole thing out of it."

"Maybe you *should* make a thing out of it," says Kim. "Or not, it's your family, I'm not going to tell you what to do. But Jesus, don't go back in there. Let's go for a walk or something so you can cool down for a bit."

Shaking my head, I shrug off her hands. "No, that would only make things worse. I can't make this worse, this is my brother's *wedding*."

"I mean, things are already pretty fucking bad, sweetheart." A tiny, shriveled part of me thrills at the endearment. "If you go back now, isn't that just teaching them that what just happened is OK?"

Yes. "No. It's just . . . what I have to do." I have to prove them wrong, prove that my mother admitting to everyone we know, plus a legion of country club waiters, that she'll never see me as a woman doesn't devastate me, doesn't mean she's *right*. It's the same reason I can't snipe at a customer service agent when they call me sir on the phone or be rude to a waiter when they tell me the men's room is on the right. The bigger deal I make of it, the more I draw attention to the very dissonance they're pointing out.

But those are things I can shrug off, they're simply a fundamental part of my daily reality. This is seismic, this is my world altering. Or rather, this is a truth long hidden finally come to light: I am not my mother's daughter. I never was and I never will be. That is my new reality.

I wish I didn't care. But I do.

"Julia." She's almost pleading. "Baby."

"I'll see you back inside," I say, lifting my psychic shovel and preparing to bury the sad, pitying look in her eyes.

"Don't do this," she says, wrapping a hand around my wrist to stop me from walking away. "Don't let them make you small."

"Jules." With perfect timing, Aiden chooses that exact moment to appear before us. "Are you OK?"

"Of course she isn't," Kim snaps. He looks taken aback but tries to draw me into a hug. I shake him off, too overstimulated as it is, but Kim catches my flinch and her eyes narrow. She faces Aiden down, bristling with anger.

"Maybe if you'd been more supportive, something like this wouldn't have happened. You clearly set the tone in your family."

No. Fuck. Not this, not now. Anything but this.

"What are you talking about?" He's so confused.

"Let's not do this, please," I beg.

"No, Julia, I can't keep my mouth shut after that." All the

empathy and compassion I've been nurturing are hardening; I can see the culmination of every lie I've told Kim. "I know about how badly you've treated her," Kim said, "and it makes me sick."

"Jules, *what* is she talking about?"

"Please, Kim, I didn't—"

"She told me how you've never really accepted her, that you thought her womanhood was some phase. That you only made her best woman out of obligation. You could have been the one person in your family who stood up for her, and maybe what happened tonight never would have happened."

She may as well have slapped him. No, I realize as he turns to me with horror on his face. *I* may as well have slapped him.

"Stop it, Kim," I say. She reaches toward me, but I flinch away, bracing myself.

"I'm just trying to—"

"I lied," I gasp, feeling winded. "It wasn't true. Aiden has never been anything but good to me. He always wanted me in the wedding."

"What are you talking about? You said—"

"No, *you* said." I hate how defensive I sound. "You assumed. And I let you, fuck, I'm so sorry." I am a worm, a cockroach, a slug. I am the lowest creature to walk the earth. "I let you believe it so you'd . . . I don't know, so you'd like me."

She recoils, and I die a little bit more inside. But even worse is Aiden, how devastated he looks.

"I'm sorry," I tell them both. Kim has her arms wrapped around herself and I can see her shutting down, going cold. A door opens and someone shouts Aiden's name and he gives me a look that says, very clearly, *I'm not done with you,* and stalks off.

"Kim," I say, ready to get down on my knees and beg for forgiveness. I will grovel until Aiden and Rachel's first anniversary if I need to.

"Do you realize how fucked-up what you did is?" Her voice is flat, and her eyes are empty. "You manipulated me. That's not normal, Julia."

"I know." Finally, I'm crying. I can't help it. Not ugly sobs like I wish, sobs that would hurt but would be healing. Just silent tears running down my cheeks. "I liked you so much and I was sure that the only way you'd be into me was if you . . . felt sorry for me, I guess. That sounds so horrible."

"It is horrible. You could have been honest, but instead, you used your fake sob story to get into my pants. That's low, Julia."

I nod.

She shakes something off, squares herself, and looks beyond me to where the reception dinner is still going on. Right, there are 150 people I know intimately just inside.

"I need . . . to not be here right now." She glances around her, eyes locking on the sun setting in the distance over the golf course. Kim kicks off her heels, snatches them up, and starts walking through the perfectly manicured grass. She stops and looks back at me over her perfect shoulder, all the warmth I kindled gone from her eyes. "Don't follow me. Go fuck yourself."

She leaves and I'm alone again, but not for long.

"Julia? You OK, kiddo?" It's my dad, the absolute last person I expected to follow me out.

"I'm fine, Dad. Just needed a minute." He nods, takes a vape out, and puffs away. He holds it out and I take it, glad for something to do—at least until I start choking on the piña colada–

scented vapor. Dad thumps me on the back, then leaves his hand between my shoulder blades, rubbing soft circles that are surprisingly soothing.

"You know," he says, "I'm not supposed to drink with the back pain medication I'm on, and I've had two glasses of wine."

"OK," I say.

"And my doctor doesn't like me driving at night. Says my eyes are going. Sure could use someone to give me a lift home," he says, poker face firmly in place. My dad does not have back problems, and his eye prescription is so fierce I'm pretty sure he sees better than I do. He's still rubbing those circles on my back, and it's so much easier to just take the out he's offering.

"I guess I could give you a lift home, though I don't know how I'd get back to Mom's."

He pulls me close. "That's OK, kiddo, the guest room is yours if you want it."

It's not really a solution to anything. Mom will have moved past any embarrassment by now and me crashing with Dad will just reignite their bitter resentment for each other, making it even easier for her to make the disaster of this whole evening my fault. And I don't want my dad to think he's scored some points with me—or more likely, against my mother. If I hadn't messed up so massively with Kim I might have spent the night in her hotel room, but since I've screwed that up . . . why not.

"Got an extra toothbrush?"

He smiles. "Sure do. An electric one, even."

I sigh. "Got any moisturizer?"

"No," he says, "but I think Aiden left some hyaluronic acid serum the last time he spent the night."

Of course he did.

"We'll leave as soon as they cut the cake," he says, rubbing my back the way he used to when I was little and had a cold.

"OK."

"Now let's get back inside," he says, taking my hand in his. He doesn't let go.

Rachel and Aiden's first dance is to a cover of Joni Mitchell's "A Case of You," which is remarkably tasteful for them—Mom had played *Blue* on the record player most Sundays when we were growing up. This is followed by Fleetwood Mac's "You Make Loving Fun," which I don't think the wedding band singer really has the voice for.

Brody and Brian suffer through dances with me before disappearing, probably off to sneak into the bar storage room or, more likely, kill lizards on the golf course. I can see rows of empty golf carts lined up through the window, backlit by the floodlights, an endless, manicured green meadow beyond. Somewhere out there Kim is hating me, deconstructing every moment we've spent together this week and seeing it through the new eyes of that hatred.

I dance with my dad, and we both do an admirable job pretending it isn't weird. When the song ("My Girl" by the Temptations, who would not be pleased with the cover) ends, Dad catches the eye of someone behind me and passes me along.

It's Aiden, slightly sweaty and *very* tipsy. "Saved a dance for your little brother?" he asks.

"Just don't step on my shoes," I say, taking his hand. "I borrowed them from a pop star."

"We asked the band to sprinkle in a few Hannah G covers," he says, laying a hand on my waist. "Rachel and I learned the choreography for 'Love Aneurysm.'"

"Congratulations," I say as we move slowly to "Wouldn't It Be Nice."

"Thanks," he says. "Can you believe it?"

"Yeah." I hadn't been able to, earlier, but here he is. My brother, the husband, all grown up. "I'm really happy for you."

"Thanks," he says, flushing. He pulls me closer. "I'm so sorry about Mom, Jules. But I'm also really fucking mad at you. What the fuck?"

"I know," I say, dropping my head against his shoulder. "I'm sorry and I'm angry and I'm fucking destroyed and god, I did exactly what I didn't want to do: I made your whole wedding about me."

"You had some help," he says. "And believe me, I'm pissed at Mom too, but I can't deal with any of this right now. It's my wedding, so I'm gonna dance with *my sister* and believe that she has a really good explanation for what just happened and hope she knows we're gonna figure this shit out when it's no longer actively *my wedding*."

"I can do that," I say, nodding against his shoulder.

"But before that, I need you to find the maid of honor so my *wife* can stop freaking out."

"Fuck."

I find Rachel by the cake, a staggering tower of frosted roses. She gives me a tight, desperate hug and pulls back to look soulfully into my eyes, something sisterly passing between us. I nod in a way that I hope implies *We'll talk about it later*. I think she gets it, because she switches into business mode. "Have you seen Kim?"

"Not for a while. She . . . we had . . . an argument."

"About what your mom said," she asks.

"Kind of. I . . . I fucked up, Rach. Pretty bad. I need to talk to her. I know I can't make anything better, but I owe her . . . something. An explanation, or a better apology, or the chance to tell me to fuck off and die."

Rachel looks confused for a moment, but looks around the room at the hundreds of people she's entertaining and snaps her fingers. Immediately one of the Rachels is beside her, holding a glass of water and her phone. Rachel sips one while perusing the other. She pinches two fingers, clearly zooming in on something on the screen.

"She's out on the golf course," Rachel says, glancing out the window, and then back to her phone. "She must have been walking for a while, she's all the way out by the seventeenth hole."

I hold in an unnecessary joke about holes. "Is that a lot, relatively? I don't know anything about golf."

"It's a lot," says the other Rachel, lips pursed. Rachel Prime glances back out the window, eyes narrowing before her face lights up with inspiration.

"I think you could catch up."

Ten minutes and a hefty tip to a groundskeeper later, I'm zooming across the grass in a golf cart, seizing up in fear every time I go over a small mound of earth and drop, experiencing the sick weightless feeling you get when an airplane briefly dips and your stomach lifts into your chest. But that feeling remains even as the grass levels out, and in fact, grows the closer I get to the little pin on my phone that Rachel had shared with me. In the blue twilight, the golf course looks lush and endless, stretching out in every possible direction. It's kind of beautiful, but then I remember that men spend their time here hitting little balls with sticks and wish fervently for it to get bulldozed and turned into a strip mall.

The green grass slopes upward into a hill, and as I crest it the harsh, fluorescent lamplight hits my eyes, blinding me for a second. When I regain my vision, Kim is there, standing beside a small hole in the ground. She is smoking a cigarette and tipping the ashes into said hole and looks completely unsurprised to see me.

I bring the golf cart to an abrupt and juddering stop and lurch down onto the grass, unsteady in my heels. Kim keeps smoking silently as I cross the distance toward her, wondering what I am going to say and increasingly having no fucking clue the closer I get.

"Hi," I say.

"I told you not to follow," she says, but she mostly sounds defeated.

I gesture to her cigarette. "Can I have one of those?"

"This was my last one."

"Oh," I say. "OK."

"What do you want?" she asks, turning to face the rising moon.

I shrug, though she can't see me. "I don't know. Probably nothing I deserve."

Her back is rigid. She looks so beautiful in the hazy blue twilight. "I hate that I was some prize to you. You used me for some kind of fucked-up validation."

"Could we think of it as gender-affirming care?" I ask, trying to defuse the tension. If anything, it makes the vibe worse.

"I don't exist to make you feel better about yourself or more secure in your womanhood or whatever. You can't treat people like that."

"I know. Well, clearly I *didn't* know. But I get that now."

She's still facing away from me, so I can't see her face, but her voice sounds different than I've ever heard it. Softer, more vulnerable. "Did you even *like* me? Or did you just have something to prove?"

"I liked you. So much. I have since I was sixteen. But the other stuff seemed more important." I watch a family of ducks floating in a small pond beyond the next hole. "I've spent the last couple of years being selfish out of necessity, as some kind of survival instinct. I think transitioning might be kind of inherently selfish."

She takes a drag from her cigarette. "It's not fair to make this a trans thing. That makes me feel like I can't be mad about it or I'm like, toxic or problematic or transphobic."

"Yeah," I agree. "But that doesn't make it any less true for me. It can be true for me and not be true for you." I take a deep breath, summoning up my courage. "You just made it so *easy*, assuming I needed you to swoop in and save me."

"I was just being nice," she snaps back, nostrils flaring.

"No," I shoot back, remembering what I'd felt underneath the rush of pleasure at her coming to my defense, both tonight and weeks ago at the fucking Cheesecake Factory. "You went out of your way to come to my rescue when I never asked you to. You assumed that I was some poor little trans girl whose family didn't love her, and I feel like shit for playing into it, but I also feel like shit that you thought it in the first place. And now I feel like shit because you weren't wrong."

Kim looks like she wants to say something, but holds it back. She nods, and I can see this information being filed away, incorporated into her. This is a lesson she's learned, as surely as I've learned mine.

"That still doesn't make any of it right, that I let it go so far. I liked you *so* much. You've probably gathered by now, but I had a *huge* crush on you in high school. That day you drove me home . . . I would have done *anything*. But I knew you wouldn't want me because you only liked girls. And now I *am* a girl and you show up again and I think, there's no way she'd be into me, but it seems like you are! But I can't trust that, because you knew me *before*, the odds were so stacked against me and I just wanted any extra help I could get. I've spent the past few years trying to convince the world to see me this way that you seemed to finally see me, and it was everything I'd ever wanted. But I shouldn't have lied to you, because I don't think the truth would have changed anything between us at the beginning. I was too fucking scared and insecure to see that you just liked me, would have liked me even without my sob story."

Even now, I can't help but hope she'll tell me I'm right. The sad, pathetic part of me still licking my wounds from this evening lifts her head, eager for any small bit of absolution.

She drops the end of her cigarette into the open hole and turns to look at me, sad and serious. "We'll never know."

"Yeah," I say, and that's it. That's all there is, and we both know it. Even if she has real feelings for me, she could never forget that our relationship was founded on a lie. And even if she forgave me, I'd always be wondering if any of it was real, or if I'd simply tricked her into falling for me.

We stand in silence as the stars twinkle down from a navy-blue sky.

"Can I give you a ride back?" I ask. "They're probably gonna cut the cake soon."

She shakes her head, pulling out a crumpled pack of cigarettes. "I'll walk."

I nod and walk back to the golf cart. The engine starts on the third try, and I give an awkward little wave. Kim, illuminated by the headlights, doesn't wave back.

Aiden and Rachel are smushing cake into each other's faces when I enter the reception hall, everyone cheering them on. I stand in the crowd around them and laugh along with everyone else, though it doesn't strike me as particularly funny. Across the dance floor, I catch Mom's eye. She smiles happily at me, but it doesn't reach her eyes. I think of Kim walking across the hazy, moonlit golf course, smoking cigarette after cigarette.

Ben joins me in the line to pick up a slice of cake. His tie is loose, his top button unbuttoned, his hair wild from dancing. He's very handsome and he gives me a little eyebrow waggle. "Care for a dance?" he asks.

It would be so easy to have my cake and eat it too, follow him out onto the dance floor, crowd up against him, and let him make me feel better, but I'm not sure easy always equates to *good*, or *right*. I give him a little shove with my shoulder and grab a slice of marble cake with white frosting, hightailing it back to my table.

Brody and Brian have returned and look to already be three slices in. Randy and Mom are slow dancing to an Elvis cover—much more firmly in the wedding singer's range, actually quite a smooth baritone—and my dad is leading a few kids on some kind of scavenger hunt in the corner. My grandparents are sitting together and chatting quietly over decaf coffee, sharing a single slice of cake, and laughing softly at some shared joke. In the distance beyond them, Aiden and Rachel are doing the same thing. My chest feels tight, my eyes are hot. None of them are perfect. None of *us* are perfect. But we're doing our best.

CHAPTER Thirty

DAD'S HOUSE IS still as small and cramped with junk as it was this morning, but clearly he'd heeded my suggestion about leaving the windows open. The smell of *lazy man* no longer lingers quite as heavily in the air.

"Oh thank god," I groan, dropping down onto a bench by the door to take the heels off my aching feet.

"I don't understand why you didn't just take those off in the car," Dad says, walking toward the kitchen to grab a bottle of water. Not very sustainable. I'll have to get him a reusable bottle.

"My friend Daytona always says that a queen shouldn't take her drag off until she's at home with the door locked."

"But you're not a drag queen," Dad says, brow furrowed.

"No, but *this*," I say, sweeping an arm to encompass the dress I was still squeezed into, the makeup on my face, and my giant blowout, "is drag."

"So that's not really you," he said, sounding genuinely curious. "You don't like getting all glammed up in a dress and high heels?" There's a question underneath the question, something like, *Then what's the point.* I can't believe I'm discussing fashion and gender presentation with the man who refused to buy me a Sailor Venus doll when I was nine.

I pull my right foot up onto the bench and start massaging the blood back into it. "Because it's what everyone expected. Or needed to see. Whatever."

Dad hands me an evil, environmentally unsound plastic water bottle and falls heavily into his favored armchair. "I don't think anyone needed you to be uncomfortable just to, I don't know, prove something."

I can't help the snort I let out. "Of course they did, Dad. That's what being trans *is*." I crack open the water and take a glug. "I'm tired. I'm going to bed."

He tells me where I'll find everything I'd need for the night and that we'd need to leave early the next morning if I wanted to have time to swing by Mom's and get ready before heading to the farewell brunch. The thought of being in that house and facing her—

I've always wanted a daughter.

—makes my stomach seize up like I'm constipated. And maybe I am, just not . . . physically. Psychic constipation.

The room is almost as I'd left it just days ago, with one glaring omission. The photo of me that had hung on the wall was gone. In its place is the ugliest piece of art I've ever seen: a giant papier-mâché Kit Kat bar, executed in wobbly detail by someone with little artistic talent or hand-eye coordination but *lots* of enthusiasm. I knew this because I'd made it in second grade.

I had no idea Dad had held on to it. I'd always wondered why this piece wasn't in my mother's cabinet of offspring art. One of the edges bore my initials, still the same even after my trip to city court two years ago to have my name legally changed: JR. Here is a little piece of my past that my dad had kept all these years as I moved further and further away from him and the version of myself he knew and understood. A piece of me that is, in a measurable way, unchanged.

I unzip my dress and get into bed. I think of how my mother would chide me for going to sleep without washing my makeup off, and that's the thing that finally shakes the ugly sobs from my chest.

CHAPTER
Thirty-One

"RISE AND SHINE, bitch."

My eyes crack open painfully, glued shut by a mixture of eye makeup and tears. At first, Daytona's presence doesn't register as odd, because we'd been in this position so many times before. Despite her hedonistic lifestyle, Daytona is an unbearable morning person and anytime we crash at each other's homes, she always wakes me up early, demanding breakfast.

None of that explained why she was waking me up now, in my father's apartment. In Florida.

"What," I croak, "the fuck are you doing here?"

She is wearing a Juicy Couture tracksuit straight out of the early aughts, hair piled atop her head, huge vintage Dior sunglasses shielding her eyes from the sun slanting through the blinds. Everything about her is at odds with the scenery, but at the same time, it makes complete sense that she's here. Daytona insisted herself upon the world, and because of that, there was no place in which she didn't belong, no space she could not command and make her own.

"I'm here to get you the fuck out of bed and play fairy grandmother." She studies her nails, claws so viciously red they look dipped in blood. "I don't have all day, and you have a brunch to get to, so let's *go*, girl."

I laugh, somewhat frantically. "No, seriously, what the *fuck* are you doing here? You're supposed to be in Atlanta, not my Dad's spare bedroom."

As if summoned, my Dad pops his head in the door, two coffee mugs in hand. "Morning, Jules. Daytona, I only had skim milk, I hope that's OK." He hands her the mug I'd always loved as a kid, whose handle was an airplane streaming an arced jet of wind.

Daytona takes the mug and cocks her head coquettishly. "That's just fine, honey. Thanks so much." To my horror, my father blushes and adjusts his glasses, handing me the other mug and closing the door on his way out.

"Have you been *flirting* with my dad?"

She sips her coffee, the picture of nonchalance. "You know I like them a little seasoned."

I gulp down some coffee, choking a bit on how hot it is. The ensuing coughing fit helps wake me up a bit more. My body feels sore, mostly concentrated in my feet, shoulders, and head. My eyes are dry and the bobby pins I'd never taken out were poking my scalp. And, right, I'd been publicly humiliated by my mother in front of a ballroom full of people last night, then exposed as a horrible person in front of the girl I was into and my brother, whose wedding I ruined by being the victim of one scene and the cause of another.

Tears start welling up in my eyes again, and I squeeze them shut to stave them off. As the world goes dark, I hear the thump of Daytona setting her mug down on the nightstand, then taking mine out of my hands and doing the same with it. Then, unthinkably, her arms wrap around me as she draws me to her crushed velvet bosom.

"I know, honey. I'm sorry. I'm so sorry." She strokes my hair and holds me as I let myself fall apart. It feels awful, but also really, really good.

Once I've cried off the rest of last night's mascara, Daytona cuddles up behind me and explains into my rat's nest hair that she'd been filling her tank at an Atlanta gas station when Aiden DM'd her on Instagram. They'd been following each other since meeting in New York, and after the disaster of last night, Aiden had wanted to make sure one of my friends knew what had happened, even though he was confused and pissed over the drama with Kim. "He knows you pretty well, girl," Daytona says as she works through the tangles of my hair with a brush. "He knows how much you need your family."

That unleashes another round of sobs, and when they're done, Daytona continues her tale. She'd only been a few hours from the state line and knew she could make it here by morning if she—

"Don't say it," I said, needing to make the joke so I wouldn't start crying again.

"*I drove all niiiiiight,*" she sings in that husky voice, "*to get to you.* Don't worry, it wasn't a *huge* imposition. I'm crashing with this *beautiful* daddy in Fort Lauderdale. We're gonna fuck in his pool later."

How could I possibly thank her for this? How could I begin

to explain how much it means that she'd come all the way here and held me while I fell to pieces?

"It's so fucked-up, girl."

Aiden had given her a sketch of the details, but I fill in the lines with every miserable moment: how good the sex with Kim had been, how conflicted I'd felt about it after, the triumph of feeling like I'd won the wedding, and the realization of how hollow that victory was when my mom destroyed it so easily. Not being able to accept Kim's support, lashing out at her. The way she'd looked at me as she realized how mean and ugly I was, the way I'd used her to prove something to myself that was, essentially, unprovable. How I'd probably irreparably damaged my relationship with Aiden.

"I thought this was my commencement ceremony, my graduation, my fucking bat mitzvah," I admit, cleaning off my face with a makeup wipe while Daytona gives me sloppy French braids. "When I walked into that restaurant last night with Kim on my arm I felt *complete*. I'd aced the test, won the race, stuck the landing."

"I can always tell you're hungover when you use too many analogies," Daytona says from behind me.

"This was supposed to be *it*, you know? I was at my brother's wedding in a designer dress with my lesbian high school crush on my arm. You don't get more unclockable than that! And then my mother . . ."

"Clocks you harder than Big Ben?"

I start to giggle, then laugh, until finally, I'm cackling loudly, uncontrollably. It's not even remotely funny in context, but right now it's either laugh or cry, and I'll take the less painful option.

By the time I laugh myself out, Daytona has finished my

braids and is unpacking the duffel bag I'd noticed sitting by the door. She begins pulling items out and finding a place for them with military efficiency: a makeup case, blow-dryer, Spanx, and a giant mason jar of Sour Diesel.

"A very cute Asian boy dropped a bag off right before you woke up," she says. "He said you keep some stuff at his place and might want it. He told me to say hi."

"Hi," I say, crushed by their kindness: Rachel, Aiden, Ben, Daytona. My dad.

Unsurprisingly, there are no calls or texts from my mom. A heart emoji from Randy, missed calls from River and Kyle. Even the twins had sent me a photo in our group chat: an image they'd photoshopped years ago of Mom, edited so that she was falling into an erupting volcano.

Daytona's back is to me as she spreads her tools out on the dresser, so it is easy to say: "Thank you. I love you."

She turns to face me, face softer than I'd ever seen it. "I love you too, bitch. Now get your ass out of bed, I'm going to make you *sickening*."

CHAPTER
Thirty-Two

DAD LEFT WHILE I was still getting ready, so Daytona drops me off in her SUV at the beachside restaurant where the farewell brunch is being held, windows down with Britney blaring from the speakers. I manage to exit the car without falling face-first onto the pavement, so things are looking up.

I shut the door behind me and face my sister through the open window. "Have fun in Fort Lauderdale," I say. "Use a silicone-based lube in the pool."

"You think I'm fucking stupid?" she asks. "Knock 'em dead, kid." She pulls away, singing loudly for all to hear that oops, she'd done it again.

The restaurant looms ahead of me, an upscale seafood place where we always used to go on Mother's Day when I was growing up. The lobby is empty when I enter, I'm early, and the hostesses are still setting up an easel with a giant photo of Aiden and Rachel on it. Beyond them, Aiden sits alone at a table while waiters deposit napkins onto place settings and busboys light the wicks of burners under tureens of eggs Benedict.

I sit down at the table beside him and he locks his phone, his air of tired happiness shifting to something more cool and neutral. The tension is thick in the air between us. I wonder if he's going to yell and tell me to leave. Or worse, tell me he's *disappointed*. But what he does is grab my right arm, lift it to his mouth, and bite.

"Fucking OW!" I shake him off and cradle my arm in my other hand. "You broke the skin!"

"You deserved it!"

He's got me there.

This is how we've settled every major fight since childhood. When we moved in with Randy and I got the bigger room. When he pulled my pants down in front of the girl I liked at sleepaway camp. When I started sleeping with Ben. Every disagreement has been settled this way, and I understand that this one is a little too big to be solved with a chomp, but it'll have to do to get us through today.

"There's just one thing I need to ask," Aiden says, resolve hard on his face. "Is that . . . what you told Kim, is that what you really think of me? Is there some part of you that believes it?"

"No," I gasp, horror blocking out the throbbing pain in my arm. "Never. I mean," I concede, "I always expected the other shoe would drop someday. And it did, with Mom. But never with you."

And because he's my brother, he takes me at my word and the doubt clears off his face. That settled, Aiden throws his arms around me. "I'm so sorry, Jules."

"I know," I say to his shoulder. "It sucks. Thanks. I'm sorry too. I was . . . not very nice."

He lets out a huff. "Yeah, I think that's an understatement."

"I apologized," I tell him. "I don't think there's much more I can do. I don't think she wants to talk to me."

"But you don't *know*," he says. "You know what happens when you assume."

"OK, Grandpa."

"Shut up," he says, flicking me on the arm the way he knows spins me into a rage. "I hope to be as cool as Grandpa someday."

"Yeah, it was so funny when he suggested you might get a divorce while blessing the challah at your *wedding reception*."

He shrugs. "He's practical. Besides"—he fixes his gaze behind me, to where Rachel is entering with the wedding planner trailing behind her—"I'm not worried about that."

"Me neither," I tell him, knowing that no matter what else happens, he and I will be OK.

An hour later I'm standing in a corner with Brody and Brian, who look young and innocent in their matching polo shirts, but I know better.

"Can you guys cover me for like, ten minutes?" I ask through a mouthful of bagel, cream cheese, and lox. I wash it down with a swig of mimosa. "I need to not talk to anyone until I have a good buzz going."

"Sure," says Brody.

"*If* you get us some booze," says Brian.

I think about it for a second. "Sure," I reply. If nothing else, I'm committed to my role as the cool older sister. And I don't particularly care if Mom gets mad.

"Wicked," they say in unison, turning to shield me as I flag down a passing server. I grab four glasses of champagne, keeping two for myself and passing off my two empties. I mean, it's *brunch*. I'm only going to be able to endure this if a lot of alcohol is involved.

"Mom was a dick last night," Brian says, turning to take a surreptitious sip of his drink.

"Yeah," I agree. "Don't let her see you drinking that, though. And if she does, do *not* tell her I gave it to you."

So much for not being worried if she gets mad. Lingering hurt and disappointment aside, I'm still conditioned to fear her ire.

He smiles, showing off the blue bands on his braces. "We can negotiate."

An aunt wanders by, and Brian turns back to distract her. Brody takes his own gulp of champagne.

"I was thinking," he says, "we have spring break in a couple of months. Could we maybe . . . come to New York and stay with you?"

I swallow abruptly, sending my champagne down the wrong pipe, and spend thirty seconds coughing as the twins pat me on the back, assuring concerned family members that I'm fine. When I get my breath under control, I look at them suspiciously.

"What's the angle? Are you going to break into the UN and cause an international incident? Deface the Statue of Liberty? Oh god," I say, "do you have some creepy Snapchat girlfriends you're meeting up with who are probably fifty-year-old men?"

Brian finishes his champagne and eyes my extra glass hopefully, but I finish the one I'd been drinking and take a sip. He sighs.

"No, we just thought it would be cool to come see where you

live and like, hang out," Brody says, oddly shy. "We could go to museums and eat pizza and stuff."

"And go to a *rave*," says Brian.

I'm hit with a rush of affection for them, remembering their squalling red faces in the delivery room moments after they'd been born, and the forts we'd built when they were toddlers. "I don't know about the rave, but yeah, we could do that. I can show you some cool spots, we can get good food, and maybe see a Broadway show."

"Can we see *Phantom of the Opera?*" Brody asks breathlessly. I recall them at four years old, strapped into car seats in the back of my Volvo station wagon, the three of us singing along to "Masquerade."

I give an exaggerated frown. "I'm sorry, buddy, it closed."

His face falls. "Damn," he says, taking another sip of champagne. "Fuck Andrew Lloyd Webber."

Another glass of champagne later, Brody, Brian, and I join the rest of the nuclear families out on the back patio for photographs. I watch Mom and Aiden pose, her eyes leaking tears until she calls for Randy to grab her bag for touch-ups.

Rachel sidles up next to me.

"Congratulations," I tell her, squeezing her into a hug. I pull away and look her up and down. "You looked incredible yesterday."

"Thank you," she says, a perfect smile on her face. Then, without changing her tone or missing a beat, "I think what you did to Kim is really shitty. What you did to Aiden too. But I know you, Julia, and I think I understand why you did it. That doesn't make it right."

I wince. "No, it doesn't. I'm sorry, I shouldn't have done it and I shouldn't have brought that into your wedding."

"You're my sister now," she says. "And sisters tell each other this kind of shit. Clean up your mess. Do better." She gives me another hug. "Now fix your eyelash and go take pictures with your brother."

"What's wrong with my eyelash?"

Mom is a looming presence just outside my periphery all through the photo shoot, and while I would love nothing more than to pound champagne and ignore her, I can feel her eyes on me and know a confrontation is imminent, so I switch to coffee in preparation. Sure enough, she approaches me on the patio when everyone inside is engaged in a slideshow of baby pictures organized by Rachel's parents.

"See," Rachel crows from inside, "Aiden was hung even as a toddler!"

"That's not appropriate," I mutter.

"Julia." Mom is standing behind me, shielding her eyes from the light. "They only serve Pepsi here. Ride with me to McDonald's?"

"Sure." Inhale, exhale. Best get it over with now. "Where's the car?"

Why does every serious discussion or major emotional moment with my mother have to happen in a car? Is it because in every situation, no matter how dire, she has a clear exit strategy? She can simply get out.

We pick her car up from valet and I assure Mom I'm fine to drive. Between the coffee and an adrenaline surge at looking into her eyes for the first time since she destroyed my world last night, I feel stone-cold sober.

"Should I take Powerline?" I ask, buckling my seatbelt.

"Military," she says, checking her lipstick in the sun visor mirror. She turns to face me as I pull out of the parking spot, checking the rearview mirror for cars. "I'm very sorry that I hurt you, Julia. You know I didn't mean to."

I make a right turn out of the parking lot onto a winding drive and stop at a red light. Cars rush by, although one little white sedan seems to *crawl*. I can see almost nothing but hands on the steering wheel, a Florida phenomenon that makes sense when you understand that people shrink as they get older.

The light turns green. I make a left.

"I know you didn't mean to. That doesn't make it better or hurt any less. And you did it in front of *everyone*." My voice cracks, and I cough as I make a right turn a little sharper than I mean to.

"Careful, please," my mother says, grabbing the handle on her door. "God, do you remember that horrible sharp right you made in the mall parking lot when I was teaching you to drive?"

Remarkably, I laugh. "Yeah, I went over the curb. You screamed *so* loudly."

She laughs too. "I was scared!" Out of the corner of my eye I can see her shake her head. "It was my fault, though. I don't think I taught you to drive very well."

My hands tighten on the wheel. "You're not a very good driver."

"No," she says, shaking her head. "I'm not." She turns her head my way. "But you are. You learned well even though I was a bad teacher."

"I had to," I say. "Didn't want to cause any accidents."

"I'm sorry," she says again. "You're my daughter, Julia, and I love you. I'm not perfect, but I love you."

And she does. I know that. I grew up with the unshakable knowledge that my mother would kill for me, die for me. But I'd also learned that wasn't always enough. Not everything is life or death, some things just feel like them. You can support someone and care for them, and show your love through words and deeds, but some truths live too deep to root out. For my mother, on some level, I will always be the little boy she gave birth to and watched take his first steps. She can tell me to wear a bra and take me out for pedicures and use the correct name and pronouns and really, truly *mean* them, but it will never erase the life we lived together for the first two-thirds of my existence. I don't want it to, nor do I want her to retcon her memories. A few years ago I might have wished that every recollection of my first twenty-five years on earth could be scrubbed from the minds of everyone who knows me, but now I understand how necessary it is to have people in my life who've known me for all of it, known every version of me. It helps me remember myself, and keep building the Julia I want to be for the rest of my life.

"I've been telling myself for years that my transition made us closer than we'd ever been," I say.

"It has," she agrees, sounding hopeful, as though we've moved past the hard part of the conversation.

"And yeah, maybe that's true, but we weren't that close before, so how much of a difference did it really make? I mean"—I take a deep breath—"I've spent most of my life too scared to really *talk* to you, so when I finally did and it was about something so monumental, that was this huge shift in our relationship, but it only got us to this somewhat even playing field. Or some kind of sports metaphor, I don't know."

"Maybe we should leave those to your brother."

"I was so grateful that you were supportive when I came out—both times, if I'm being honest. I have one friend whose parents won't ask if they're dating anyone and another friend whose parents pretend she doesn't exist. I've always felt so lucky that I got this baseline acceptance from you that I was afraid to ask for anything more."

"What more can I *do,* Julia? Really, tell me, what can I do more than love you?"

"You can love *me,* not the me I might be if I lived up to your standards for womanhood. Or even just . . . personhood. You never criticized me for *wanting* to be a woman but ever since, you've been judging me for the *kind* of woman I decided to be."

That's the truth of it, and we both know it. We sit in silence for a moment, but of course she has to break it.

"You're right," she says.

I don't think she's ever said those words to me. "Come again?"

"I love you, Julia, and I *know* you, because you're my child. But I don't . . . understand you, any better than my mother understood me. You've made all these choices for your life, and I want you to have everything that you want. I try as much as possible to guide you when I can and stay out of your way the rest of the time."

"I'm twenty-nine years old, Mom."

"But you're still my baby."

When we were little, Mom used to read Aiden and me a book called *Love You Forever,* and the mother's refrain from the book was one she'd repeat to us in tender moments. "I love you forever, I'll like you for always. As long as I'm living my baby you'll be." When I was eight, twelve, even twenty, it was enough.

"I can't keep trying to be the daughter you've always wanted," I choke out. "The daughter you have *has* to be good enough."

"You are," she says, voice thick. Her hand comes down on mine on the steering wheel. "I promise, you are."

It doesn't erase or excuse what happened at the reception. It was so public and shameful. I still feel . . . dirty, in a way, and caught out. I feel like a fraud, and the world has made me feel that way so many times. But my mom never had. Until now. Something has been broken between us. I don't think I'll ever see her the same way again, and an ugly part of me almost delights in the symmetry: this must be how she felt four years ago, when I told her I wasn't the person she'd thought I was for twenty-five years. And thinking about it that way, as if it's an even trade, lets me see the compromise we're both making. If she can try to let me be the daughter she never had, I can try to let her be the mother I always wanted.

"It's OK, Mom. I love you too. Don't do it again." She doesn't look any more reassured by the words than I feel saying them. I pull into the drive-thru and open the window. "One large Diet Coke, please."

CHAPTER
Thirty-Three

SOMETHING VIBRATES INSIDE my bag. It's a call from Daytona—a regular phone call, not FaceTime, which is unusual.

"Hello, Daytona."

"Hello, doll. Having a good time?"

"Not particularly." Brunch is winding down, but someone's put on a playlist of early-nineties pop music, leading to some very uncoordinated mimosa-fueled dancing. No one wants the party to end, but I'm ready to go home. "But I did what I came to do."

"Got the girl?"

"No," I say. Speak of the devil: Kim dances with Rachel, sexy as hell in jeans and a blazer, cool and composed and closed off to me forever. "I saw my brother get married. I made a toast. I ate kugel. My job here is done."

"Good girl," she says. "I'm proud of you. Although I'd be prouder if you were too busy dancing to answer the phone."

I laugh, leaning back in my chair. Brody and Brian leave the table for parts unknown. "Give me time, I'll find some lonely busboy or sweet-talk one of the bridesmaids into giving me a spin. Eventually. Or I'll leave alone and die an old spinster."

"Must you be so melodramatic? Sylvia fucking Plath over here. Need to find a nice oven to stick your head in?"

"As if," I say, faux aggrieved. "My suicide would be much sadder and more glamorous. Pills, perhaps. Or drowning. I could fill my pockets with stones and walk into the sea like in *The Awakening*."

"Yeah, I skipped that day in English."

"But you got the reference, so I think you're lying."

"I can just picture you there, all sad and morose with your half-eaten crème brûlée."

I look down at my plate. "How did you know it was half eaten?"

"You're probably biting your nails again, ruining that manicure your mother paid for, the way you do when you're *really* going through it."

I had, in fact, been chewing on my thumbnail quite aggressively.

"You're probably wishing you'd gone with a nude color instead of black," she says, knowingly. I look around wildly. "And you're wondering who added Celine to the queue."

"There were nights when the wind was so cold" crackles over the speakers. I stand, swinging right, then left, searching past the tables, dancing bridesmaids, and towers of smoked fish. Daytona continues speaking into my ear, providing commentary on unfortunate dress and hair choices as I bob and weave through the dancers. I reach the edge of the floor, where Rachel now dances with Aiden, both moving slowly, completely incongruous with the music.

"Oh, honey, how many times do I have to tell you? The shoes stay on until you get home."

The voice isn't just in my ear. It's here. Daytona is here, standing just behind the newlyweds. She wears a short red dress with a dangerously high slit, her hair swept to one side so she can hold her phone to her ear. She is incandescent and improbable, and I want to cry just looking at her.

"I must admit," she says, still talking into the phone, "not *everyone* here is a total lost cause. Your brother is kind of cute, and you already know how I feel about your dad."

"If you fuck my dad I will never forgive you."

Her grin is wicked, per usual. "Yes, you will."

My answering smile feels just a bit manic. "Yes, I will."

"But wait," she says, hamming up a look of shocked surprise. "Who is that on the edge of the dance floor? A striking woman in red, mysterious as the night itself, too lovely for words."

"And yet you're still talking."

"Could this beautiful stranger be the woman you've been waiting for? Not for sex, of course—she has a previous engagement with a certain older gentleman."

"I'm going to hang up."

"You're sad and brokenhearted. This woman is clearly out of your league on every level, and she doesn't even *like* women. But you think, what the hell." Daytona hangs up her phone, dropping it onto a nearby table along with her bag. She struts her way toward where I stand alone, but not for long. "Maybe there won't be sex," she allows.

"I surely fucking hope not," I say, grabbing her hand and squeezing it. Her nails dig into my palm and the pain grounds me in this moment.

"Maybe there won't be perfect mothers or gorgeous lesbians." She starts to lead me into the fray, heels clacking even over the voices singing along with Celine Dion.

"There will *always* be gorgeous lesbians," I counter.

She leans against me, pressing a lip to my cheek. I can smell the sweet tuberose of her perfume, wrapping around me in a cloud of comfort. This is home, I think. Daytona's hand in mine, the people around me, this stupid city with its strip malls and golf courses. It's not perfect, but it's mine.

My sister wraps her arms around my waist, starting to move as that wicked smile blooms once more on her face. "But by god," she tells me, leading me into a twirl, "there will be dancing."

And she's right.

CHAPTER
Thirty-Four

"AS CLEARLY STATED on your receipt, Born to Bride does not accept returns on items that have *clearly* been worn." There's more of Lorraine's horrid pink lipstick on her teeth than her lips, which have been turned down into a grimace since I walked into the store.

"I only *tried it on* at home," I insist again. We've been doing this for at least five minutes already. "That's why it has those deodorant stains." Maybe I shouldn't have drawn her attention to those.

"Not to mention you're outside the thirty-day return policy," Lorraine says, sneering at me from behind the counter.

"By one day!" I've only been back from Florida for a week. One week of ignoring Mom's calls, double tapping Aiden's honeymoon photos, and staring at my text thread with Kim, trying to figure out what to say, if it's even worth saying anything. I'm guessing she found someone else to take to that party.

"Listen," I say, leaning over the counter toward Lorraine,

"can't you just bend the rules this *one* time? The dress is in pristine condition!" She snorts. "*Near* pristine condition." I attempt pleading puppy dog eyes. "I could really use the money back." Things are still precarious between Everett and me after our discussion upon my return. He says we're taking it one day at a time, but he's certainly not in a rush to give me any more responsibility, meaning a raise—and a generous Christmas bonus—are probably out of the cards. I'm accepting it as penance for my various sins.

"Fine," she says through gritted teeth. "Just please, if you have another wedding to attend, *shop somewhere else.*" She yanks the dress laid on the counter and starts typing away at the register as I breathe a sigh of relief. Looks like I'll be making rent this month after all.

"Thank you. And don't worry, I'm *never* going to a wedding again. They're miserable."

She looks around furtively. It's Tuesday morning and the shop—like most of the mall—is empty. Now sure the coast is clear, she sags against the counter, going from poised to exhausted in half a second.

"*Tell* me about it, honey. I spend every day of my life talking to people about their weddings, this one day they think is going to be special enough to make up for how empty and meaningless the rest of their lives are." She's clacking away at the register again, processing my return, but her motions are lethargic, robotic. "They come in here and buy dresses they can't afford to marry men who will divorce them. The brides torture everyone: the bridesmaids, their mothers, *me*. Insert your card, please."

I do.

"But they torture themselves most of all. Am I going to be too fat on my wedding day? Will he think I'm beautiful? Will I be able to hold on to this one moment for the rest of my life?

"I'll let you in on a secret, honey: weddings bring out the worst in *everyone*. Everyone is stressed out and hungry and worried about spending too much money to act like rational human beings. People say things they don't mean at weddings, they make bad decisions when the booze is flowing. I assume it was an open bar?"

"Of course. God, can you imagine?"

We share a shudder.

"If the marriage lasts, they'll only remember the good parts. And maybe they'll have kids, and kids always help smooth things over. If they don't, no one is gonna wanna remember the wedding anyway."

She tears off my receipt and hands it to me.

"You'll be fine, honey. Now go buy yourself something nice with your refund." Her face smooths over, back into business mode, as the front door rings open behind us. "Good morning, how can I help you today?"

There's an Auntie Anne's across the corridor from Born to Bride, and I buy myself a piping hot cinnamon pretzel, which burns my fingers but tastes like a memory. I walk slowly, aimlessly through the mall, pausing occasionally to check a window display or pop inside a store. Thanksgiving is next week, but there are already Christmas lights decorating the cavernous hallways of this temple to consumption. My phone buzzes in my bag.

"Do you still like whales?" my dad asks.

"Yes, whales are cool as hell. Why?"

"Maybe we can go to the Natural History museum, I haven't

been there since the seventies." Dad is flying in to Boston next week to spend the holiday at his brother's house upstate. I'll see him there on Thanksgiving and he'll drive me back to the city on Black Friday and spend the day with me. We've been trying to figure out things we can do together that won't drive one of us crazy.

"It'll be super crowded." I can already imagine the sheer amount of screaming children. "But yeah, that would be cool."

"You were obsessed with whales as a kid. You had this little set of toy whales and you wouldn't play with anything else for months."

"Yeah, I remember. I threw one of them through a window when you and Mom told us you were getting divorced. The glass exploded everywhere."

I expect an awkward silence but instead my dad laughs, loudly and gleefully.

"I forgot about that! Oh my god, I felt so bad for you, kid," he wheezes. "But it was really funny!"

He's right. It is funny. One of my most crystal clear memories of foundational emotional trauma, and it's really fucking funny now. That's nice. One day, I'll laugh about the wedding too.

For now, I'll shop. There's gotta be something in Hot Topic that will give my mother a minor stroke.

Three
MONTHS LATER

MY LEAST FAVORITE part of winter in New York is how hot it always is inside. I dressed for the twenty-degree February weather, but now I'm overheated in the boiling-hot basement we're all shoved into.

I've lost Kyle and River in the throng, but onstage, Daytona is giving go-go realness, shaking her ass and whipping her hair as a monotonous techno track blossoms into Madonna's "Ray of Light." I can't help but start to wiggle myself out of the funk I've been in all night—all winter, if I'm being honest.

My only dance move is classic white girl, running my hands up my torso and lifting them over my head, tossing my hair side to side. I've been growing out my bangs, and they stick awkwardly to my sweaty forehead, but I allow myself not to care for the moment and give over to the music. Or at least to the ketamine River and I did in the bathroom twenty minutes ago.

I'm so used to being in my head and all I want is to let go and be in my body, every imperfect inch of it. I sing along at the top of my lungs, but even Madonna isn't enough to keep me from noticing *her* weaving through the bodies toward me.

The lights overhead bathe Kim in blue as she reaches me. It's that point in the night—morning, really—when you don't want to look at anyone too hard because we've all sweated most of our makeup off and everyone's pupils are a bit too dilated, but Kim looks as unruffled as ever in a black T-shirt, tight black jeans. Wow, she looks incredible. I'm nowhere near as put together, but I am wearing a pair of Proenza Schouler boots River pilfered from Hannah G's closet in the days following her cancellation—a series of eleven-year-old-tweets with a veritable orgy of slurs that had absolutely *not* been sent anonymously by a disgruntled stylist who had been pushed out of one too many sprinter vans, thank you very much! The boots are black and heavy and my mom would hate them. I wear them almost every day.

I slow my awkward gyrating down a bit as she reaches me, but don't stop swaying entirely because honestly the room is spinning a little, and Kim nods her head to the beat as her eyes sweep over me. That's a good sign, I don't think she'd dance during a confrontation. We just stand there dancing for a moment, which is very surreal but also kind of sexy. It's working for me.

"I'm still sorry," I shout over the music.

"I know," she shouts back, and for a moment I think that's it, which would be fine. But she moves closer, lets the crowd around us push us up against each other so we're really dancing together. I remember what it felt like to be under her, over her. I remember her arm around my waist. I remember her staring off into the moonlight on a golf course in Florida.

She ducks down to place her mouth against my ear. "I missed you," she says, breath hotter than the swampy air around us.

"I missed you too," I tell her, tentative. With the storm of her anger and my thorny defensiveness feeling very far away, I let myself follow the impulse to rest my head into the crook of her shoulder, breathing into her neck. She smells like cigarettes and sage. Tentatively, I wrap my arms around her.

It can't be that easy. Although, I suppose, none of this *was* easy.

"Is this . . . are we . . ."

"I don't know," she says, hands wrapping around my waist. Mine twine behind her neck. "Let's find out."

It's too hot in here. Sweat is trickling down my neck. My feet are aching in a pop star's stolen boots. But I'm holding the whole world in my arms.

And I feel like I just got home . . .

ACKNOWLEDGMENTS

I am endlessly, overwhelmingly grateful to everyone who encouraged, supported, and took care of me as I wrote *Best Woman*. Thanks to Ryan Streit for thousands of minutes on the phone. Thanks to my mother for telling me to trust myself. Thanks to Maddy and Alex for teaching me how to be a sister. Thanks to Zach and Sharri for giving me hope for the future in Elliott. Thanks to my dad for bringing me to the library. Thanks to Fran Tirado for encouraging all my best and worst impulses.

Thank you especially Grandma Harriet and Grandpa Stan for every Broadway show, every trip to the bookstore, every Sunday at the Polo Club, and every peanut butter and jelly sandwich. You always believed I could, so I did.

Endless gratitude to my incredible agent, Jessica Spitz, for believing in me enough for the both of us. Thank you also to my UK agent, Emma Luong. Thank you to my editors, Jesse Shuman and Sally Williamson, and the teams at Ballantine and Transworld, for making this the best version of *Best Woman* it could possibly be.

Thank you, Madonna and Julia Roberts, for existing and hopefully not suing me.

To my therapist, I would not be here without you.

To all trans people everywhere: We are yesterday, today, tomorrow. We get to write our own stories. I love you so much.

ABOUT THE AUTHOR

Rose Dommu is the author of the Substack newsletter *Mall Goth* and host of the podcast *Like a Virgin*. A former journalist and retired international party girl, Dommu produces work that brings queer communities together through pop culture. She lives in Brooklyn with her alarmingly large collection of shoes.

Substack: @rosedommu
Instagram: @rosedommu
X: @rosedommu

ABOUT THE TYPE

This book was set in Fairfield, the first typeface from the hand of the distinguished American artist and engraver Rudolph Ruzicka (1883–1978). Ruzicka was born in Bohemia (in the present-day Czech Republic) and came to America in 1894. He set up his own shop, devoted to wood engraving and printing, in New York in 1913 after a varied career working as a wood engraver, in photoengraving and banknote printing plants, and as an art director and freelance artist. He designed and illustrated many books, and was the creator of a considerable list of individual prints—wood engravings, line engravings on copper, and aquatints.